The Apprentice Journals II: Gemini

By
J. Michael Shell

Contents © J. Michael Shell, 2016.
Cover art © Vincent Sammy, 2016.

No part of this publication may be reproduced or copied, in print or in any other form, except for the purposes of review and/or criticism, without the publisher's prior written consent.

Published by
Dog Horn Publishing
45 Monk Ings, Birstall, Batley WF17 9HU
United Kingdom
doghornpublishing.com

ISBN 978-1-907133-92-3

Cover design by
Adam Lowe

Typesetting by
Jonathan Penton

UK Distribution: Central Books
99 Wallis Road, London, E9 5LN, United Kingdom
orders@centralbooks.com
Phone:+44 (0) 845 458 9911
Fax: +44 (0) 845 458 9912

Overseas Distribution: Printondemand-worldwide.com
9 Culley Court
Orton Southgate
Peterborough
PE2 6XD
Telephone: 01733 237867
Facsimile: 01733 234309
Email: info@printondemand-worldwide.com

The Apprentice Journals II: Gemini

Table of Contents

The Apprentice Journals II: Gemini   p.7

I.	Very Smart Babies	p.9
II.	My Sister's Puppy	p.10
III.	The Birthday Present	p.13
IV.	Spearl's Education	p.18
V.	Childhood's End	p.24
VI.	Smith's Crossing	p.31
VII.	Thirest and Trouble	p.41
VIII.	Changing Plots	p.51
IX.	Homecoming	p.56
X.	The Last of Fun and Games	p.62
XI.	The Beginning of Dread	p.67
XII.	Dark Star	p.76
XIII.	Traces of Love	p.88
XIV.	Traces of Horror	p.94
XV.	Fierae Blood	p.98
XVI.	A Long and Winding Road	p.107
XVII.	Star City	p.126
XVIII.	Blitz' Prophecy	p.141
XIX.	The Tinkerers' Coup (Traces of Pain)	p.149
XX.	The Apprentice	p.153
XXI.	Traces of Pain Revisited	p.158
XXII.	The New Apprentice	p.164
XXIII.	Tool's Warning	p.183
XXIV.	Traces of Madness	p.190
XXV.	Traces of Mystery	p.198
XXVI.	A Very Brief Summary of a Very Long Life	p.201
XXVII.	The Final Chapter	p.203

> "There is another element, the elementals of which inhabit all. They are the Luminae, who as yet remain silent. When they reveal their will, all must attend."
>
> —Blitz
>
> From *The Third Account* by Spearl the Historian, Final Chapter—"The Death of Blitz."

As life in this body pales and fades, it is not death I fear, and perhaps the word "fear" is ill chosen. Even "regret" doesn't ring true. Let's just say I'm annoyed that I find myself unable to produce the final chapter of my *Third Account*. If I do expire before I manage it, perhaps someone will end that book for me with a brief and unremarkable chapter called, "Finally, an Ending from Spearl!"

Sorry. I try to avoid these morbid moods, but they seem to be an inescapable symptom of old age. And perhaps I'm calling prematurely for that final chapter. Perhaps I'll experience the eccentricities of *extreme* old age. Either way, I am leaving *The Third Account* unfinished for the time being.

It truly amazes me, and is flattering beyond words, how many people have read the first and second *Accounts*. Books are still so rare and expensive, despite my own efforts to improve capability in that arena, yet my histories remain more popular than the very fine and entertaining fiction being written these days. Even so, and again I am touched by this devotion to my work, I know that the *Accounts* are not particularly "colorful," and I admit that this was by design. They are as I titled them, *Accounts*, and I tried my best to keep them free of the emotion that accompanied my witnessing, and occasional involvement in the history I've accounted for.

Which is why, at this late date in my time on World, I've decided to start a new book—no, let's call it a *journal*. I was never truly an Apprentice, though my father insisted I was. Still, I always wished my histories could have been presented as an Apprentice Journal, with all the spontaneity and emotion, the fears and joys, the unabashed *honesty* that was so evident in my father's journal. But I was a historian, and remained true to that calling.

Now my histories are written (sans that final chapter) and I long to simply tell my tale as I so vividly remember it. Not the history of the hero Spaul, but the story of my father. Not an enumeration of the deeds of the aneke'lemental lady Pearl, but the story of my mother and her *human* family. And then, of course, there's my sister, who I loved so dearly even as she frightened World itself. "The Witch Queen," "DreaKin," "DreadStar." All those names she wore throughout her brief and tragic, splendid life, while to me she was always little Star; the starshine in my father's eye, the dearest daughter to the mother who tried and failed, then tried again, to protect her—to *save* her. Though I miss my most beautiful sister more than I can write, a strange feeling always accompanies my thinking of her—a feeling that I will see her again before I die. I would trade all my remaining days to have that feeling come true.

So here it begins, not the journal of a great Apprentice, but the remarkable tale of an unremarkable man. What better place to start than the day we were born.

I
Very Smart Babies

My sister and I became aware the day my mother rose from her sea, and Blitz, who had become the first Starshine, took her place there to begin our education. Actually, it was my sister the first Starshine educated in the womb. But we were twins, snuggled together inside our warm mother, and we loved one another too intensely not to share, too vehemently to keep any secrets. My sister, however, was an Apprentice from the day we were conceived—a *female* Apprentice, an *aneke'lemental* Apprentice, and a shykik to boot. Though I heard every lesson our Fierae mother gave to her, lessons that Star understood at an elemental level, it was all, as the saying goes, Greek to me. Still, I learned, in the womb, every Inglish word, old and new. On the day I was born, had my vision not been so blurry, I could have read any book aloud, though my voice was barely a squeak. I could have walked if my muscles hadn't been womb weak, and I already knew the faces of Father and Mother and Grandfather Tool. I was one very smart baby, but no more than an uncomprehending infant compared to my sister.

Still bloody from birth, the first thing Starshine did was exit her body and call to her Fierae father—her other self. I say other self because on the day Star was born, the first Starshine left my mother's mind-sea and sailed away on the sea of my sister. On the day she was born, those two Stars became one.

My sister Starshine was a wild force from the day of our birth. It took all of Mother and Father's skill to tame her for even the short span that she remained tame. A span that might have been longer, and given World an aneke'lemental completely different from the one Star became, had dark forces not intervened. But let's not go there yet. First let me tell of the darling sister I loved, and our family, once so happy and close. Let me remember the joy before I recall the dread.

II
My Sister's Puppy

Though Blitz had ridden a southward traveling cold front to witness the arrival of the first born aneke'lemental, he refused communication with Star. In fact, he reached out with a tendril bolt and zapped her back into her bloody little body. Somehow I was aware of exactly what had happened, and, when it caused her to cry, squeaked with tiny laughter. "Why are you laughing?" she sniffled.

"Because you sound just like a newborn baby," I told her through a smile.

After a moment, and several more sniffles, Star began laughing, too. Somehow, we crawled, or wriggled, into one another's bloody arms and laughed together lying there between our mother's legs. Almost immediately, Grandfather Tool scooped us both into a soft blanket and said, "Dese granbabies *talkin'*."

Then I heard Mother say, in a voice weakened by pain, "What are they saying, Papa?"

"Dey's hard to hear, kinda squeaky like, but it somethin' 'bout bein' babies."

"Spaul!" Mother called. "What are they saying?"

But it was Grandfather who answered, "He down on de floor. Done faint away cold when de granbabies come."

"Well splash some water on his face, Papa!" Mother scolded.

"I got granbabies to clean! *You* ain't doin' nothin'."

"I just gave birth to twins!" Mother roared.

"Any more comin'?" Grandfather asked.

"No!" Mother told him. "Those two were enough!"

"Den you done. See you can bring dey daddy around."

After a moment I heard my mother softly laugh and say, "Oh, my poor Spaul."

Mother recovered quickly from delivering us into World. Father came to in Mother's arms, but almost fainted again when I recognized his blurry face hovering over me and said, "Hello, Father."

Starshine didn't help when she piped in, "Oh! Is that Papa? Why is everything so fuzzy?"

Our first few days were, I think, difficult for us, and strange. The newness of everything, juxtaposed against our knowledge and awareness, dealt us both joy and frustration. Mostly it was our bodies that frustrated us, as they functioned in every way like the newborns they were. For instance, Star's tummy had a tendency to regurgitate a bit whenever Mother fed us. Once, when we were still but a few days old, this reaction occurred. We were side-by-side in the double cradle Grandfather had built for us, and somehow Rummy had gotten into the room. In a moment, he was in our cradle with us licking Starshine's milk-dribbled cheek.

It's hard for me to describe the joy of hearing my sister's delighted laughter. It was such a wonderful sound that I actually *felt* it. The next thing I knew, Rummy was encased in a whirring cocoon of Zephrae, hovering over our heads like a living mobile, and Starshine was squealing in her high pitched voice, "Can I have him Grandpapa? Can Rummy be mine?"

Grandfather was out in the barn tending to his stillery, but Star could make her voice travel for miles with help from her Zephrae. Before long, Grandfather came running into the room shouting, "Star callin' me! Star callin' me!"

Then he saw Rummy silently barking inside his Zephrae cocoon. "Can I have him, Grandpapa?" Star asked again.

"He yours, darlin'," Grandfather said, wiping sweat from his brow with an old red kerchief. "Give you my heart, you as' for it."

Then he knelt down and kissed us both on our foreheads. As he was leaving the room, he suddenly stopped, turned back and said to me, "Dat ol' muley out in de field, he yours, Spearl. Hurry up get big, I teaches you to ride him."

"Thank you, Grandfather," I said.

Grandfather Tool left the room shaking his head and chuckling, "Dem granbabies *talkin'*."

Before long, we were walking as well. Starshine actually taught me leg exercises that we did lying in our cradle. Once, I was wondering why she wanted so badly to walk when she could easily summon up mag-lines and fly around the yard. Immediately, she answered my thought. "Because," she told me, "if I put you on the lines it would hurt your hands. I want to walk so *we* can walk."

"Doesn't it hurt *your* hands?" I asked her.

"No. I'm aneke'lemental and can charge my hands."

"I wish I were aneke'lemental, too," I told her.

"If I could make us both aneke'lemental," she said, "or make us both human, I'd make us human."

"And give up all the things you can do that I can't?" I asked.

"I'm also shykik," she told me. "And I have a bad feeling, Spearl. Like something is coming for me *because* I'm aneke'lemental."

"I won't let anything hurt you. Not *ever*!" I told her, vehemence laced into my squeaky voice.

"Don't say such things!" Star scolded. "If something *is* coming, don't you dare get between it and me. If you ever got hurt because of what I am...well...I don't know *what* I would do, but it would be *bad*. Search your memory. Do you remember Drea?"

That name conjured up not just memory but a terrible feeling. "You wouldn't become Drea, would you?" I shivered.

"Drea would be a lamb compared to what I'd become if someone hurt you!" Then she plopped down onto her butt like the unsteady toddler she should have been, and began to cry. "You're the only part of me that's human," she whimpered. "I love you more than anything."

"More than Rummy?" I said softly, plopping down beside her and stroking her hair.

"No," she smiled, touching a finger to my nose. "Grandpapa gave me Rummy. I *have* to love him more."

III
The Birthday Present

Star and I were inseparable, which meant Star and *Rummy* and I were inseparable. At least until Father made my gauntlets. After that, there were times when Rummy got left behind.

Star and I were almost five by that time, and looked like pretty normal, though agile for our age, children. When we were walking, talking infants, I think even Mother and Father, and especially Grandfather, were a bit astounded by us.

Just before that fifth birthday, Father found me one day hiding from Star behind the barn. Actually, hiding from Star involved more than just being somewhere she was not. I also had to hide my thoughts from her, which wasn't easy.

"Spearl!" Father said, poking his head around the corner of the barn to startle me. Then he sat beside me and said, "Your sister's frantic looking for you, you know."

I frowned, but didn't answer. If I had, Star would have found me instantly.

"It's okay," Father told me. "Your mother has her occupied. It must be very hard keeping her from finding your thoughts."

"I can't do that," I told him.

"Then how...?"

"I have to not think at all. It's the only way."

"Well," Father smiled. "That's got to be pretty hard, too?"

"It is. How does Mother keep her from hearing?"

"Your mother is aneke'lemental, too, Spearl. She just wasn't born that way. And I don't think she *can* keep Star from hearing. I think she *asks* her in some special way. Star isn't listening right now because your mother is asking her not to."

"But she has to *keep* asking, doesn't she?"

Father smiled and said, "You know Star. And, yes, asking like that is tiring. So why don't you tell me why you're hiding from your sister before Mother tires and she can hear you again."

"I'm holding her back, Father," I said, and tears filled my eyes, though I willed them not to fall.

"What do you mean?"

"Do you remember how she got so much taller than me, but then stopped growing till I caught up? Starshine could be six feet tall if she wanted to, but she stays little because I'm little. And she won't ride the lines because I can't ride with her."

"Not good for the hands," Father chuckled.

"Yes," I told him. "I can remember when yours were so badly hurt and the first Starshine fixed them."

"It still amazes me how you have all those memories," Father smiled.

"I don't really *have* them. I kind-of have to *look* for them. It's Star who *has* them. I feel sorry for her."

"Why is that?"

"Because there are times when she isn't sure who she is. The memories are too close for her."

"Slipped in the traces," Father whispered.

I looked for that memory, and when I found it said, "Something like that, but not as bad as the first Starshine had it. It's more like Star can't tell which traces are hers."

"She needs you, Spearl. And you *don't* hold her back. She holds onto you because you anchor her. You keep her from getting *really* lost in the traces. Besides, both of you are growing fast enough. Your mother will *not* be happy with a six-foot tall, five-year-old Star. As for riding the lines, we'll see what we can do. Okay?"

"Okay, Father. She's coming."

"Can you hear her thoughts, too, Spearl?" Father asked, furrowing his brow.

"No, but I can tell when she's listening to mine."

"Is she always listening?"

"Not since I asked her not to. I asked her to *never* listen, but she just laughed and said, 'I have to listen sometimes, silly'."

I don't know where he got enough magnetite, or how he made the little finger and palm sized ingots, but I suspect it was mother who sewed them into a pair of leather gloves that fit me loosely, but well. On our fifth birthday, Father gave the lodestone gauntlets to Star and me. "They go on Spearl's hands," he said, "but they're for both of you. Now you can ride the lines together."

I don't think I'd ever seen Star as happy as she was at that moment. She wrapped her arms around Father's neck and wouldn't let go as tears streamed down her face.

That day was not the first time I'd been on the lines. Beyond her own concern for my hands, Father had forbidden Star from ever, even for a moment, placing me on the lines. He knew that a few experimental moments on the mag-lines wouldn't harm my hands, but Star was an Apprentice, and Father was vehement about teaching her never to place a human in the way of harm if it could be helped.

But, of course, Starshine had her own rules, and once lifted me onto the lines about ten feet off the ground. "Now lean forward and slide!" she called to me.

I was scared, especially since I couldn't even see the lines that were holding me. I could feel them, though, and trusted Star. She'd raised me up steeply, and I slid down fast and ended up tumbling when I reached the end of my ride. Star came running to me, panic stricken, until she heard me laughing to beat all helluva. "Don't you dare tell Papa," she said, helping me up onto my strong, toddler legs.

"You *know* I wouldn't," I said, angry that she'd even think such a thing.

"I know," she said, hugging me close. "I was just scared I'd hurt you."

"You could never hurt me, Star," I whispered into her ear.

With my lodestone gauntlets, Star and I became terrors of the mag-lines. If Father or Mother had ever seen us, floated up a hundred feet in one of Star's Zephrae cocoons and then dropped onto the lines for a hair-raising ride...well...I'm glad they never did. But I think Mother knew. I once overheard her say to Star, "Spearl is smart, Star, but he's a little boy. A little *human* boy. He can't even see the lines you ride him on."

"I make the lines go to his gauntlets, Mama!" Star told her in a frustrated voice. "And he's *more* than just human. I can feel it."

"I don't even sense Apprentice in him, Star," Mother said softly. "Not a bit."

At that, Star became dangerously angry. When that happened, sparks would dance on her fingertips and her eyes would glow. "You know *nothing!*" she screamed at Mother. "You're not even true *aneke'lemental.* You just had Fierae squirted into you like semen when you consorted with Blitz!"

I thought Mother was going to slap her when she said that. I thanked Jess she didn't, as Star was furious. I think part of it had to do with the fact that Blitz refused to communicate with her. Somehow, though, I believe he was always nearby. Whenever Star tried to come out of her body, something would zap her right back in, and it always made her cry.

Mother regained her composure quickly, which probably saved her being injured. Then she said softly, "It hurts that you think of me that way, Star. I love both your fathers, but Blitz is very much like a father to me as well."

Slowly the light faded from Starshine's eyes, and tears replaced it. Then she whimpered, "He won't even speak to me, Mama."

"You have to trust him, Star. I promise you, there is a reason."

"What is it?" Star cried, folding herself into Mother's arms.

I couldn't hear what Mother whispered into Starshine's ear, but I never again saw her try to come out of her body.

Star grew only, and exactly, as tall as I did. By the time we were seven, we'd ridden the lines hundreds of klicks in all directions. Once we stayed at the beach for three days, swimming and calling out fish to cook on our fires. When we finally arrived home, Mother and Father were relieved, and then terribly angry. Father had never spanked me before, but that day, as Grandfather put it, he tanned my hide.

Starshine was furious, but Father looked defiantly into her glowing eyes the entire time he was tanning me, and she didn't intervene. Instead, she marched over to Mother and demanded to be spanked as well. When Mother obliged her, Starshine shouted, "Harder! You spank me harder than Spearl! I made him do it! It was my fault!"

"No it wasn't," I insisted, pulling my trousers up over my scarlet butt.

"Oh, I think it probably was," Mother said, bearing down on Star's reddening little bottom.

Then Grandfather showed up and all spanking ceased. "Who made dem gloves?" Grandfather yelled. "What you 'spect gonna happen? Next time you spanks dem granbabies, I tan *both* y'all hides! Come here, chillen," Grandfather said, gathering us into his arms. "You promise Granpapa right now you never stay away like dat again. Rummy done cried every night y'all was gone."

"Did *you* cry, Grandpapa?" Star asked.

"'Course I did, every night."

When Star heard him say that you'd have sworn she was nothing more than a fragile little girl. She cried so hard she could barely get the words out, but over and over she said, "I'm sorry Grandpapa. I'm sorry Grandpapa," as she clung to him fiercely.

"I'm sorry, too, Grandfather," I said.

"You de man," he told me, his face as stern as he could make it with Star soaking him in tears. "Women folk gets carried away, men folk gots to do what's right. You gots to keep care of Star, tell her when she doin' wrong, not do wrong with her. You understands? 'Cause if'n dey's a next time, *Granpapa* gonna do the spankin'! Den you *really* be spanked."

"I promise, Grandfather."

"Good! Den all forgiven. 'Cept y'all coulda brought Granpapa a fish. Y'all knows Granpapa likes a fish."

"I'll get you one tomorrow, Grandpapa," Star sobbed.

"Oh no you won't!" Mother scolded. "You two aren't to leave this yard for a week!" Then she held out her hand and said, "Give them to me, Spearl. Right now."

With my head down, I walked over and handed Mother my gauntlets. Quietly, almost apologetically, she said, "Stay in the yard for a week and I'll give them back. Okay?"

"Yes, Mother."

Then she looked angrily at Star and said, "Go to your room, young lady. Grandpapa or no, I may not be done with your spanking."

Mother did go into Starshine's room that night, and I heard Star yell, "You knew the whole time! Did you think I wouldn't see your Zephrae?"

Then I heard spanking again, and was amazed that Star let her do it.

IV
Spearl's Education

We had just turned ten, and Mother had sewn my lodestone gauntlets into a larger pair of gloves—beautiful gloves made of calfskin, which Father had gotten from Mr. Smith on one of his trips to Smith's Crossing. Mother had dyed the leather dark red and embroidered a yellow Fierae bolt onto the back of each one. The only one prouder of those gloves than I was Star. "You look so *handsome* riding in those," she told me. "They go so well with the color of the mag-lines."

"What color *are* the lines?" I asked her.

She was about to tell me, but stopped. After a moment, she said, "You'll know when you see them."

"I'm not going to see them, Star. I'm not *aneke'lemental*. I'm not even Apprentice."

"Don't you dare say that, or you'll make it true," Star insisted with a little bit of angry light in her eyes. "You've been on the lines so much that they know you. Put on your gloves and call them up under your hands."

"I *can't*," I insisted.

"Just *do* it," Star insisted right back, stamping her foot for emphasis.

With my gauntleted hands outstretched, I closed my eyes and called to the lines.

"Why are you closing your eyes?" Star asked in an exasperated tone.

"I don't know," I told her. "It just feels right."

"Well...do what feels right," she conceded.

Suddenly, and very clearly, I could see my red gauntlets and their embroidered Fierae bolts. I couldn't see my arms, or anything else, but when I raised one hand a bit, the glove I was seeing raised as well. Then fat blue lines that seemed to pulse with light rose up under my palms. "They're blue!" I called to Star.

"Yes!" she squealed. "I knew it! You've called them up! Do you feel them?"

"Yes!"

"Swell them, raise yourself off the ground."

I did, and up I went. At that point, I opened my eyes and could no longer see the lines. But they were there, holding me firmly aloft.

"Now call to the Zephrae to push you along!" Star said excitedly.

Of course, I could not. I couldn't even try, because I had not the slightest idea where to start. Finally, I said to Star, "Tell me how."

"You *know* how," she insisted. "It can't be taught or told. Just *do* it."

But there was simply no way. To this day, I can close my eyes and see and call the lines, but it's pretty much my only trick.

When I told father about my new ability, he was ecstatic, and insisted from that day on that I was an Apprentice. "But it's all I can do," I told him.

"You know," he said to me, conspiratorially. "Your grandfather is an Apprentice, too, though he doesn't know it. I've never told him—and don't you, either—because he'd think I was making fun of him. But did you ever notice when he kills a yard-bird how he thanks it?"

"Yes, I have."

"Well, they *answer* him. Their light, as it leaves, always says, 'Tool is welcome.'"

"And that makes him an Apprentice?"

"Yes!" he told me. "Because you either *are* or you *aren't*. And even if you can only do one thing, you *are*. What makes one an Apprentice, Spearl, is that the Elementals are aware of you. If the leaving light of a yard-bird can hear your grandfather, then so can the Elementals. People who aren't Apprentice are invisible. Tool is not invisible, and neither is Spearl."

I understand, now, the wisdom of my father's words. But back then, I just thought he was trying to make me feel better about the fact that Star had so much talent while I had none.

I still have the Fierae-bolt gloves Mother made me. I can still call up the lines. And on the day I discovered that the lines were blue, Starshine worked a piece of majick that is still in effect today. When I simply could not call to the Zephrae to push me along, Starshine "convinced" them to gather at my back and blow whenever I call out loud, "Star says push!" and then to stop me when I say, "Star says stop!"

"How did you do it?" I asked her when the trick worked.

"Don't you ever tell Mama or Papa, Spearl. Swear on your love for me."

"I swear, Star," I said angrily, "but you *know* I wouldn't."

"I do know, but this is serious. I've *compelled* them, forever, to obey those commands from you. Only use it when you must, because it pisses them off something awful."

"Is it dangerous for me to use it?" I asked.

"No, it just pisses them off. No use making them mad if you don't have to. And it doesn't make them *that* mad."

"Like the first Starshine made them?"

When I said that, Star giggled and her eyes went distant, as if she were reviewing that memory. Then she smiled and said, "I wasn't exactly in my right mind when I did that."

"That wasn't you!" I yelled at her.

Then her eyes seemed to regain their focus and she said, "When *she* did that. I said *she*."

I was about to argue with her, but thought better of it. I remembered what Father had told me about being her anchor, and said, "You are my sister Star. If you ever forget that, it will kill me sure as a Fierae bolt."

"Don't say such things," she said with a pout that suited her little girl face.

"Then don't *make* me say such things." I insisted. "Don't go traipsing around in the traces."

For a moment, I thought she would cry. But she smiled instead and said, "You're so wise. What would I do without you?"

"Oh, I don't know," I said. "Maybe call down the moon and punch him in the eye."

"I'd call down the sun for you, Spearl, and all the stars. You take care of me."

"Come on," I said. "Let's ride to the beach."

"Yes!" Star squealed. "And get Grandpapa a fish! It's been weeks since we brought him a fish."

"A markaral?" I asked.

"No, a big Dorado."

"I think he likes markaral better."
"Yes, but Dorado are prettier."

Star said I took care of her, but she was also making sure I could take care of myself. She taught me all manner of ancient fighting techniques, including how to wield a sword. We made wooden ones to practice with, but one day Star gave me a present. It was a magnificent short sword made of bright green stone. "It's ceramic," she told me. "Incredibly sharp, and it will never lose its edge. It's a slashing weapon, and quite effective. But don't stab with it. It might break against bone. Once you know how to use it, and where to slash an opponent, you'll never need to stab. Humans can be drained of blood very quickly if you open the right veins."

"*I'm* human," I told her.

"Yes, but you'll be the one slashing."

After staring at the incredible and beautiful weapon for a bit, I looked Star in the eyes and said, "How did you make this?"

"How do you know I made it?" she said with a coy smile. "I might have bought it in Ginny."

"Not *this*, Star. You didn't buy *this*."

"There are some things, Spearl..." she began, but then stopped. With all her memory, she couldn't find the word, so I provided it.

"Secrets, Star," I said, and the sadness on my face reflected back to me from hers.

"Yes," she said softly. "There are some things..."

"There are *no* things," I insisted. "Not if you trust me."

For a long while Star stood with her head bowed and her eyes closed. I could almost feel the wrenching debate going on in her mind. Finally, she looked up at me and her eyes were glowing. I could actually feel the heat radiating from her face. "I trust you, Spearl," she said, her voice gone elemental. "Stand back."

I took a few steps away from Star, but she said, "Stand *back*! Keep going till I tell you to stop."

I jogged away from Starshine quite a distance before she said, "Okay. Shield your eyes." Then she turned and faced a tall pine standing alone nearby.

It was something like fire, but white and streaming. As best I could tell, it came from her eyes, but little Fierae bolts were also running down her body, coming out of her fingertips and diving into the ground. The pine exploded and threw boiling, flaming sap in all directions. What reached Star sizzled away to mist before it could touch her. In a moment it was over and a pile of smoldering ash lay where the tree had stood. It took a few seconds, but the lectrics stopped flowing out of Star, and her eyes cooled. Then she turned and, for the first time, *thought* to me, "That was a little bit. I can focus it even smaller to make things, like glass or ceramic, but I wanted you to *know*. No secrets."

I was pretty much frozen in place. I didn't know what to say or do. I was happy Star didn't keep these secrets from me, but part of me was wishing she had. When I didn't move, or say anything, Star walked to me and said aloud, "The *knowledge*, though not the power, to make your sword is available to you, but you have to 'traipse through the traces' to find it." Then she took the little sword from my hands and said, "Its name is 'Gryn.' It has no elemental awareness, but is kin to the lines. Learn to visualize it the way you do with the mag-lines, and it will come to you. Practice with it, and you may be able to throw it and guide its flight with the lines. The longer it is with you, the more it will come to know you. I'm honestly not sure myself of all the possibilities. I have access to so much, but I can't claim to understand it all."

It took a while, but I finally found my voice. "Thank you, Star," I told her. "Not just for 'Gryn,' but for trusting me. Still, I have to ask. I've seen that power in your eyes when you were angry. I was afraid once that you might harm Mother. Father I don't worry about, he seems to have some power..."

"It's love," Star said softly. "Even when it's stern or commanding, it's still love that he holds over me. Please don't ask me to explain..."

"I won't, because I know. But what about Mother?"

Star looked away from me, but I could see the tears welled into her eyes. "I love our mother," she said quietly, almost to herself. "But there is something...some *envy* that plays with my temper. Sometimes, Spearl, I am torn by emotions that are not my own."

"The first Starshine," I said, and it was not a question.

When I said that the tears literally sizzled out of Star's eyes and left like little fogs lifting. Then she said, sternly and defiantly, "I am Star, daughter of Spaul and Pearl, granddaughter of Tool and

Sia. Loving sister of Spearl. I will *never* harm my family. I will *never* harm our mother." Then the light left her eyes and, smiling wickedly at me, she said, "No matter how much she pisses me off."

V
Childhood's End

Other than the bodies we wore, Star and I were never really "children." There was much about us, for a long while, that was child *like*, but we simply knew too much to remain even the semblance of children for long. My father was tall, and Mother by no means short. By the time I was thirteen, I was as tall as Mother, and so, of course, was Star.

Starshine had become, at age thirteen, a woman. My memory contains a fully formed vision of the first Starshine, who was, believe it or not, recognizably different from Mother. Being honest, I would have to say the first Starshine was more beautiful than Mother. Starshine had forged herself into what would be most beautiful, most pleasing to my father, and I am my father's son. But my sister Star, with her soft, strawberry and copper mane of curls, her red plum lips and amethyst eyes, was very nearly painful to look upon—especially if you were her brother.

Star was one of a kind—aneke'lemental—and I can tell you that the entirety of that race, that species, that *element*, was beautiful beyond description. And though it hurt, I was glad I was her brother. I feared for the sanity of any man whose love for her (or desire of her) went unrequited. Surely it would haunt and drive him mad.

Star came into her womanhood very quickly. It seemed to me that she was one day my skinny, athletic playmate, and the next a magnificent lady. Even her eyes—not their appearance, but the way she looked at things, the way she blinked, had become beautiful. She also started using some kind of oily charcoal to line those eyes and darken her lashes. She made colored powders with which to dust her eyelids; blue ones and lavender, green and sparkly white. One day I walked in on her applying her powders and blurted out, "Are you trying to incite your brother to incest?"

"Spearl!" she squealed, turning wide eyed to search my face. Then she smiled her most wicked smile and said, "I would never deny you anything. And since we aren't even the same species, calling it 'incest' would be contraindicated."

"Jess help me," I muttered, turning on my heels and getting the helluva out of there. I made it a point, after that, not to stare at her overly long.

Mother never said anything about Star accentuating her beauty. In fact, had Star and I played at sex, I don't think it would have bothered her. Mother was very much Fierae, and her Fierae sensibilities at times overruled Apprentice notions. *And*, she was very powerful. She once told me that, even though the first Starshine was gone from her sea, she could probably call up Drea, or something akin, in a dire emergency. She also said it would be very dangerous, and could kill her. But Star was able to turn it on and off at will. Mother was a power, Star was a force.

Star was always careful with Father—the way I was careful with her. I was grateful for it, especially after our conversation about her alien emotions. While every Apprentice knows that jealousy is foul and greedy, I know that Mother had eyes only for Father. And while she would never have denied him any pleasure, if he'd chosen to take it with another girl, I think she would have been jealous. I know that's a terrible thing to say about my mother, but I am honest. Had the first Starshine ever peeked out of Star and engaged in that seduction, something deadly may well have ensued. Such are the results of jealousy, especially when mixed with aneke'lemental passion.

If Star ever fought with anything beyond daughterly love, it never showed. Anyway, it would only have upset Father, as it would have if Star and I had dallied. Father was first, last and always an Apprentice, and every Apprentice is taught that incest jeopardizes the gene pool. It is against the rules.

Not long after we turned thirteen, as a mild winter began hinting spring, we were separated for the first time. Father came to me one day and told me we were going on a trip to the Lizzy-Anna Purchase by way of Smith's Crossing. Pearl and I had never gone south to Smith's during our mag-line adventures. It wasn't a "day trip," and after our three-day excursion to the beach (and the indignity of the spankings) we always returned home by nightfall. The idea of going to meet Smith, a friend of Father's, and to stay at the Crossing, not to mention the journey into the Purchase, excited me greatly. I also knew Smith had pretty girls to rent, and all my knowledge and memories were of little use against the raging of my adolescent body. With that thought in mind, I began wishing that Mother and Star weren't coming. As if he had Star's ability to hear my thoughts, Father said, "Star and your mother will be traveling in the opposite direction." Then he smiled and added, rolling his eyes, "They're going to Ginny to shop."

Suddenly, memories began assaulting me, and I said, "I know it's been over a decade, but what if someone recognizes Mother as 'Queen Starshine' up there?"

"Trust me, Spearl, even the Ginny Stud herself wouldn't recognize your mother if she didn't want her to. She can confuse the perceptions of people around her if the need arises. So! The men will go south and the women, north. There are things to say strictly between father and son, as there are things between mother and daughter. Also there are things I would say to you Apprentice to Apprentice."

"And Mother and Star aneke'lemental to aneke'lemental?"

"Roger that."

"Who is Roger?" I asked, confused.

"Sorry," Father answered. "It's an ancient expression Thirest used to use. It means 'correct'."

"Will you tell me of Thirest on the trip?"

"I will take you to his bunker. You'll see him as I saw him, though, of course, he'll be dead."

"I'll miss Star," I admitted. "And Mother," I hastily added.

"I know. Your sister is beautiful beyond words, and it must gnaw on you some."

"Father!" I protested too vehemently.

"My, but that's a raw nerve," Father smiled. "Beauty inspires desire, Spearl, especially when adolescence addles ones chemistry," he said, tousling my hair. "But you are an Apprentice, and I know you understand about..."

"The rules," I finished for him. "*Incest*. Can we *please* change the subject?"

"Yes," Father laughed. "The subject is preparing your pack. We leave in the morning."

"Does Star know?"

"By now, I'd think, yes."

"Then I want to spend the rest of the day with her."

"You've spent *all* your days with her. You two will survive a couple of weeks apart."

I found Star arranging her pack. "So you know," I said.

"Yes," she answered without looking up. "Father was right, we'll survive a couple of weeks."

"How do you...?"

"I traipsed through your traces. He actually brought up desire and incest. Our father is brave and honest." Then she turned to me with unreadable eyes and asked, "Do I hurt you, Spearl? Do you *need* me?"

"I love you," I told her. "And sometimes your beauty is overwhelming. But you are my *sister*, and, no, desire does not conquer that love."

"I'm glad," she said, returning to her pack. "It would be strange, I think, if you did need me that way. Because I would, you know. I wouldn't let you..."

Placing my fingers on her lips, I said, "Stop. You'll never need to show me you love me too much. And I may just rent a girl down at Smith's, so I'll be well taken care of in that regard."

"*Oooooh!*" she said, squinting her eyes and scrinching her nose. Then she shoved me gently and said, "I'll be *jealous*!"

"Don't say such things," I said softly.

"Can Spearl no longer take a joke from his sister?" she smiled.

"Spearl can," I smiled back.

"Then come here and I'll guide you through the traces so you can hear what Mama said to me. It's only fair."

"Can you do that?"

"*Spearl! You* can do that without me, if you only *knew* you could. My traces are as available to you as yours are to me. We're practically the same mind." Then she got that frustrated look on her face and said, "I can't *teach* you these things, you simply have to *do* them. But I can *take* you. Are you ready?"

"I guess," I said, not sure what was going to happen.

Nothing happened. After a moment, Star, still folding clothes into her pack, said, "So, what did you think?"

"About what?" I asked.

Frustration again appeared on Star's face and she rolled her eyes. "Come *here*!" she commanded. Then she placed her palms against my temples, not gently, either, and I was suddenly looking at Mother and saying, "He loves me as a sister. He's an Apprentice."

"I knew that, but your father was concerned."

"Papa said something like that?" I screeched.

"Of course not," Mother told me. "But he knows what desire is, and he knows how beautiful you are and that you're the only girl, much less beautiful girl, for miles. I think the concern I felt in him was for Spearl's sanity."

"You think I'm driving my brother insane?" I protested.

"Do *you*?" Mother asked, pointedly. "Is your bother driving *you* insane?"

I was seeing and hearing through Star, but I was also aware of her thoughts and feelings. If Mother had asked, "Is your father driving you insane?" Star would have been sorely tempted to break her oath never to harm Mother. Finally, I said, "Mama, if I thought I was driving my brother insane, I'd bed him in an instant and think nothing of *incest*!"

"And if he were driving *you* insane?"

"I'd tell him and hope he'd do the same."

Mother rose and took me into her arms. Kissing my cheek, she said, "I love you, Star. I love your honesty. And I will be honest with you. I'm happy, as well as impressed, that you and Spearl are able to love as brother and sister, because I know the bond between you is fierce. But I am also Fierae—more Fierae than you think."

"Mama, I'm sorry about what I said..."

"Don't be sorry," Mother interrupted. "That was a long time ago. And you kept control of your anger, which must have been difficult. But I *am* Fierae, and will never condemn you for being true to yourself in that regard."

After a little silence, I asked, "So where are we going?"

"To Ginny to shop."

"Doesn't sound very much like a Fierae thing to do," I smiled.

"Do you not want to shop?" Mother asked, eyebrows raised.

"Of course I want to shop!" I insisted.

"Then it *must* be a Fierae thing to do."

Suddenly Star snatched me off that trace and I was again in her room watching her pack. "That was amazing," I told her.

"It should be commonplace," Star said matter-of-factly. "But what did you think of the conversation?"

"I think you and I have had it to death, it's been put to rest, and from now on they should mind their own business in that regard."

"You think it's none of their business?"

I thought about that for a moment, then said, "I guess, as an Apprentice, Father believes it's his business."

"Then, as Papa's life-mate, and an aneke'lemental, it must be Mama's as well."

"Enough of this shite!" I said, losing my temper.

Grabbing Star by the wrist, I dragged her out of her room and into the kitchen, where Mother and Father were sitting. Star was giggling as I said to them, "We *have* not, *are* not, and *will* not. *Ever!* Aneke'lemental, Fierae and Apprentice sensibilities be damned, we are brother and sister and it would freak us out to have sex with one another. Are there any further concerns?"

"State them at your peril," Star giggled, "because Spearl is sorely pissed."

Mother smiled. Father looked at Mother and shrugged his shoulders, after which I dragged Star out of the kitchen shouting, "That is the end of it!"

"End of what?" Grandfather said, coming though the front door.

"Unrequited love," Star told him, giggling to beat all helluva.

"*What* quite a love?" Grandfather asked.

He never got an answer, as I dragged Star into her room and swung her by the arm till she landed on the bed. She had the most amazing look on her face as I said, "Now I *really* need one of Smith's girls."

"That's the first time you ever really thought about it, isn't it?"

"There are some thoughts I seriously wish you wouldn't hear, Star," I told her.

"I didn't need to hear it. You should see the look on your face."

"I think I'm seeing it on yours."

"You are," she told me, her beautiful eyes wide with it.
"See you in a couple of weeks," I said, getting out of there with no time to spare.

VI
Smith's Crossing

"Would you like to eat a mush rat?"

"I don't think so, Father."

"Oh, don't be like that. You've got to try new things."

"Have *you* ever eaten a mush rat?" I asked.

"I ate one the night before I met your mother. Or was it the night before the night before?"

"I don't know, Father. I don't have memories of you before you met Mother."

"Hmmm. So it's your Mother's memories you have."

"And the first Starshine's. I can also get into the traces a bit, traces of knowledge and such, but I can't get into other people's traces without help. Star says I have access to all of them, especially hers, but so far I haven't found my way in."

"If I'd met your mother before I ate the mush rat, and shared it with her, you'd know what it tastes like, wouldn't you?"

"Yes."

"Well, I'm glad I didn't. You're in for a treat. Come on, let's make camp and find us a fat one!"

Father and I hiked a lot, though we rode the lines some as well. For the most part, our rides were short—water crossings and such—but we also took longer rides to "make some time" as Father said. When we did that, Father used a trick to keep both our hands from being injured.

What he would do was call up three lines, one on either side of us and one between. Then he would take one of my gauntlets and put it on his outside hand. The other was on *my* outside hand. Between our inside hands, which would be on the center line, Father placed another lodestone. The naked lodestone was on the back of his hand, onto which I would place my palm. Even though Father's palm was directly on the center line, the lodestone on the back of his hand gave him some protection, and protected me completely. When I asked him why he didn't put the lodestone under his palm, with my hand on the back of his, he told me our hands would become stuck together for a time. "I didn't mind with your mother," he said, "but you and I would find it quite inconvenient. Besides, I'm afraid the line *could* reach around and tug on your metals."

After a long ride, Father's hand would be a bit red, and was probably sore, but Mother had placed markaral liver in his pack, and that seemed to heal him pretty quickly.

Mush rat wasn't as tasty as Father claimed, and I think even he didn't find it as good as he remembered. But it didn't matter, because the following day we traveled on into the night until we came to Smith's.

Smith's Crossing was really just an inn and a few outbuildings. "Why is it called Smith's Crossing," I asked Father. "We haven't crossed anything that I noticed."

Father laughed and said, "Smith started calling it that a few years back—thought it sounded good. And it does. *Smith's Crossing*," he said with exaggerated pomp. "Famous from one end of Smith's Crossing to the other!"

It wasn't that late, and a few stragglers were still munching hushpuppies and drinking wine. When he saw my father, Smith beamed and came running (or waddling, as he carried quite a belly under his filthy apron) over to greet us. "Spaul!" he shouted. "My old friend! And this has to be Spearl! I should knock you over the head for not bringing him here before this. Why, he's a full growed man already!"

"Not quite," Father laughed.

Then Smith lowered his voice to a conspiratorial level and said, "But I'll bet he's old enough to want a young lass to warm his bed, eh?"

Smith grinned hugely as Father shook his head and chuckled. "That's entirely up to Spearl," he said. "But I'm pretty sure he won't want his *first time* to come right after an exhausting hike well into the night. I'm pretty sure he'd rather be well rested, and have had a chance to talk with his father and ask any questions that might be on his mind."

"First time, eh?" Smith grinned even wider, if that were possible. "Well, he might just want to jump in and see what happens!"

"Again, that's totally up to Spearl," Father said, giving me a somewhat pointed look.

"I *am* tired," I said. "And very hungry. Have you ever eaten a mush rat, Mr. Smith?"

"I have *never* served mush rat in my establishment, lad. Squirrel, yes. Gator when I can get one. But you haven't lived till you've had one of Smith's special steaks off'n a cow."

With his thumbs hooked into his sospensors, Smith beamed with pride and Father said, "Bring two, bloody, with pups and whatever else you think Spearl might like to try."

"A girl?" Smith chuckled, staring holes through me.

"I'm so very hungry, sir," I told him. "And I don't know if I should do it right after stuffing myself with food."

"That's one of the things he might want to ask his old man," Father told Smith with a wink. "So let's wait till tomorrow to think about girls, and concentrate on eating."

"Sure enough!" Smith roared, pounding his fist on the table. "You're a wise man, Spaul."

Smith's cow steaks were excellent, and *huge*. Though I'd never loved a girl before, I had my doubts as to whether I could have done it (especially for the first time) as full as I was.

While we were eating dessert—apple-blackberry sauce—Smith came over with a piece of stone on a pewter platter. "Do you know what this is, lad?" he asked me.

I had the memory of it, but smiled at Father and said, "No." Father knew my lie was a polite one, and winked his understanding.

"That there is a bona fidey stone off'n Mason Dicksem's wall!" Smith announced. "Carried to me by yer own dear Papa not long before you was born. Brung yer pregnant Mama with him—huge as a house she was, and beautiful as sunshine! Had a grand ol' time of it, didn't we, Spaul?"

"*You* did!" Father laughed. "You beat us every night at cards, and took a pretty pile of silver for your efforts!"

"Hmmm. Don't seem to recollect that part, Spaul," Smith pretended. "Shall we teach young Spearl to play?"

"You can corrupt my son tomorrow, Smith. Tonight we are stuffed and bone weary. Two rooms, if you please, with washbasins full. We stink."

"Have 'em ready in a minute," Smith said, marching off to see to our accommodations.

I was surprised when Father ordered two rooms, and I'm sure he could see it on my face. "Yes," he said without my asking. "Two rooms. I was serious when I told Smith it's up to you about the girl."

"Have *you* ever rented a girl?" I asked.

"No, I haven't. Do you have memories of Rufus Bowagad?"

That name inspired in me feelings akin to hatred. "The slaver," I said.

"Well, you probably don't have a memory of a conversation I had with him, as your mother wasn't present at the time. But I was arguing with him against slavery, and he asked if I'd ever rented a girl at an inn. As I said, I hadn't, but I'd never thought about it being wrong until a slaver asked me that question."

"Do you think it's wrong?"

"I honestly don't know, Spearl. Rufus pointed out that an innkeeper might rent his daughters in order to feed his sons, and who had the right to judge his means of survival."

"But he was a *slaver*."

"Yes, and he had to be stopped," Father said quietly. Then a sad expression stole over his face and he added, "I've often wished he could have been helped instead." After an extended silence, Father came out of his reverie and said, "The *point*, Spearl, is there are some questions that defy answers. Renting a girl? I don't know. I know Smith won't *make* his girls rent out to anyone they are opposed to, or afraid of. In fact, Smith is picky about who he'll rent his girls to at all. And I'm sure he has a girl who would like to be rented to you. But you have to make up your own mind about this. Perhaps it would help you with...other circumstances." Then he quickly raised his hands palms out and added, "Circumstances I have *no further concerns* about! So that's it. That's the talk. Thirest once told me doing it could be dangerous, which was an understatement in my case. Loving and love, life and living—they are all dangerous, Spearl, but you won't want to miss them, either. So decide. I don't even need to know. It's between you and Smith, and perhaps you and one of his girls. Now let's get cleaned up and get some sleep. One way or another, you've got a big day ahead of you."

She was very young. When I asked, she told me she was fourteen, but I doubted it. She didn't look older than I was to me.

I had thin sleeping shorts on when she quietly entered my room. "Hello," she said in a shy little voice.

She was pretty. Actually, she was cute. Slowly she came out of the baggy dress she wore until she stood before me in a pair of shorts quite similar to what I was wearing. I noticed she was trembling, then realized I was as well. "I'm sorry I got such little titties," she said in her hushed voice.

"I think they're very nice," I told her.

"Thank you," she said, her eyes lowered shyly.

A prolonged silence ensued during which neither of us moved. Finally I said, almost in a whisper, "It's my first time. What should we...?" Then my question petered out.

"We should climb into bed, I guess," she told me.

We lay down side by side, but I was quite frankly scared to death. Kimberly, as her name turned out to be, was trembling awfully. Finally, she said, in a quivering voice, "It's my first time, too."

"Are you scared?" I asked.

"Terribly so," she admitted.

"Me, too," I told her. "What if we don't, you know, do it *all*. What if we just sort of get our feet wet, if you know what I mean."

"'Kay," she agreed, relief in her voice. "You could try out touchin' my titties," she offered.

I put my arm around Kimberly, and with my other hand caressed her little breasts. "Does it feel good?" I asked, quite genuinely curious.

"Yes," she said. "You could try out kissin' me," she added.

As I touched my lips to Kimberly's, she dove an exploratory hand under the blanket and found what she had apparently decided to get hold of. After a second or two, she smiled through our kiss and said, "You done squirted. It's so *warm*."

I slept well, that night, but woke up several times to find Kimberly snuggled against me. The "squirting" had felt good, but holding Kimberly's warm, sleeping body felt even better. There was love in that feeling, though not binding love. And for just one moment, my mind pretended it was Starshine I held, and the love I felt became intense, but also conflicted. I rose up on an elbow to look down at Kimberly and get the image of Starshine out of my mind. Kimberly opened her sleepy eyes and stared up at me. "Whatcha lookin' at?" she asked through a yawn.

"You're very pretty," I said.

"You're pretty, too," she told me, closing her eyes and slipping back into sleep.

We stayed three nights at Smith's. Once I had bedded (sort-of) Kimberly, Smith never brought up the subject of renting again. I guess he figured I'd ask if I wanted more.

I have no doubt that Father knew, even if Smith didn't charge him for my first encounter. If nothing else, Kimberly wandered out of the kitchen several times during our stay, blushing at me to beat all helluva. I may have blushed back.

I considered having her come to my bed again while we were there, but if she had, I knew we'd do more than get our "feet wet." We were both over the trepidation—perhaps she even more than I. "Doing it" no longer scared me, but I was absolutely petrified that while we did, I'd have another pretend encounter with Starshine. Renting a girl to ameliorate desire for her seemed to have been a mistake. Before Kimberly I was sure I did *not* want to dally with Star. Afterward, I feared I did, which I suspected wouldn't make it any easier to avoid.

I was wrong. It was coming to terms with my desire that defeated it, not pretending it didn't exist, though I have to admit, Star and I danced mighty close to the edge of that cliff on more than one occasion. To this day, I wonder if it wouldn't have been better just to do it and have it over with.

As we were leaving Smiths for the Lizzy-Anna Purchase, I wandered out by a corral fence to look at some cows he had in there. Father and Smith were exchanging farewells and laughing about something. Then Kimberly came out with an oily looking bag in her hand. "Go ahead, darlin'," Smith told her.

Kimberly jogged over to where I was standing and held out the bag. "Some hushpups for yer trip," She blushed.

Then I heard Smith say to Father, "My poor, 'parted sister's girl. They kinda cute together, ain't they? 'Bout the same age."

"She's a darling," Father said.

Kimberly handed me the pups and turned toward the inn. At the last moment she spun around and planted a kiss on my cheek. "Thank you," she whispered. Then she ran back and disappeared through the door.

"I think she mighta took a shine to yer Spearl," Smith said with his thumbs in his sospensors. "If'n he gets to pinin' for her, I'd let her go, though it be hard, to such a fine lad as yours."

"If he pines," Father told him, "I wouldn't think of keeping them apart."

With that, Father finished his good-byes, and we quickly left. An uncomfortable silence permeated our air for several kliks. Finally, I said, "I didn't. Not exactly."

"Spearl," Father began, "you don't have to..."

"But I can if I want, can't I?"

Father smiled and said, "Tell me."

I recalled my encounter with Kimberly, leaving out only a few minor details—specifically the detail concerning Starshine. I also didn't mention the squirting. I think what I really wanted Father to know was that I had, under the circumstances and to the best of my understanding, done the right thing. Nobody was harmed, and I was sure Kimberly was well pleased that her fears had been taken into consideration. Nothing had occurred that she hadn't wanted.

After I finished the tale of my first encounter, Father said nothing for quite a while. Finally, he turned to me, smiled and said, "She's cute. Smith says you can have her if you like."

"*Have* her?"

"Take her home with you, you know, *keep* her."

"She's not a puppy!" I protested.

Father laughed to beat all helluva. After a bit, he choked off his laughter and said, "We can avoid Smith's on the way home if you like."

At that point I had to laugh as well. "That might be a good idea," I said. After a moment I added, "But she *is* cute."

"Very," Father smiled.

At the Southern Edge, we stopped and looked out over the dots of swampy land that constituted the Florida. "We could have turned west much sooner," Father told me, "but I wanted you to see this. They say it was once a huge land mass, all above the sea. The Ancients managed to sink it with their teck. No one goes in there, now. It's full of crocs and gators and giant pyraton snakes."

"I thought the elementals washed it away with hurrakin parties."

"Yes, they did," Father said. "But the Ancients warmed World, which also warmed the seas and raised them up. They made it much easier for the elementals to cavort with greater and greater enthusiasm. You know, with all the traces Star has access to, we should really find out more about what happened. There's so much we don't know."

"Maybe I'll find a way to get into those traces someday," I said. Had I been shykik, I might have added, "and become a historian."

"Shall we get the Zephrae to take us up for a better look?" Father asked.

I had never seen Father do Mother and Star's trick of the Zephrae cocoons by himself. "I didn't know you could do that," I told him, surprise in my voice.

"It took a few years," he told me, "but your mother finally managed to teach it to me."

"Star says you can't teach those things. She says you have to just *do* them," I said.

"Well," Father told me after a brief silence, "I think she's right. It isn't that your mother *taught* me the trick, it's more that I learned from being with her so many times when she did it. There's really nothing to see or hear when someone is executing it that will help you. You have to *feel* what the Zephrae are feeling, if that makes sense. Then you have to communicate, in a language all your own, until they begin feeling that way again. Even that is a simple way of explaining what can't really be explained."

"I can't see or hear or feel the Zephrae. I have no awareness of the elementals," I said, a sad, almost lonely, feeling coming over me.

"Remember what I told you, Spearl, about being an Apprentice. Trust me, the elementals are aware of *you*. So do what you *can* do. Become what you *can* become. If Star says you have access to the traces, find your way in. Even your mother has little access there, though I'm guessing she can enter her children's traces, and traces of knowledge. And Star only has the access she does because Starshine sails her sea."

I was shocked when he said that. *I* knew because Star had told me. But it was one of the many secrets I'd sworn to keep. "How do you know that?" I asked.

"Even the amazing color of your sister's eyes can't hide what I sometimes see looking out of them. But enough of my compromising your secrets," he said with a wry smile that caused me never to underestimate him again. "Let's fly a bit and look out over this foreboding place."

He took us up very high, and the Florida *was* foreboding. "I think I see crocodiles," I said, pointing.

"Put on your gauntlets," Father grinned.

"What...?"

"Just do it. Don't worry about me, this will be brief."

I obeyed, and Father gave me quite a surprise. He was a master with the lines, and called them up under our hands. When his Zephrae dropped us onto them, we slid down steeply out over the Florida. Somehow, he had twisted those lines so that they carried us out a ways, then banked, then rose up and went down over and over again. All the while, the wind was rushing past us so fast it pushed tears from our laughing eyes. Father looked over at me and screamed through that wind, "For all their Teck, I'll bet the Ancients that lived here never took a ride like *this*!"

Finally, the lines banked back toward the edge and deposited us on the ground where our packs lay waiting for us. I couldn't get the grin off my face or the love out of my voice, when I said to my father, "That was *amazing*!"

After a good, long hike, Father and I "made some time" on the lines. We camped close to the sea and called out a fish, which went well with my gift from Kimberly.

As we ate, Father told me about this part of World. "The sea here was once called the Oily Gulf. No one I've ever talked to remembers why, but I can tell you there are a lot of tar-balls on the beaches around here. If we ride the lines a good bit tomorrow, we might make it to Thirest's bunker."

I wasn't sure how to voice my anxiety, so I finally said softly, "I've never seen anyone dead before."

"If it bothers you," he said matter-of-factly, "you don't have to go in. But he'll simply look like he's sleeping. I placed him on cedar bows, and the elementals take turns preserving him exactly the way I left him. You know, it's funny—they won't fix disease, or what disease has wrought, but they are more than happy to preserve the dead if you know how to ask."

"Star says the elementals don't understand death."

"Does she?" he asked me. "Do you? Why do you suppose we go through the process of dying, only to come back with no memory, to start over again? Seems silly, doesn't it?"

"Maybe bodies just aren't made to last and we need new ones."

"But why do we lose our memories?" he pressed.

"Maybe we'd get bored?" I said, half jokingly.

Father smiled and said, "Or maybe we're *afraid* we'd get bored."

That really got me thinking. "If that were so," I said, "wouldn't it imply that we somehow set things up this way?"

"What a fine question, Spearl," Father said with something like pride in his voice. "Don't ever stop asking such questions."

After a bit, I said, "I can't help but notice you didn't have an answer."

"No," he chuckled. "But I haven't stopped asking."

VII
Thirest and Trouble

Thirest's bunker, from the outside, was not much more than a big mound of dirt covered in cut flowers—some fresh, some long dried. On one side there was an excavation that led to a sturdy, wooden door. "It looks like somebody's been remembering him with flowers," I told Father.

"Seems that way," he said with a puzzled look.

"Did he have a lady friend?" I asked.

"I don't think so," Father smiled. "Not all, but many Apprentices are drawn to their own gender. I never knew Thirest to have *any* relationships, but I have a feeling he was like most. If he had a lover, or even so close a friend, I'd want to meet them. Regular humans weren't fond of Thirest because he was very strict about the rules. But he truly believed the things he did were for the benefit of humankind."

"Did Apprentices like him?" I asked.

"Yes. Apprentices loved Thirest because he was *above all* one of them. He was also a very strong, even powerful, Apprentice. But we aren't many, Spearl. Still, at the few gatherings he and I attended together, it was easy to see he was well and truly loved. Now, I need to converse with the elementals here so we can get in. Give me a minute."

Father sat down, closed his eyes, and placed his hands on the ground. After a minute, the door to Thirest's bunker seemed to creek. Then it eased open a bit. Father sighed and stood. "Let's go in," he said.

Immediately I was amazed and said, "Where is the light coming from?"

"Look at it," he smiled. "You tell me."

"I *think*," I said, "everything is glowing."

"Very good," Father said, putting an arm around me and giving me a hug. "But it *is* hard to tell that, isn't it. I asked the Terrae to do it. There are even Terrae in Thirest, now. Over time, they will inhabit an abandoned body. They are preserving him for me."

I walked over to the small bed on which Thirest lay amidst cedar bows and gardenias. "He's so *young*!" I exclaimed. "He looks no older than you are, Father." Father had allowed himself to start aging again not long after we were born. "Why did he die?"

"I don't know," he answered. "I found him one day sitting against a tree. He had a strange look on his face, and seemed barely able to move. "Place me in my bunker, Spaul," he whispered. "Remember what I taught you. Preserve me well."

"I knew what he meant, but I didn't understand, and asked him what was wrong. All he would say was that it was time. He died lying right there exactly as he is now. He said he loved me, and then he died. His light left in a flash."

"He taught you well, Father," I told him. "He's preserved perfectly. He's beautiful." And he was. Thirest had been a very beautiful man.

Suddenly a startled look appeared on Father's face, just as I realized Star was listening to my thoughts. "Something's wrong," he said.

"What is it?" I asked.

"Your mother was just listening to my thoughts. She hasn't done that since before you were born."

"Why not?" I said.

"Because I asked her not to."

"I've asked Star not to, but you can guess what good that did. She was just now listening to me, too. I felt it right before you felt Mother."

"Something's amiss. They were checking to see if we're alright."

"Can't Mother speak in your thoughts? Star can speak to me. Why wouldn't she tell me if something were wrong?"

"Because they don't want us to do what we're about to do."

"What's that?"

"Go like helluva up there to find them!"

Then I heard Star speak in my mind. I think the distance was confounding her a bit, but I managed to hear, "Don't come. We are well."

"Star says they're okay, Father. She says not to come."

"You know your sister, Spearl. What do *you* think we should do?"

"Go like all helluva!" I told him.

We rode the lines hard until I screamed at Father to stop. "Do you want to lose your hand?" I yelled.

When he stopped us I looked at his palm and saw that it was starting to bleed. "Eat this," I said, reaching into his pack and pulling out some markaral liver. "Then take my gauntlets and go! I'll go east until I come to the 95. I can find my way home from there."

Father smiled and put his good hand on my cheek. "I'm not letting you hike through half of Two-Carolines."

We'd been taking a crow's path from Thirest's bunker, and were a little west and a bit past Smith's. "I'm going to light a line from here back to Smith's. You can be there before dawn tomorrow. You stay there till you hear from your sister. I'll bet Kimberly will be glad to see you," he smiled.

"But I'm *worried*!" I said.

Vaguely, I could hear Star say, "Don't worry."

"For all intents, Spearl, I am your Finished, and I'm telling you, as an Apprentice, to go to Smith's and wait. What will you do?"

Without hesitation I said, "I will go to Smith's and wait."

Father called up a mag-line, twisted it toward Smith's Crossing, and caused it to glow a bit. "Can you see it?" he asked.

"I can see it now," I said. "But when the sun comes up…"

"You'll be at Smith's by then if you hurry." Then he grabbed me into a hug and said, "I'm proud of you, Spearl. Try not to worry. Tell Smith I said to take care of my son till I return. Now go," he said, donning my gauntlets.

I watched Father call up his lines and gather a screaming chorus of Zephrae at his back. He was out of sight in seconds, and I started to walk. I kept listening for Starshine, but she said nothing else. Finally, when I was almost to Smith's, I just barely heard her say, "Coming."

When I showed up alone, Smith immediately surmised that something was wrong. "Some sort of 'Prentice emergency, ain't it?" he asked, his face painted with concern.

"We're really not sure," I told him. "Father went to find out and sent me here."

"You look like you been walkin' all night," Smith told me. "Sit and I'll get some eggs and bacon. You look scared to death, but don't you worry. Whatever's about, yer papa will take care of it, I know. And ol' Smith gonna take good care of *you*, so don't fret. Just you sit here and catch yer breath. Food's comin'!"

Smith hadn't been in the kitchen a minute when Kimberly came out with a little mug of wine. There was a look of true concern on her face, and she didn't blush. "Uncle says drink a little of this," she told me. "It'll make you feel better. Don't worry, Spearl, everything will be okay. Please don't fret."

"I'm alright, Kimberly," I told her. "Maybe just a little worried."

"Everybody calls me Kimmy," she said. "I wish you would, too."

"Okay, Kimmy," I said, and then she *did* blush.

In short order, Smith came out with a huge breakfast and said, "I got chores that won't wait. Kimmy, you stay with Spearl and see that he eats. I'll get the other girls to share your chores this mornin'. Spearl is your chore, so see that he eats and don't fret. He needs anything, you come find me. Okay?"

"Yes, Uncle," she answered.

When Smith had gone off to do his chores, Kimmy said, "You eat, now, or I'll get my hide tanned. When yer done, I'll get my Old Maid cards and we'll play. Ever played Old Maid?"

"No," I told her.

"Uncle made me my cards, and it's fun. It'll keep you from frettin'. And later, we can go see my new kittens. They're just the cutest li'l ol' things."

I had to smile. Kimberly, it seemed, wasn't at all as shy as I'd thought.

I had walked all night, and after breakfast, a game of Old Maid, and playing with Kimmy's kittens, I was exhausted. I knew Kimmy was trying to keep my mind off my worries, and her concern touched me. Little tendrils of love were winding their way into my heart.

It wasn't quite noon, but Smith said, after feeding me again, to take the room I'd had when Father and I were here and get some rest. I lay on the bed, dead tired, but troubling thoughts kept me awake. Then I heard the door open and felt Kimmy crawl into bed.

She snuggled up close, kissed me on the cheek and said, "Go to sleep." I did.

When I awoke, I noticed that Kimmy was gone. Then I heard Star's voice in my head say, "Who's Kimmy?"

Her voice was strong, and I thought, "Where are you?"

"With Mama and Papa. We're on our way to get you. Papa's been lecturing me about how I shouldn't listen to your thoughts, and now Mama's joined in. Maybe they're right. I'm going to have to hear *your* thoughts...I mean, hear what you have to *say* about it. Should I get into your traces and find out about Kimmy?"

"*Please* don't, Star," I pleaded, absolutely panicked that she'd know how I'd thought of her while holding Kimberly.

"I won't," she said quickly, obviously feeling my distress. "But you're going to tell me, aren't you?"

When I didn't answer, she said, with a little pleading of her own, "Will you tell me what you can?"

"Yes," I answered, relieved that she seemed finally to be taking my privacy more seriously.

"Good. Now pay attention. I'm going to try and guide you into my traces so you'll know what's going on, or at least know what I know. Hopefully, we can do this without my having to grab onto your head. And don't worry, I haven't been so amorous as you, so you won't be embarrassed. Now relax. Drift back along my voice and see me."

Suddenly, I saw Star's face, then I was looking out through her eyes at a shiny, silver bracelet set with little blue stones. "That's pretty," Mother said as I held it up. "But it's a bit big. Kind of clunky."

"For *Spearl*, Mama," I said.

"Yes," Mother agreed. Then she laughed and said, "It would definitely look better on Spearl than on you."

Suddenly I felt it. I looked over at Mother and her eyes were wide. She'd felt something, too. "They've come," she said, her voice gone elemental.

"Who are they, Mama?" I asked, speaking *and* feeling Star's fear.

"It has something to do with Fargus," Mother answered.

Then I felt it and gasped. "You're *marked*!" I said to Mother, taking her hand in mine and looking at it intently. "Can't you see it, Mama?"

"No!" she told me. "What *is* it?"

I closed my eyes and placed Mother's hand on my cheek. Suddenly, shykik visions came to me like ghosts flying through my mind. "It cut you," I said, my voice tinged with Fierae lectrics. "A prison jar. What does it *mean*? I can't understand it!"

"The little glass jars Fargus used to trap elementals. Calm down. Search your memories."

"Masons!" I screamed, the shykik visions coming faster and harder. "They've come! Dire plans! An Apprentice accompanies, very strong, a Finished with terrible cunning. Mama! They've found you!"

I was in some sort of panicked state—not in my right mind. The visions were coming too fast, were too dire and dreadful. A glass cage, torment and rape. Single-minded evil justifying its means with dubious ends. I could feel the fire rising in my face, my eyes. I could feel terrible fear and anger welling up in me. "To ash!" I screamed, as Mother tried to drag me away from the booths and bobarkers of Ginny.

"No, Star!" she was crying, but I could feel the fire escaping me.

Suddenly, Mother and I were high above Ginny, cocooned with heat and rising fire. "Let it settle!" Mother was screaming. "Star, it will kill me!" Then she dropped out of the cocoon onto the lines and slid away from me.

Seeing Mother falling away caused the visions to stop. I regained control and damped down the fire. "Mama!" I called. "Wait!"

Mother looked back and saw me, eyes cooling, following her on the lines. She smiled and had the Zephrae stop her. I slid up next to her and also stopped. Though she wore a smile of relief, Mother said, "You *must* separate the shykik from the Fierae, Star! You almost cooked us both!"

"I don't think fire can hurt me, Mama," I said.

"Are you sure?"

"No."

"Do you really want to find out?"

"No."

"Do you want to turn your mother into crispy bacon?"

"Sometimes," I smiled. Mother squinted her eyes at me and I said, "No, Mama, I don't want to fry you."

"Then we work on this until it's under control, okay?"

"Yes, but what about…"

"Don't think about it, Star! It might take you again. You might have seared all of Ginny! We'll figure this out when we've gained you some control. Right now, listen for your brother, and I'll listen for your father. Make sure they're alright."

"They're at Thirest's bunker," I said. "They seem to be…"

"Fine," Mother finished with a sigh of relief. "Oh shite. Your father felt me. Now he'll worry."

"Spearl always feels me when I hear him. Nothing I can do about it, and, yes, they're worried. —*don't worry, we're well*— I don't think he can hear me! —*don't come, we are well*— Okay, he heard me that time, but guess what."

"I know, they're coming," Mother said. "Let's go! We should all be together, anyway. Something dire is stalking us."

When she said that I grew dizzy and said, "You are marked!" I was slipping back into that trance.

"Star!" Mother screamed, and the fire calmed back down. "*Please* think about something else. Can you charge my hands for me?"

"Can't you keep your hands charged, Mama?" I asked, but as I extended my own charge to her I realized she couldn't.

"I've always needed a little help with that, sweetie."

I was about to ask, help from who, when it came to me. "Blitz," I said. "Why won't he talk to me, Mama?"

"I don't know, Star," she told me. "He refuses even to speak of you, as if it causes him pain. The only thing he's ever told me is that you must never come out of your body."

"But why? And how could it harm Spearl?"

"I don't know, and as much as I am Fierae, I can't pretend to understand them. But I do know this, they are trying to plot traces."

When Mother said that, I felt startled and a bit faint. Finally, I said, "How can they plot traces? They'd be building irresistible futures. It's not possible."

"I don't know," Mother said, and I could see the pain in her face, in her eyes just trying to contemplate this impossible thing.

"Don't think about it, Mama," I told her. "It can't be done. Even shykik premonition isn't irresistible. Things are waiting to happen, but none of them can insist."

Suddenly the pain left Mother's face and she said, "Those are concerns quite beyond us right now. Let's find the boys and try to determine what it is that's coming for us."

"Coming for *you*," I thought, feeling my ire and flame stirring. "You are marked."

It took me some time to recover from following Star's trace. Feelings stayed with me that I didn't understand, and I found myself contemplating the idea of "plotting traces." Thoughts and ideas seemed to be coming from Jess knew where. It was Kimmy who brought me out of that reverie, when I saw her face very close to mine. She seemed upset.

"Spearl! Spearl!" she was calling as my eyes focused. "What's wrong?"

Suddenly, she seemed like the prettiest thing I'd ever seen, and I smiled. Kimmy's worried look vanished, and she smiled back. Then she gave me a little shove and said, "Don't scare me like that. You looked like you done left for good and all."

I was barely a moment from taking her into my arms, when she pecked me a little kiss and said, "Come on down for supper. Uncle's got it all laid out." Then she jumped up off the bed and I noticed she was blushing. "Maybe afterward we can take a walk by the cow-pond. It's awful pretty down there at night, if'n you take care 'bout the cow patties." Then she turned and skipped out of the room.

For a moment, I sat and could see her face again so close to mine, until I heard Star say, somewhat impatiently, "Where have you *been*?" Then I heard that giggle of hers and she said, "Oh! So *that's* Kimmy!"

I was panicked and angry, and sure Star had traipsed through my traces with Kimberly. But she calmed me, saying, "I *didn't*. But I couldn't help seeing her face in your thoughts just then. She's pretty. And you *will* tell me about it! No secrets!"

"Nothing happened," I thought to her.

"*Something* happened," she said, and I could almost see her grinning.

"Just hurry," I thought, "before something does happen."

I could feel her drifting out of my thoughts as she said, in what sounded like a whisper, "No secrets."

Smith had huge cow steaks and all sorts of vegetables heaped onto the table. "You lookin' better, Master Spearl," he said, those thumbs in his sospensors.

"Mother and Father are coming," I told him.

"Ain't even gonna ask how you knows, but I'm guessin' you got some of yer Papa's 'Prentice in you."

"Very little, I'm afraid," I told him. "I can't thank you enough for taking such care of me. And Kimmy, too," I said, smiling at her sitting there next to me, which inspired her most glorious blush ever.

For dessert, Smith brought out a sweet potato pie, and dollop-ed what he told me was "whipped cream" onto it. I'd never tasted anything so delicious, and said so. "That there is Kimmy's favorite, too," Smith told me. "Why don't you two chillen go walk off yer supper. Yer 'scused from chores tonight, Kim, since yer takin' such good care of Spearl. Git, now, 'fore I change my mind and strap aprons on you both."

Kimmy took me through a pasture that dove down to a little pond. "Mind you don't step in a cow flop," she said, nudging me playfully with her shoulder.

We sat in a little patch of grazed-short grass. The moon was a sliver that reflected in the water like a shimmering slice of silver melon. After a moment, Kimmy leaned against me and I put my arm around her. That little bit of moonlight softly lit her straw colored hair. Her skin seemed nearly as white as the whipped cream, and her blue eyes were so pale they looked like clear little ponds shimmering in her tender face. I could barely hear her as she whispered, as if on an intake of breath, "You could try out kissin' me again."

She was soft and warm and, at that moment, all I wanted in World. But it wasn't those things that were causing me to love her. Star was also all those things, and far more beautiful. But Kimmy was like *me*. She was human, and she cared about *human* Spearl. As we kissed I felt a love different from anything I'd ever known.

Love I'd never felt even for Star. Then I noticed Kim had started to tremble again, and she whispered, "If you want, you could do it to me now."

I immediately thought of Star again, and feared for my, and Kimmy's, privacy. "When I do it for the first time," I told her, "I want it to be with you. But let's wait a bit. I'm still worried about my family," I said, which was true, but in more ways than I was admitting. "Will you wait?" I asked her. "Because I'll do whatever you want. If you need me now..."

Kimmy placed her fingers on my lips and I saw a tear shimmering in her eye. "I need just what we have, Spearl. I need whatever you decide. I never felt like this before, I promise, and I ain't never rentin' out again. You were the first and the last. But I'll sorely miss you when your mama and papa takes you home, and I don't know how I'll keep from dyin'."

"Don't worry," I smiled. "I don't have much Apprentice in me, but there's one trick I *can* do, and it'll get me here pretty quick. And I'm going to ask your uncle if I can come back and see you, so you'll know I'm really coming. Okay?"

"And when you come back?"

"Yes," I told her. "But in a nice bed, with no cow patties around."

"I'd lie with you in a briar patch," she said, putting her head on my shoulder.

We sat there by that pond for hours. I can't tell you how tempted I was to love her...if it hadn't been for Star. She and I were going to have to come to an understanding. I could no longer abide her intrusions.

VIII
Changing Plots

When Kimmy and I came up from the cow-pond, we expected to find the inn dark and everyone asleep. But things were well lit, and we could hear voices and clinking mugs. Then I recognized Mother's voice saying, "You won so much at cards that night I was afraid Spaul and I would go home naked!"

"Oh, I'da left y'all *somethin'* to wear!" Smith roared, and I could tell he was in his cups. When Kim and I walked through the door, he said, "Here's some lovebirds now!" Then he placed his hand over his mouth and said, "Ooops, I done drunk too much wine."

There was something between Star and I that I still have trouble explaining. When I saw her standing there next to Mother, my heart leapt and I could see what I was feeling beaming from her face. Without any control or cognition, we ran to one another and embraced. "We survived," I whispered into her ear.

"Barely," she said into mine. Then she released me and said, "You'd better tend to your little girlfriend. She looks like someone just carved out her heart with a spoon."

Taking Star by the hand, I dragged her over to where Kimmy was standing. It hurt me awfully when I saw that she was trembling. "My *sister*!" I blurted out. Then I gathered my wits and said, "Kimmy, I want you to meet my sister, Star. Star, this is Kimmy." The relief that overcame Kim sent a tear sliding down her cheek. "Kimmy's been taking care of me," I said.

"I can tell," Star told me. "And she's so *pretty*. And you're *lovebirds*."

"Uncle's just a little bit drunk," Kimmy said softly, but her blush wouldn't be restrained.

Then Star leaned in and whispered to her, "I'm *glad*. Spearl deserves a girl as pretty as you."

"*Me?*" Kim exclaimed, and there was relief in that exclamation. Relief, I think, that Star seemed to approve of her. "When I saw Spearl huggin' the most beautiful girl in World, I almost wailed out loud."

"You're very kind," Star said, pretending modesty. "Why don't we girls go talk about my brother. I'll get us a mug of wine to share."

"'Kay," Kimmy said, smiling hugely, as if to say 'She likes me!' "You can come see my kittens."

"Can I have one, do you think?" Star asked.

"'Course you can. They're old enough."

"You better go give Mama a hug, Spearl," Star told me, as she and Kimmy walked away hand in hand. Star scooped up a mug of wine as they left, then looked back at me and winked.

There was a lot of wine drunk, and I think there was Maria in Smith's pipe, because I saw Mother and Father take a puff off it once. Star and Kimmy returned with a kitten each. At some point, Star got me alone and said, through her wicked smile, "So, you *haven't*, then. And, no, I wasn't in your traces. Girls talk to one another, Spearl, and wine makes us chatty."

"Please be nice to her, Star," I begged. "*Please*."

"You ask her if I've been nice. Go ahead, right now. I'll bet she loves me like a sister. But not as much as *you* love me. How much do you love me, Spearl?"

"How much wine have you had," I asked.

"Quite enough," she said, tossing her head back. "I'm going to bed. Father got me my own room, which means you must have *your* own room. Better lock your door tonight. There are pretty girls everywhere thinking about you."

Perhaps you have to love someone as much as I loved Star to become as angry as I was with her that night. When I *did* lock my door, Kimmy was already in my bed. She had had some wine, but not, it seemed, as much as Star.

I never thought once, or at least I no longer cared, about Star invading that trace, as Kimmy and I made our first love together. If it was clumsy, neither of us knew. When it was over, Kimmy kissed me hard and said, "Now we have to do it again."

Though I had no problem with that idea, I asked, "Why do we *have* to."

"'Cause my cousin Janie says it don't hurt at all 'cept the very first time, and I want to see."

52

"Did it hurt?" I asked.

"Just a tiny bit when you first put into me. After that it was very fine. Please do it again."

I tried to kiss her, but ended up grinning on her lips. "What's so funny," she asked, mock frowning.

"You don't ever have to say *please*," I told her. "All you have to do is smile for me." When I said that her eyes welled with tears and I asked, "What is it?"

"I love you, Spearl," she whispered. "Please say it back."

"You don't have to say please for that either," I told her. Then I locked her into our embrace again and said, "I love you, Kim."

I woke early and left Kimmy asleep in my bed. It wasn't quite dawn, and the inn seemed to be still asleep. But when I came down from my room, Mother and Father were sitting at a table, talking quietly and drinking tea. Mother's back was to me, but when Father saw me coming down, she turned and said, "You're up early. I'm guessing you stayed away from the wine."

"Apprentices should beware of intoxication," I told her, and Father smiled hugely.

"You look like a man with something to say," he said, furrowing his brow.

I hadn't expected this conversation. I'd come down to think about what I would say. But you can't plot traces, and this future had arrived. I took a deep breath and said, "I don't want to pine, Father. I've decided to keep her."

Mother's eyes grew wide and she looked at Father. "Keep who?" she asked. Then realization spread over her face and she placed her head into her hands. "Oh, no," she said.

"I love her," I announced.

"You aren't fourteen," Mother said through her hands.

"You know better than that, Mother."

"Well then, *she* isn't fourteen, yet!"

"How old was your mother when she and Grandfather found one another? How old were you when you left with Father?"

"I was almost seventeen!" Mother exclaimed.

Father laughed and said, "If only I'd known you were so *old*!" Then he took Mother's chin in his hand and said, "Spearl has made a decision, Pearl. I will *not* be party to keeping them apart."

But Mother said, gravely, "Something is coming, Spaul."

"Something is always coming," he smiled.

"Star is fragile right now..."

But father cut her off abruptly and said, "How could Star be anything but happy for her brother. Look at him, Pearl. *Look!*"

When Mother turned to me, Father said, "Will you watch him pine? Will you keep him from that pretty little girl he loves?"

Mother sighed and said, "No. Papa would tan my hide."

"So would I," Father smiled.

Mother smiled back and made a sound I can't quite describe. Then she asked, "Smith's daughter?"

"His poor 'parted sister's," Father told her.

Mother laughed into her hands, then sighed and said, "Better get her up and packed. We're leaving early."

I ran over and kissed her, then grabbed Father's hand and squeezed. "Thank you," I said.

I was about to run upstairs and tell Kimmy when I felt Star. She was coming. She was furious. From the top of the stairs she looked at me and said, "You *lied*!" Then she marched down toward me shouting, "Secrets, Spearl! Secrets!"

"Starshine!" Mother said sternly, but Star continued marching out the door.

"I'll go after her," I said, hot on her heels.

She hadn't gone far, was out by the corral fence where I'd gotten hushpuppies and a kiss. "You've been through the trace, haven't you?" I asked. Without waiting for an answer, I said, "Did you enjoy it? Was Kimberly to your liking?"

She'd had her back to me, but she spun around and said, "I couldn't finish. As soon as I realized what was happening, I left. It was making me sick!"

"That's vile, Star. It was the most beautiful moment of my life, the most loving feeling, and it made you sick?"

Tears didn't just well up in Star's eyes, they began flowing like streams, like rivers. Then she ran to me and threw her arms around my neck, bawling in great heaving gasps. "I'm sorry, Spearl. I don't know what's wrong with me. I want you to be happy. And she's lovely, really. I *do* love you too much. I can't separate Fierae from shykik, I can't separate Fierae from human. I feel like I'm losing you and I simply can't bear it."

After a moment of holding her tightly, I steeled myself and said, "Go back to that trace, Star. If you have to, go to Kimmy's trace..."

"Spearl!" she interrupted, and I thought for a moment she would slap me.

"I'm sorry," I said. "I don't know what to say. I don't know what you want."

"I don't know either," she said softly. "But I'll not be a voyeur. This is my fault, Spearl. You've always tried to be a good *brother*, and I've always pretended it was *you* who wanted *me*. I'm Fierae, Spearl," she said, crying harder, speaking in gasps. "And now you've found someone human, and my heart is broken!"

For some time I held her as she cried terribly, hysterically. Finally, she calmed down and eased herself off my tear soaked shoulder. "Don't tell Mama and Papa," she whimpered. "*Please*."

"Have I ever, Star?"

"No," she said. "You're a good brother." Then she wiped her eyes on my shirttail, kissed me on the lips and walked away back into the inn. If I hadn't had Kimmy upstairs for comfort, I'd have stood there alone and cried.

IX
Homecoming

When Grandfather Tool saw us all coming, he jumped high off the ground, looked up at the sky and hollered, "Thanky!" Then he ran to Mother and hugged her. He had Father by the shoulders when he noticed Kimmy holding my hand. "And who *dis*?" he asked after giving Star a kiss.

"This is Spearl's friend Kimmy," Father told him.

"Ah, Spearl, she a darlin's darlin'!" Then he took her away from me and hugged her as if she were long lost kin. "Welcome home!" he said, putting an arm around her and the other around me. "Come in de house! I done cotched two rabbit today. Gonna kill two bird and we all have a feast! Welcome home, y'all. Welcome home, darlin's!"

Grandfather's obvious love for Kimmy made me love her that much more. After our feast, I heard him in the kitchen with Mother, saying, "Gonna have *great* granbabies! If'n only Sia knew."

"She knows, Papa," Mother told him. "And don't count great granbabies before they're hatched."

But I heard Grandfather chuckle and say, "Can't see it? What kinda shykik you? She cookin' up great granbaby one right now."

"What makes you..." Mother began. Then she stuck her head into the dining room and saw me sitting there alone with a piece of pie. "Where is everybody?" she asked.

"Star and Kimmy are introducing their kittens to Rummy. Father said something about a tiny taste of corn, and I'm right here, if I count as somebody."

"Of course you do, sweetie. But go find Kimmy and bring her in for pie."

"She already..." I began.

"Bring her in for more," Mother insisted.

Suddenly, the conversation in the kitchen clicked in my mind and I started shaking. I ran to find Kim, wanting desperately to *know*.

I can't even remember my pretext for bringing her back into the house, but I think I said something stupid about Rummy being too old and those kittens might hurt him. Mother was waiting with slices of pie, which she handed to Kim and Star. "We already..." Star began.

"Have more," Mother told her. Then she took Kimmy by the shoulders and, looking hard at her face, said, "I think you've gotten a little sunburned, sweetie. I'll get you some aloe later."

Mother marched back into the kitchen, and I heard her say, "She is *not*!" Grandfather laughed to beat all helluva, and Mother said, "*You* are *bad*!"

For all of a week, Kimmy and I were like the very best of childhood friends, but with a wonderful secret between us. Star was nearly always with Mother. They were working on something together. Sometimes, while Grandfather was leading his muley around the yard with Kimmy on its back, I'd sit outside Star's door and listen to them. They were usually talking very seriously, but sometimes they argued. Occasionally, I'd hear Star weeping. Sometimes Father joined them. When that happened, there was no arguing or crying.

One morning, I rose early and left Kim asleep in our bed. Father was just getting up as well. He seemed still to be tired. "Father," I said quietly. "Can we talk?"

"Of course," he told me. "What's on your mind?"

"I feel like something's going on and I'm being left out. I know about what happened with Mother and Star in Ginny. Has it something to do with that?"

"Yes," Father said without hesitation.

"I know I don't have any talent to offer, but I want to help."

"It has nothing to do with your talent, Spearl. You and Kimmy are so happy, and we just don't want to spoil that. You two pretty much *are* the happiness around here right now."

"Nothing will stop us being happy, Father. I want to help."

"Then you will. Your mother is trying to get Star under control. Her shykik abilities are so strong they send her into trances and her Fierae side responds to her visions. It's very dangerous."

"What about the trouble they've seen coming?"

"Your mother and I have been working on that. She and Star also did some things, things I'm not sure I approve of, to throw our enemies off the scent, so to speak."

"What?" I asked. "What did they do?"

"Come on," he said. "I was just going in. We'll catch you up."

Father had been right about Kimmy's and my happiness. We'd been living on a pink cloud while my family sat under a dark one. It wasn't until I walked into that room that I realized I hadn't seen Star at all in three days. The sight of her startled me.

She was gaunt and thin. Her beautiful curls hung in oily ringlets. There were dark circles beneath her beautiful eyes. She seemed, just sitting there, to be angry and nervous. Still, when she saw me she leapt up and we embraced. "Where have you been?" she whispered in my ear.

"I'm here," was all I could think to whisper back.

Father got right to the point. "They are Masons," he began. "They've managed to come across the sea. Apparently, they sent a lone spy not long after Fargus marked your mother." At this point, Father shook his head and chuckled derisively. "This spy found his way to Ginny, right about the time practically every woman there was bearing a child. The tales he heard about "Queen Starshine" confused, but also excited him. We think he might have been able to track your mother by the mark Fargus put on her. But he was alone, and not more than a weak Apprentice. His task had been to gather information, and, if he was able, to kidnap your mother and sail with her back across the sea. But, as I said, he was weak. He was told that the 'Queen' had perished in a blaze. He inspected the remains of the cottage and found no bones. He was unsure. He suspected you mother was still alive, but he also thought she was the Starshine he'd heard about, and he was afraid. He'd seen the remains and results of Star's majick, and knew he was no match for this 'witch,' as the people of Ginny called her.

"Still, he searched for a sign, a *feeling* from that mark. He followed our path north to Mason Dicksem's line. But your Mother and I rose high above the line in a Zephrae cocoon, then rode lines a long way into the south. He lost our trail and became lost for years looking for her in the north. But not long ago, he wandered south again, and finally felt the calling of that mark. He knew your mother was alive, and decided, again afraid, to return across the sea and report. He was old and tired with those years of wandering and longed for home. But when he reported to his masters, those Masons, they began building a ship, and preparing a small army, more like a gang, to come and take your mother by force. They are somewhere near Ginny now, but they're a bit confused.

"It seems your mother and Star, with help from the Fierae, have managed to place a mark on the hand of every woman who is about your mother's age, *everywhere*."

"Not *everywhere*," Mother corrected.

"For hundreds and hundreds of klicks, all around!" Father said, his eyes wide. "Anyway, it will take them some time, but they'll almost assuredly find a way to tell the difference. They have a very cunning Finished with them."

"But how do you *know* all this?" I asked.

Star had taken her seat again, and Father looked over at her with sad eyes. It was Mother who answered. "Star can get into the traces, Spearl, you know that. Getting into traces of knowledge is easy for her, but getting into *people's* traces, people other than family, is very difficult, and very taxing. That's what we've been doing. That's how we know. But between that and working to control her abilities, well."

"You *let* her do this?" I asked, incredulous. "You *did* this to her?"

"Where were you?" Star whispered, looking down at her hands. Then she looked up at me with her eyes dimly glowing. "If you had climbed down off your little human wench..."

"Star!" Father exclaimed, and she quieted.

"Where?" she whispered, looking down at her hands again.

I left the room, angry, and Father followed. I turned on him and said, "How? How could you allow this?"

"I wasn't really aware of what they were doing until a day or two ago. Your mother told me they were trying to control Star's abilities, which was true. But she failed to mention...well. It's over now. Apparently, Star has gained some control and..."

"She was barely in control just now!" I shouted.

"She needs rest and sleep and food. I'm going to start making medicine for her today so she'll sleep long and hard. And you and

Kimmy are going to the beach to get sea-fish liver, lots of it."

"How can we go to the beach alone, Father? It's sixty or seventy klicks?"

"You're going to do our three-lines trick. And be careful what you say now, because I've heard you use Star's majick to call the Zephrae. Don't worry, I'm not going to ask how she did it, but I have a pretty good idea."

"What about the center line? What about my hand?"

"The lodestone will be *under* your palm, and Kimmy's hand will be on top of yours. I checked with your mother, and found that your hands will only be stuck together for a minute or two after you leave the lines. Apparently, ours had been stuck for much longer because your mother wanted it that way." When I smiled, Father said, "Yes, your mother was quite an imp back then. Be thankful Kimmy is merely a darling."

"But will the lines reach around and hurt her?"

"Your mother says no, but stop and check every once in a while. Look at her eyes, not her hand. See that she doesn't grow weak or faint. And both of you eat fish liver while you're at the beach. You'll have to spend a night there."

"We *might* could do it all in a day," I told him, "though Star's Zephrae only push at one speed, which isn't very fast. I'm also not as good as she is at calling fish."

"But you *can*, can't you? And you say you have no talent."

"Even Fargus could call fish," I told him.

"Yes," he said. "Maybe you're touched by the wee folk. Anyway, I want you to stay one night. Give Star a couple of days rest from you two. I won't say my daughter is jealous, but she feels a great loss. She misses you."

"But I've been right here," I said quietly, knowing it was very nearly a lie.

"I know, Spearl," Father said sadly. "And don't you dare let this affect you and Kim. That girl loves you dearly, and she's good and decent." After a moment he asked, "Do you truly love her, Spearl?"

"I can't even answer that with words, Father. She is *like* me, and loves me *for* me. And did you ever notice how pretty she is, especially in the moonlight?"

Father laughed. "She is *very* pretty, Spearl. I love her like a daughter."

"A human daughter," I said softly.

"Yes," he said with a sad smile.

X
The Last of Fun and Games

It took me a while to call up three lines. Father and Mother were seeing us off, but wouldn't help. "I don't want you to get down there and have to walk back," Mother said.

Once I managed it, I knew I could easily do it again. It was just a matter of figuring it out. Mother and Father waved as we slowly picked up speed, and I actually heard Mother giggle and say, "They're so *cute* together!" Soon, we were out of sight.

Kimmy seemed a little anxious at first, but when we got up to speed and she started laughing, I thought she'd never stop. At one point she shouted, "I got me a majickal boy, pretty as springtime! Eat yer heart out, cousin Janie!"

I had to laugh, but I shouted back, "Not so majickal. Most of this trick is thanks to Star."

When I said that she stopped laughing and said, very seriously, "I'd love you, Spearl, if'n you couldn't get up off yer arse!"

With the help of Star's Zephrae, we made it to the beach in half a day. I was surprised, really, that we'd done it so quickly. "Can you swim?" Kim called to me, stripping off her clothes in very short order.

"Of course I can swim!" I told her, coming out of my own and chasing her into the sea.

After we swam a bit, we stood in the tiny surf and I told her a bawdy little tale about a girl Apprentice and a boy Apprentice playing at love with Naiadae in the sea. "Then he carried her out of the ocean, and she said, 'Don't ever do that to me again, unless I absolutely beg you to'," I concluded. Then I added, "And they lived happily ever after."

Kimmy squealed her delight, then threw her arms around my neck and said, "Yer just gonna hafta do it to me the ol' reg'lar human way." I did.

Mother had given me earthen jars with big cork stoppers to put the fish livers in. They were cold to the touch, as Mother had majicked them that way. Kim absolutely refused to eat any liver. When a memory came to mind, and I told her she could eat it off my tongue, she said, "That's gross!" Then she added, "Not yer tongue, but yer tongue with fish liver on it."

I had a thin blanket in my pack, and we dug a cool little bed in the sand and spread it out. We were so happy, and so comfortable with one another, that we never dressed the entire time we were there. That night, as I held Kim in our dugout bed by the dying embers of our fire, I said, "We'll call out more fish in the morning—we have one more jar to fill—then we'll head home."

Kimmy rolled onto me and said, her face very close to mine, "Yer gonna *love* me in the morning, then we're gonna swim, then yer gonna call fish. I'll help."

"And how will you help?" I asked, giving her a kiss.

"I can tell where they are, specially the big 'uns."

"How do you do that?" I said, not sure whether or not she was kidding.

"Mama was Madama, used to read the cards, and she sometimes knew things that was gonna happen. I ain't got it so good as she did, but I always been able to tell where a big fish is gonna be. Uncle used to call me the fishin'-est little brat on two legs."

"You're not a brat," I said, kissing her again.

Then she became serious and said, "If I ever am, Spearl, you just tan my hide. Please promise me if yer ever mad with me that you'll give me a lickin' 'fore you stop lovin' me."

"Okay," I said, grabbing her up and throwing her across my lap. Then I lay my hand on her pretty bottom and said, "Are you ready?"

She was laughing to beat all helluva, but managed to say, "But I ain't *done* nothin' yet!"

"Well, *do* something," I said.

In a flash, she scrambled out of my lap, straddled me, and pushed my shoulders down into the blanket. "How 'bout I do this," she said, reaching down and joining us.

"Kim!" I exclaimed, as she started rocking back and forth. "You won't get spanked for *that*!"

In the morning, after loving and swimming, Kimmy showed me that she really could tell where the fish were. "Them ones you call markaral are swimmin' in a bunch just over there and about the width of this beach out in the water."

I wasn't actually sure how I called the fish out, but it mostly seemed like I did just that—*called* them. *Finding* them was always the hardest part. With Kimmy finding them for me, it became easy.

When the first one came flying out of the water, Kim squealed and ran to it, kneeling on it to stop it flouncing. "Be careful," I called. "They have teeth, you know!"

With the fish secured under her knees, she laughed and said, "Don't be a ol' fussbudget!"

"A what?" I called, and she laughed even louder. Then I stood and started toward her saying, "What did you call me?"

Her eyes grew wide and her grin enormous as she squealed again and ran away from me. But she didn't try hard enough to escape me, and I threw her over my lap and gave her the loveliest little spanking. That ended in another love-tussle, until we were so sandy we looked like big fried yard-birds. We dove into the sea to wash off, then came out and called up one more fish. Believe it or not, the exact same thing happened again.

Mother had sewn a long, thin pocket, sort of a sheath, on the outside of my pack. It was where I kept "Gryn." I asked Kimmy to get it for me so I could open up our fish and get their livers. As she handed it to me, she asked, "Where'd you git such a beautiful knife?"

"It's actually a short sword," I told her. "Star made it. Its name is Gryn."

"You named your knife?" she asked.

"Short sword," I said, opening the first markaral. "Yes. It's a *majickal* sword."

"How so?" she asked.

I stood with Gryn, which was dripping fish blood, and said, "Let's see." Then I stuck it into the sand with my hand about a foot away from the handle. I closed my eyes and called to it, kind of a cross between calling lines and calling a fish. Suddenly, and surprisingly, it was in my hand. Kimmy's eyes went wide, and her mouth dropped open. Then her lower lip quivered and she said in a voice filled with distress, "What're you doin' with me, Spearl? I'm just reg'lar human Kimberly, and yer a sure-as-helluva 'Prentice." Then she started crying, and said, "How long till yer bored of me?"

For some reason, this made me angry, and I grabbed her by the shoulders and said, "Don't you ever say that again, or I *will* tan your hide. Because it means you don't trust me. Do you think I've been lying to you? *Do* you? Is our loving a lie?"

"No," she whimpered.

Then I hugged her to me and said, "I know a couple of tricks, Kim, but I'm as regular human as you are. Shite, I can't even find fish the way you do. How long till you're bored with *me*?"

"Long as I draw breath, I'm gonna love you," she said into my ear.

"Me, too," I told her. "Do you believe me?"

"Yes," she said, as I wiped tears off her lovely, sunburned cheeks.

With our jars full and our packs ready, we took one more quick swim and then got dressed. "Ready to ride?" I asked.

"Ridin's fun. Can we do it more, once we're home, I mean?"

"Yes. We can go see your uncle, if you like."

"And show cousin Janie?" she asked, excitedly.

"I'll take her for a ride," I said.

"A *short* ride."

"Very short," I assured her.

I had no trouble calling up our three lines. In no time, we were heading west as fast as Star's Zephres would move us. We were just coming up out of the low country to where the land was drier, when we saw some men camped a little north of us. They looked as if they didn't belong, as if they were somehow foreign. I could see that a few of them wore swords, and there were several bows stacked against a tree. "I don't like their look," Kimmy shouted.

"Me neither," I told her. "But they're far enough away. We'll be past them in a minute."

Then I noticed that one of that group was far from his friends, and far closer to us. Suddenly, the others started yelling to him and he ran to maneuver himself right into our path. "Turn us away!" Kimmy cried.

"I can't change the lines that fast!" I told her.

"What'll we do? He's gonna snatch us up!"

"Keep your hand on mine!" I told her.

I'm not really sure how it worked, but I called to Gryn, and it came out of my pack to lay itself, business end forward, on our center line. Then it started sliding away from us toward the man blocking our way. I'm not sure if the man could see it, but the others did, and started yelling to him. Still, he didn't move. He was awfully close to us, but closer to Gryn. When my sword was almost to him, it began spinning furiously on that line. A moment later, it sliced his belly open like a split watermelon. Blood spurted out in bucketsful, and he fell away out of our path. As we went by him, Gryn spun itself clean of blood and then slid back into my pack. Several arrows flew by us, shot by those other men.

Kimmy watched the bloody mess of the man as we passed, and I said, "I'm sorry."

"Better we done to him 'fore he done to us," she said.

I was surprised by those words she'd chosen, that she'd said, "we," and I knew right then that everything we did after that would be done *together*. It was the first time I thought of us as "life-mates."

We rode our lines non-stop to home. When we were in sight of the house, I felt Star, and she came running out to greet us. She looked better than she had when we left.

"Something's wrong!" she was screaming. "I could feel it!"

When we stopped and slid off the lines, Star grabbed me into a hug and said, "I wanted to hear you, to run to your traces, but I was afraid. I *don't* want to ruin you and Kimmy! I promise, Spearl, I promise!"

Star *looked* better, but she was shaking, and her poor mind seemed fragile as ever. "You won't," I told her. "We *know* you love us."

"I do!" she said, letting me go and hugging Kim. "I do love you both. Now tell me what happened."

"I think *you* should tell *us*," I said. "Go into my traces—go into our ride home. There were men..."

As soon as I said that I could tell she was gone to the trace. It only took a moment or two before she was back. Light came into her eyes and she said, "It's *them*!"

XI
The Beginning of Dread

I expected to see Mother and Father come running out of the house. When they didn't, I said to Star, "Where are they?"

"Gone with Grandpapa to the big pond over the ridge. Mama looked in on you two once with her Zephrae, and said you might be a while coming back." As Kimmy blushed, Star smiled and said, "I guess she saw that the fishing was good. They've gone to catch me pond-fish livers."

"How do you feel?" I asked.

She looked at me and her eyes flashed brightly. "I feel *angry*!" she said, her voice going elemental. "They shot arrows at you! Their intentions were *not good*! Their time left alive is compromised."

I knew nothing would stop her going. "Star!" I shouted, as a huge chorus of Zephres gathered around her. "Star!" I screamed. "If you go without me, I *swear*..."

She looked at me with those glowing eyes, and her lips tensed into a line. Then she called in an elemental voice so loud it hurt my ears, "*COME!*"

"Spearl, don't you dare!" Kimmy screamed.

I slid Gryn out of my pack, and ran to Star. As I did, I pointed to the ridge and called to Kimmy, "Find Mother and Father. Go!"

Star cocooned us, and took us up hundreds of meters. Then she dropped us onto the lines and we went faster than I'd ever gone. She had something blocking the wind, and with nothing to slow us, and no screaming air, the ride seemed like a dream—or maybe a nightmare. It seemed like no time at all until we could see those men. I looked at Star, and thought she might just explode. "We need answers, Star," I told her, "not death! Put me down, then hover over them. They won't harm me with you up here."

"Not going to happen!" she said in that terrible voice.

Thinking fast, I said, "Do you want Grandfather to tan my hide? Remember what he said about my taking care of you if you're going to do wrong! Well, this is wrong, Star!"

Believe it or not, she smiled and seemed to settle just a bit. Then she said, her voice a touch more normal, "Alright, Spearl, you are the man. We'll do it your way. But if they *twitch* toward a weapon, if they make the slightest move against you...well...you *know*. I'm sure you know."

Star set me down fifty meters from that gathering of men, then hovered that far above their heads. I saw one look at a bow leaning against a nearby tree. "If you do," I shouted to him, "you'll be a tiny pile of ash before you touch it."

"Who is that, then?" one of them called in a strange accent.

I pointed Gryn toward Starshine and said, "That is Star of the Dread, a Fierae goddess. She put me here to ask you questions, which you will answer."

"That's the blade as killed Tommy!" one of the men shouted.

"Don't be stupid, now," I warned. "You've come across the Great Pond, haven't you?"

"That's so, and we ain't all!" one of them yelled. "We got dreaded blokes as can kick yer arses!"

"But they aren't here now, are they?" I said. "Where are they?"

"Lookin' fer *that*!" one of them shouted, pointing at Star. Then he moved so quickly I could barely make it out. Apparently he was hiding a bow behind his back. In a single motion he brought it around, and the next thing I knew, an arrow was in my shoulder and sticking out my back.

"NO!" I heard Star scream, and then all I could see was fire. All I could feel was heat.

The conflagration was still roaring when Star dropped down and cocooned us in Zephrae. Then she rose up and I could see a black circle of ash where those men had been. Star was hot to the touch, and her eyes were glowing like white hot coals. I could see her struggling for control, doing her best to settle her fire. "Can you hold the lines?" she asked me.

"Yes,"

"Where is your other gauntlet?" she asked.

"On Kimmy's hand." For some reason, that seemed funny and I laughed. I was feeling a little faint.

Star grabbed my hand and turned it palm up. Her own hand felt hot on mine. "We weren't on that long," she said. "No real damage. But you *can't* hold the lines, can you?"

"Feeling a little fuzzy," I said.

"Climb onto my back, *now!*" she roared.

I did, and hung onto her the best I could. The Zephres dropped us, and the rest was literally a blur.

I woke up in my bed with a tight bandage wrapping around my shoulder and back. There was a tiny round spot of red in the center. My other shoulder felt wet, and held Kim's sleeping head. The door to my room was open, and I heard Star say, "He's awake."

Then everyone came into the room. The commotion woke Kim, who looked at me and started to cry. "Don't you ever do that again," she wept, "or I'll give you a lickin'."

"How do you feel?" Father asked.

"Ever been shot through with an arrow?" I asked.

"I'm getting him something for pain," Mother said, turning on her heels and leaving the room. She went quickly, but I saw the tears in her eyes.

"You see that!" Kim said, still weeping. "You made yer mama cry!"

"I don't want *anybody* crying," I said, wrapping my good arm around her and pulling her to me. Then I whispered in her ear, "It's only my shoulder. Don't be a fussbudget."

"I'm gonna git you fer that," she wept.

"Tonight," I told her.

Star heard me and said, "It *is* night. You've been out for two days."

"Most of that was your mother's potions," Father told me. "I had Star flash-burn the arrow out of you, which cauterized the wound pretty well, but I'm guessing it was painful."

"It's pretty painful, now," I said. "But I don't remember anything after..." then it all came back to me, maybe a dozen men incinerated in a flash.

Mother was back in the room and held up my head to drink something foul tasting. "Don't think about it now," she said, seeing the distress on my face.

"Star," I said.

"They *shot* you, Spearl," she exclaimed. "I should have made them suffer!"

I saw Father's hand move reflexively, and was sure he was going to slap her. But Mother put her arm around Star and led her out of the room. As she left, she looked back at Father and shook her head.

Grandfather was the last to leave, other than Kimmy, who would not be moved. Before he left, he put his hand on my good one and said, "You was doin' *right*, wasn't you, Spearl?"

"I was trying," I told him.

"Comes to what's right," he said, "tryin's doin'."

When they were gone, Kim lay her head on my shoulder again and began crying softly. "I'm okay," I told her. "I promise."

"I ain't weepin' for you," she said. "I'm weepin' for *me*. Yer mama told me no lovin' for at least a week."

"Don't worry," I chuckled. "We'll get around that."

"Oh no we won't," she said, wiping away her tears and stifling her sniffles. "We ain't goin' 'gainst yer mama. You need all yer strength to heal, she said. But after that week's up, yer gonna need all yer strength to make up for that week!"

Father and Mother and I went over what happened time and again. Mother mostly kept Star away from those conversations. One night, after I told them, for the thousandth time, about Kimmy's and my ride home on the lines, Mother asked, "Where *is* that knife of yours?"

"Short sword," I told her.

We were in my room, and my pack was sitting against a wall. Without even realizing I was doing it, I held out my hand and thought, 'Gryn.' In a flash, I was holding it in my hand. Father smiled, but Mother frowned and told him, "That was *not* Apprentice majick."

"Then what...?"

"Look at the color," she said. "Where have you seen that very color before?"

"It does seem familiar," he told her.

"Bring it outside, Spearl."

We went out into the night, and Mother said, "Hold it up and call to it."

When I did, Mother and Father looked at each other with surprise on their faces. Mother said, in a hushed exclamation, "Linea Clipses!"

"What?" I asked.

"Can't you see them?" Father asked.

I looked closely at Gryn, and decided it might be glowing ever so slightly. "Is Gryn glowing?" I asked.

"Yes," Father said, "but you can't see the lines, can you?"

"There are fat lines the color of Gryn between World and the moon," Mother said. "Gryn is somehow tied to them"

"That could be dangerous, couldn't it?" Father asked.

"*Could* be?" Mother told him.

Then Star, who had joined us without our knowing, said, "Beautiful, aren't they?" I turned and saw that she was looking up into the sky. "If you try to take it from him, try to hide it, it will destroy any barrier to get back to him. Bury it a thousand meters deep, and the lines will tear open World to let it out. It knows him now. Had Spearl seen the arrow coming, Gryn would have carved it to splinters. Soon it will see these things *for* him. I told you once, Mama, that I would protect him."

"Star," she said, "You have to unmake this thing." But when Mother said that, the ground trembled, and for just a second I thought I saw green flashes in the sky.

"Shall I unmake World, Mama. This thing is *done*. To unmake it would call down the moon." Then she turned and walked back into the house.

Star wasn't kidding about Gryn always finding me. If I walked more than a hundred meters away from it, I would find it in my hand. One day, Mother came to me with a beautiful leather scabbard and belt, both died green. "You're going to have to carry it, Spearl. You can carry it in your pack when you're traveling, but I'm afraid it might harm someone trying to get to you if you go off and leave it behind. Do you understand what a dangerous thing your sister has wrought? I've been trying to find a way to undo it, but it seems hopeless."

"Can you ask the Fierae about it?" I said.

"Blitz was adamant about doing nothing. He used words I didn't know, but I got the idea."

"What did he say?"

"He said, 'Don't fuck with it'."

Like Star, I knew all Inglish words, old and new, and couldn't help laughing.

"What does it mean?" She asked.

"It means don't swerve with it," I told her, knowing she'd remember that word.

"How could you…"

"Forget it, Mother. It means leave it be."

Then Mother got the serious look on her face that always frightens me. "Spearl, your father and I are going to be leaving for a while."

"Oh?" I said, waiting for the big foot to fall.

"We want you and Kimmy to go to Smith's while we're gone, and we want you to take Star with you. Maybe from there you could all make a journey, perhaps to Thirest's bunker. You might even visit the House Town pile."

"Are you done?" I asked.

"Done what, sweetie?"

"Beating the bush around. You *know* I'll do what you and Father ask of me. I may not have a nit's worth of talent, but I follow Apprentice ways, and if anyone's *Finished*, it's you two. So tell me exactly what's going on and it will save me the time and trouble of finding out for myself, which you know I will. I have a twin, if you recall, who will do anything for me. I'm guessing, whatever you're up to, she probably knows already."

"I truly hope not. I can keep her out of Spaul's and my traces, but I'm not sure if I can keep her out of yours. In fact, I doubt it."

"I don't think she'll go to my traces unless I ask her to, Mother. In that regard, she's trying to behave. She knows how much I love Kim. Actually, I think it *scares* her how much I love Kim."

"What I'm afraid of, Spearl, is how much Star loves you."

"Well," I said, "she has a serious aversion to being a voyeur, and she'd have to step pretty lively in my traces to avoid *that*." Then I felt myself blush as I realized what I'd just said.

Mother smiled and said, "Yes. Well, then."

After a little silence, I said, "You're plotting traces, Mother. Tricky business. You never know, maybe I can help. Spill the beans."

"Beans? Oh yes, something your father heard from Thirest. That man must have been a walking book on ancient sayings."

"So?" I pressed.

"We've decided those Masons, or whomever they are, need saving. They're no match for Star. We went to the sight, the place where you were shot, and there was *nothing*. Not even bones. There were sandy places that had been turned to glass. We need to get those idiots onto their boat and back across the sea before they do something stupid and Star turns them all into a bit of ash."

"But can you and Father handle them without Star?" I asked.

"If they made me angry enough, Spearl...well, let's hope it doesn't come to that. Save them from Star and deliver them to Drea."

"You can't become Drea anymore, Mother. Not without Starshine on your sea."

"*Half* of Drea was Blitz before she became Starshine, and I am much more Fierae now than I was then. Anyway, and trust me on this, even half of Drea would be twice anything they could conjure, though it would be a dangerous piece of majick to perform, perhaps deadly dangerous. Things would have to be dire indeed for me to try it."

"They've heard of a female Apprentice, Spearl, and have decided they could take a lovely boat ride across the sea, snatch her up, and take a lovely boat ride home. Hopefully I can convince them, while they still have bones, to go back and not, what did Blitz say? Not *fuck* with me."

"So you want me to get Star out of the picture?"

"The farther she is from your father and me, the less likely she'll become aware of whatever goings on are going on. If there *is* a fight, I'm afraid she'd want to be in on it. As far as she's concerned, they are *all* to blame for that arrow in your shoulder. Yes, I want her out of the picture."

"See," I said. "Wasn't that easy."

"You've got to be careful with Star, Spearl. I almost wish you hadn't found your love for Kimberly."

"Mother!"

"Oh, Spearl, honestly! *Incest?* Apprentice rules? Love is above rules. And though Blitz won't tell me what their plan is, what traces they're 'plotting,' it's possible the Fierae meant for you and Star to be together. You're the only one, the only thing that can calm her, that might could tame her."

"If that's the trace they tried to plot, it makes a good case that it can't be done. If the Fierae plotted Star and I together, circumstances certainly did, quite easily, foil them. Everything conspired to bring Kimmy and I together. Even Star played a part. And now that we *are*, I can tell you that nothing could have stopped it."

"Fate I don't understand, Spearl, but if you believe you and Kim were fated, I won't argue. I've seen you together. I saw her devotion to you when you were wounded. And I'm not saying I want you and Star together that way. All I'm saying is things might have been better if you'd *both* wanted it that way."

"Or if we'd both been born human," I said.

"Yes," Mother said. "What beautiful human twins you'd have been. But you aren't, Spearl, and more and more I'm beginning to suspect that *neither* of you are. The Fierae are both male and female. You two may have been their attempt to create a Fierae-human. I've heard Star say more than once that you two are very nearly the same person."

"Same mind, is what she said to me."

"If what I suspect is true, Spearl, your sister is like a ground charge trying to get to her air charge. Trying to get to *you*. She can see you, even touch you, but she can't join, can't become whole again. It would be a torment you and I could never imagine."

Neither of us said anything for a moment, and I think we both knew Mother's speculating was probably true. Finally I whispered, "My poor sister."

"What lovely human twins you'd have been," Mother sighed.

The plan, though this time the word "plot" is more appropriate, was for Kim, Star and I to leave for Smith's without Star knowing that Mother and Father were heading north as we did. Star seemed physically better. In fact, if it were possible, I'd say she'd grown even more beautiful. Her eyes were almost always ever-so-slightly glowing, and she was flawlessly and silkily the color of caramel candies. Sometimes it seemed her skin glowed as well.

Once, just before we left, Kimmy and I were out feeding old

carrots to Grandfather's muley. It was dusk, and the light of day had gone a rusty amber. Star walked out of the house dressed scantily, as was becoming her custom, and I heard Kim's little, startled gasp when she saw her in that light. "I ain't never been much partial to girls," she said softly, "but that kind of beauty is soul-touchin'. I'm gollam glad she's your sister."

"Watch your language," I scolded. Then I pulled her to me and said through a kiss, "It's unbecoming from such a pretty girl."

Star played along when told of the "adventure" we were to embark on, but I had no doubt she knew *at least* that all was not as advertised. "I'd love to travel into the Purchase," she told me, "and to see Thirest's bunker. And we *must* go down, as you and Papa did, and look out over the Florida—maybe take Kimmy for a ride on the lines to see crocodiles. Unless you think it would scare her," she smiled.

"It wouldn't scare her because she trusts us, Star," I told her.

When I said that, it seemed the light in her eyes dulled just a bit and she said, softly, "I mustn't break that trust."

XII
Dark Star

Kimmy and I shared the lodestone, and Star rode beside us on her own lines. "Mama's right," she called to us once we got started. "You two *are* cute together!"

As Star was with us, we could easily have ridden to Smith's in a day. But we'd decided beforehand to camp one night and arrive at Smith's the following morning. When we stopped, I told Kimmy, trying my best to keep a straight face, "I'll catch us a mush-rat for dinner."

"Oh no you won't!" she announced, just before I started laughing. "I got all sorts of goodies for us to eat in my pack!"

While Kimmy was unpacking our dinner, Star said to me, "I'd eat a mush-rat with you." It actually startled me how seductive she'd made those words.

A little taken aback, I said, "You wouldn't like it. I was only kidding."

But she gave me a smile that truly worried me, as I remembered Mother saying, "It would be a torment you and I could never imagine."

We hadn't brought a tent, as Star had promised the weather would stay fair. Even if it hadn't, she could easily keep rain from falling on us. After our dinner, Star stoked the fire up a bit, and pulled a big jar of wine from her pack. "Let's pass this around," she said, her smile gone a bit feral, "and I'll tell a story."

"That sounds like fun," Kimmy said, grabbing onto my arm and giving it a squeeze.

When we'd all had a swallow or two of Star's strong wine, she began her tale. "Though they usually stay hidden," she said in a hushed and tantalizing voice, "the Fairae in these woods are notorious for stealing boys. One night, not long ago, a boy named Jasper was traveling along the Ninety-five, when he stopped for the night at this very spot. But before he lay down to sleep, he saw little lights flickering in amongst the trees—*just like those*!" she said, pointing behind us.

Star's tale telling voice was haunting, and Kimmy started and looked back to where she was pointing. Sure enough, little lights were sparking there in the darkness. "Fairae," Star breathed.

Kimmy grabbed hold of me tightly, but giggled. She didn't know Star as well as I did, of course, but was aware, especially when she saw my smile, that she was creating those "Fairae."

"Jasper became hypnotized by those lights," Star continued, "and walked off into the trees to get a better look. Now, most people don't know this, but Fairae, and their cousins the Fire Sprites, can breathe ether into the noses of pretty boys who wander into their demesne."

"What's ether?" Kimmy asked in a hush.

"Something that makes you very sleepy," Star told her in a seductive voice.

"What's Demesne?" Kimmy asked.

"Their domain. Jasper wandered *into* their domain, and became sleepy and faint breathing their ether."

"Uh oh," Kimmy squeaked, hanging onto me tighter. Star seriously had her going.

"Before long, Jasper had to sit down, so dizzy was all that ether making him. When he did, a tiny, beautiful girl with shimmering dragonfly wings hovered in front of him."

I have no idea how Star managed this next part, but for just a second or two, a shimmering apparition of a tiny girl with wings hovered in front of our eyes. Had she somehow placed this picture in our minds, or had she arranged it with the Zephres and Naiadae?

Kimmy, now embracing me tightly, looked up to see my reaction. When I smiled at her she relaxed a bit, then whispered, "That Fairy girl ought to put somethin' on."

Star continued without missing a beat as her little apparition faded away. "Fairae don't wear clothes," she said, "and they had a mind to get Jasper out of his."

At this point Kimmy was becoming enthralled with Star's tale. After taking another sip off the wine jar, she asked, "What was they gonna *do* to him?"

"Well," Star said, after causing our fire to dim just a bit, "Fairae girls like to dally with human boys, but it's very hard for them to do because they're so tiny. What they needed was a human girl they could inhabit in order to play with the boy they'd caught. But Jasper had come alone.

"The Fairae, however, are very patient, and have songs with which to call humans to them from far distances. Soon they were singing a song to call a girl so they could play with Jasper. Listen, you can hear it."

"I can hear it," Kimmy whispered, and I noticed her eyes were staring into the distance.

"Before long, a very pretty girl walked into the Fairae demesne, and they lighted on her, linking their little minds to hers."

Suddenly, Kimmy's grip on me loosened, and I noticed she was sweating. But when she moaned, I could see she was actually dripping with Star's Naiadae, and beginning to squirm.

"Play with our captive boy," Star continued, her eyes wide with devilry and her grin as wicked.

"Star," I said, but she kept on.

"Come out of those clothes and play," she grinned, as Kimmy started untying the thin blouse she wore.

"Star!" I insisted.

Suddenly our fire leapt up high and bright, and Kimmy came out of her trance. "Wow," she said, wiping her brow. "That was some story. Yer the best story teller, Star."

"Yes, I am," Star said, grinning at me.

"Take me to bed, Spearl," Kimmy said. "I think I drunk too much wine. I've done sweat myself soaked."

I looked over at Star and shook my head disapprovingly. Then I made up a bed and lay Kimmy down on it. "How do you feel?" I asked her.

"Too much wine," she said, blinking her eyes sleepily.

I held her in my arms, but in less than a minute she was asleep—too much wine or too much Naiadae. I wasn't sure which, but I wasn't happy. I probably should have just let it go, but I was angry and decided to go talk to Star. She was waiting for me.

"What are you doing?" I asked her.

"Getting ready for bed. How 'bout you?" she smiled.

"How long would you have let that go on?" I asked.

"Until you stopped me," she said matter-of-factly. "If you'd been inclined to play the part of Jasper, who knows, you might have enjoyed it."

"I thought you weren't going to be a voyeur," I said, anger, perhaps mixed with just a touch of fear, entering my voice.

But Star dismissed it as a joke. "Oh, I wouldn't have, really. It was just harmless fun. She won't remember it at all, I promise." Then her look became serious, and she said, "She won't wake till morning. Come sit by me and talk a bit."

At this point, I felt like I was the one having a bit of ether blown up my nose. I went and sat next to her on her blanket and said, "You played with Kim as if she were a toy, Star, and she's *not*. Are you playing with me right now?"

"No," she said through a little pout. "How could you think that of me?"

"Then what is it you want?"

Star's face very suddenly became pleading, and I immediately felt sorry for her. "*Please*," she whispered. "I *need* you, Spearl. It feels like something trying to claw its way out of me."

The love I knew for Star—and still feel to this day—was immense, and my heart ached for her. The look on her face was nothing less than anguished. But she really *wasn't* doing anything elemental to me, and I said, "There may have been a time, Star, when I could have done this...if you were...tormented. But Kimmy wouldn't understand."

"She'd deny you," Star asked in an incredulous tone, "if you felt desire to dally with another girl?"

"I don't think she'd be jealous of play," I said, "if that's what you're suggesting. Who knows, maybe she'd play, too. But I *have* no such desire, and if it were *you* I desired, it would hurt her. She knows the love you and I have, and it would be too much for her if we had that, too."

"Then we won't tell her," she said, taking my face in her hands and kissing me.

I was sure there was nothing elemental in that kiss, and that's what worried me. Before I knew, my arms were around her and I was returning it. But my mind began a furious debate, saying, "Rules!" At the same time, it said, "You must do this for Star." It said, "Kimmy will be hurt!" as my hands pulled Star to me. Then I heard my father say, "You *are* an Apprentice, Spearl."

What part of my mind won, I can't be sure, as the very ferocity of the debate caused me to hold Star away from me and then get to my feet. "I love you, Star, but I can't do this," I said. Her skin was definitely glowing. She'd been hot to the touch as we'd embraced. "And I think it would probably kill me if we did," I told her. "You're already very nearly too hot to handle."

"That's just *human* heat, Spearl, and it's all for you. I'd never harm you."

I started to walk away, but heard her crying. I didn't dare take her into my arms again. "I'm sorry, Star. I really am," I told her.

"I know," she said, stifling her tears. "I'm sorry, too. Forgive me?"

"Nothing to forgive," I said, though, considering what she'd done to Kim, that wasn't exactly true.

The next morning Kim seemed unaffected by Star's tricks. In fact, she was well rested and anxious to continue our journey. As we packed up our bedroll, she said to me, quietly, "I'm sorry I got myself so wine sleepy last night. I missed lovin' you out under the stars. But maybe it's better we didn't with poor Star all alone."

Why I said what I did just then is a mystery to me. I've often wondered if Star's "fairy" had placed the thought in my head, or was the thought simply too enticing to stay out. "What if Star wasn't my sister, and I'd wanted you *both* in my bed last night?"

Kimmy's reaction was strange. She seemed to be thinking about it quite seriously. After a bit of this thinking, she blushed, looked up at me through her lashes, and said with a strange little smile, "Gol*lam*, it's a good thing she's your sister."

I never have investigated how they managed it, but Mother and Father got word to Smith that we were coming. Though no food was as yet laid out, he had a table set with a clean, white cloth, fine white candles, and what had to be his very best china. He was so happy to see us, he actually grabbed me into a bear hug and picked me right up off my feet. Then he went to Star and said, "I don't dare squeeze you, darlin'. I'm afraid I'd get carried away and break you. You're as lovely as your mama!"

"Go ahead and squeeze me, Uncle Smith," Star said, and I remember thinking, "Uncle Smith" was a bit much. "I won't break. Ask Kim."

"Don't you make her mad!" Kimmy warned.

Smith gave Star a little squeeze, taking care to keep his dirty apron away from her. Then he marched over to Kim, looked down at her and said, with a serious look, "Have you been behavin', girl?" Then he turned to me and said, "You haven't had to tan her hide, have you, Spearl?"

Kimmy blushed and looked at me, her eyes begging that I not tell about our time at the beach. "Not yet," I said, to Kim's relief. Then I added, which *really* made her blush, "But I'm afraid she might like it."

Smith guffawed, then gave Kimmy her hug. "I ain't never had to tan this one," he said, pulling her off the ground. "Not one of my daughters as 'spectful as this 'un. Don't tell 'em I said that, o' course."

Smith fed us till we were about to burst, then insisted we go look at our rooms. He had Kimmy's and mine made up with sheets dyed pale blue, and new indigo curtains on the window. There were flowers everywhere, and the smell was intoxicating.

I'm not sure how he managed it, but Star's sheets were the same color as her eyes, and the room was full of lilacs. Star seemed genuinely touched, and wrapped her arms around his girth, dirty apron and all.

"Now, don't get yerself dirty huggin' ol' Smith," he said with a little blush of his own. "You chillen go play in the pasture. I got chores."

When Smith retreated to his kitchen, Kimmy said, "Y'all 'mind him of yer mama and papa. He loves them dearly, you know."

"Mama says he loves taking their silver at cards," Star smiled.

"That, too," Kimmy grinned. "But you ask Spearl 'bout how Uncle worried when he came here all alone 'cause Papa had gone after Mama and you," she said, falling into her habit of calling our parents her own.

"I will," Star smiled. "I'd like to know *all* about that time. I'd like to know how you two became such lovebirds."

"Ain't nothing to tell," Kimmy said shyly. "I loved this boy the very moment I set eyes on him."

"Me, too," Star chuckled, "though my vision was a little blurry at the time."

The three of us walked down through the pasture to the pond. It was a very warm day. The water looked clear and cool, and was rippled by a tiny breeze. Suddenly, Star announced, "I'm going for a swim!"

In a moment, she was out of her clothes and diving into the pond. When she came up, she called, "It feels *so good*!"

Kim and I looked at one another, but said nothing. Finally, Star called, "Don't tell me you two are gonna be *bashful*."

Kimmy's eyes widened at me, and she said, "*I* ain't bashful!" In a minute she was in with Star.

There was nobody in that pond who hadn't seen me naked. I followed Kimmy in. But I had my reservations. I knew what Star craved, though, as Mother had said, I couldn't know the extent of it. But it seemed to me she was taking every opportunity to press the issue. I honestly began to fear that she'd try to seduce Kimmy. Then I thought about those Naiadae that night of the Fairae tale, and my concern heightened.

But nothing other than splashing and horseplay occurred in the pond, much to my relief. After we let the breeze dry us a bit, we got dressed and walked out to visit the cows. All in all it was a pleasant afternoon that gave me some hope about Star's condition. Perhaps she was done playing elemental tricks. Actually, she was. Instead she resorted to a far more potent trick—the truth.

That night, Smith was showing me a card game. It was getting late, and I suddenly realized I hadn't seen Star and Kimmy in quite a while. "Where are the girls?" I asked.

Smith looked around and said, "Don't know."

"Well," I told him, "I'd better go find them. I'm going to be traveling with them for a while. If I let them, they'll end up conspiring to have their way the whole time."

"And they'll get it, more'n likely," Smith smiled.

"Ain't it so," I chuckled, hoping like helluva that he was wrong.

I left Smith playing a one person game called, "Solitary." "Sleep well," he called as I went up the stairs.

Kimmy's and my room was empty and dark, but I noticed light coming from under Star's. At first I heard nothing from in there, but when I listened carefully, I thought I heard the soft sounds of weeping. I placed my ear closer to the door, and heard Kim and Star crying gently. "I'm so sorry," I heard Kimmy whisper to Star.

"It's the truth," Star wept. "But I want you to ask Spearl. I want you to know I wouldn't lie to you about this."

"I'll talk to him," Kimmy told her. "But I don't know what we can do. We have to talk, and I need to think."

"It's all I can ask," Star said.

When I opened the door, Kimmy was holding Star, who was crying on her shoulder. Seeing me come in, Kim kissed Star on the forehead, then came and led me out of the room. "What's wrong?" I asked.

"You know," Kim told me, leading us into our room. "And I wish you coulda told me. Don't get me wrong, I don't blame you for not tellin', but it musta been a hard secret. It musta hurt you somethin' awful."

"What did she tell you?" I asked.

Star had told Kimmy *everything*. About how she wasn't human and was living as half a person. She told her she needed me so badly, she was afraid it might kill her. It was an incredible admission for Star to make to Kim, and I could find no word of it that wasn't true.

I knew there were parts that Kim didn't understand. She barely managed to pronounce "aneke'lemental." But I had no doubt that she believed Star, and felt terrible for her and her predicament. I was expecting, at any moment, for her to tell me to go in there and love my sister, and I'm not sure what I'd have done if she had. Instead, she surprised me and said, "We got to find Star a boy, Spearl."

When I laughed, she said, "What?"

"It's *me* she wants, Kim. It's *me* she needs."

"I know I ain't smart, Spearl, but I ain't stupid either. I *git* all that. She's a neklamental, and she's cravin' her other half. And *you*, bein' her twin, are that other half. But *we* are *human*, Spearl. You and me both know what yer papa'd say. Unless it's what *you* want, too." she said, her voice dropping off to a hush. "Is it, Spearl?" she asked, her eyes starting to mist.

"If that's what I wanted, Kim, it would have happened long ago. I only want you," I told her.

Then she looked down at her hands and said, "I wouldn't get jealous, you know, if you ever took a notion to play, you know, with another girl. But I wouldn't be able to help it if it was Star. 'Cause if you ever love Star, it'd just be a matter of time till you forget all about me."

"I'd never..." I started, but she interrupted.

"If Star ever gets whole with you, please send me on my way, 'cause you *know*, Spearl. You *know*. And when that day came that yer eyes set on me and didn't see a thing, it'd squeeze my heart right out of my chest."

"I never did it *before* I found you, Kim. I'm certainly not going to now that I have."

"Then let's find her a boy."

"I don't think..." I began, but was interrupted again.

"Well it sure as helluva couldn't *hurt*!" she insisted.

"How many boys do you know?" I asked, grabbing her and pulling her to me.

"Not many," she giggled. "But cousin Janie knows a passel."

The following morning, I heard Kim say to Star, "We need to be alone a bit, okay?"

"Okay," Star agreed.

Then Kim grabbed my arm and said, "Let's go. Star's gonna play Old Maid with cousin Meg."

"Where are we going?" I whispered.

"To see cousin Jane."

Janie, once she'd had a little ride on the lines, would have stood on her head in a cow-pie if we'd asked it of her. She was, to say the least, awed. Kimmy took her by the arm and walked her a little ways off. When she asked the question about a boy for Star, Janie looked back at me, and I heard her say, "Is she half as pretty as her brother?"

Kimmy punched her on the arm and said, "I *ain't* sharin', so git it out of yer head." Then she looked at me and smiled.

"So? Is she pretty?" Janie pressed, rubbing her arm.

"She's the gollamest most pretty thing as ever lived, no shite. But she's shy, so think up somebody that'll be...you know...gentle."

"Is it gonna be her first time?" Janie asked.

"*Yes*, it's gonna be her first time! That's why I want somebody gentle."

"'Cause it hurts that first time, don't it?" Janie said with an I-told-you-so look.

"I reckon, if you get some clodhopper that just shoves it in like he's buggerin' sheep!" Kimmy said, to which both of them squealed with laughter.

Finally, Janie said, "I know just the boy. I'll send him around after supper tonight. But you better make sure she's gonna put out. I don't want him comin' back 'spectin' me to take a squirt 'cause Spearl's darlin' sister changed her mind. I got a good thing goin' with Charles that lives up on the hill, and I don't want to mess it up."

"Don't worry," Kimmy said. "You just make sure he promises to be gentle."

When we got back, Star was actually playing Old Maid with Smith's daughter. When the game ended, Kim said, "Come on upstairs, Star. I've got a surprise for you."

When I joined them on the stairs, Kim said, "Maybe Star and I should talk about this alone."

"Oh no you don't," I said with a smile. "You got me into this, you aren't leaving me out of it, now."

"Let Spearl come," Star said. I think she was anticipating an entirely different surprise.

The girls sat facing one another on Star's bed, and Kimmy took her by the hands. I sat in a little chair against the wall, trying like helluva to get the grin off my face.

"Tonight," Kim began, "after supper…a boy's gonna come callin' on you."

"A boy?" Star said, her eyes gone wide.

"I know it ain't what you been cravin', Star, but Spearl and I talked, and there's just too many reasons that ain't gonna happen. So *please*, give this a chance. If'n yer chawin' at the bit, so to speak, it sure as helluva can't hurt."

"You mean you want me to…" Star began. Then she looked over at me, trying for all I was worth to stop grinning. "Maybe you should go play Old Maid," she said.

"You're not going to be *bashful*, are you?" I smiled.

Star turned right back to Kimmy and said, "You want me to *do it* with this boy?"

"If'n y'all go halfway, it's liable to just make it worse," Kim said, giving me a sideward glance that made me wonder about our first encounter. "Yer in a bad way, sugar. You need to hook up the buggy and ride."

At that point, laughter was squeaking out of me. Kim looked over, eyes squinted, and said, "Go!"

I jumped up, knocking over my chair, and scurried out of there. I managed to stay silent as I listened through the door.

You'd think all this would have made Star angry. This was not what she'd had in mind when she told Kimmy the truth. But Star had a very human side, which I believe was often at war with her aneke'lemental self. I could tell, from my perch at the door, that she was actually touched. Not only by the fact that Kimmy was trying to help her, but that she was definitely loved by this pretty little girl who so loved her brother. I heard them, through that door, become confidantes. "Janie told me he's pretty as a peach," Kimmy told her. "A little older than us, but he ain't gonna be pushy. You just tell him to go slow, and it'll hardly hurt at all."

"It *hurts*?" Star asked. Then she must have searched her memories, because I heard her say, "Oh. First time."

"But only for a second," Kimmy told her. "Then it gets real fine. His name is Wil, which is short for Wilbur. You take him down to the pond. There's a full moon tonight, so it'll be romantic as all git out. You can go for a swim after, then do it again."

"Do it twice?" Star asked.

"Definitely. Don't hurt at all the second time."

After a little silence, I heard Star say, in a pitiful, pleading voice, "I love you so much, Kimmy. I really do. Couldn't you, couldn't we—you and me and Spearl...?"

"If'n Spearl ever brings another girl into our bed, I only pray she's half as pretty as you are," Kimmy said. "But you're my life-mate's sister..."

"Life-mate?" Star said in a strange, startled voice.

"I really think so," Kimmy said. "And I swear, you *feel* like my sister, Star. I just *can't* go to bed and do all that with my sister. Can you understand?"

"My *sister*?" Star repeated. Then I could hear her crying. After some silence, she said. "I *do* understand. And I'm so sorry, Kim. I'm so, so *sorry*."

"You didn't do nothin' to be sorry for," Kimmy told her. "Weren't nothin' you could help."

That night, Kimmy and I half-heartedly played Old Maid waiting for Star and Wil to come up from the pond. Everyone else was asleep. She finally came in, alone. When she saw us she put on a smile.

Kimmy ran to her and said, "Where's Wilbur? If that peckerwood skipped out on you..."

"No!" Star told her. "It's late and I sent him home. I think we wore each other out."

"So you *did*!" Kimmy squealed. "Did y'all do it twice?"

"Three times!" Star told her, which had me beginning to smell fish. "He was gentle as a lamb," she continued. "It hardly even hurt the first time."

Then Kimmy said softly, "Do you think it helped?"

Star looked over at me, and I saw her eyes flash. Then she looked away as if she were embarrassed. Giving Kimmy a big hug, she said, "I feel *so* much better! Now I just want to sleep."

"I guess *so*," Kimmy smiled, giving her a last squeeze. "Doin' it three times and all!"

XIII
Traces of Love

Though Star had access to traces of knowledge, which I myself later learned to enter, getting into other people's traces is very difficult. Star once told me, and I later found out for myself, that human traces look like a great bowl of noodles, all the same pasty color, all tangled and wrapped with beginnings and ends hidden in the pile. All except traces of immediate family. Those tend to stand out, as though they're a color of their own.

Whether it is the blood relationship of family, or the special love family members know, I'm not sure, but many years later I became able to find my way into my parent's traces. Star's I gained access to sooner, perhaps because she'd already helped me in a number of times. Still, it was some years before I found the trace of Star's rendezvous with Wilbur. When I did, I laughed, and then I cried.

Wil had arrived at the inn with a little bunch of posies. He was a handsome fellow, who probably enjoyed great fortune with girls. But when he first saw Star, he became a tongue-tied mess. Before long, Star scooted him out the door and on their way to the pond.

Kimmy had been right about that moon, and Star actually felt the romance of it. She believed, when she and Wil left the inn, that she was going to be taken in love. She'd resigned herself to it. If nothing else, she'd do it for Kim.

When they sat on a little blanket by the pond, Wilbur slipped his arm around Star, and actually found her trembling. "I know it's yer first time," he told her. "But don't worry. I won't do it till yer ready."

Deftly, Wil slipped his hand under Star's blouse. The feeling of being touched like that surprised her. Her trembling became intense, as she felt herself becoming excited. Wilbur ran his hand down onto her belly, and she let out a little gasp. When she did, Wil grabbed a handful of curls and gently eased her head back. Star closed her eyes as he kissed her, taking and giving that kiss with abandon. But in the middle of it, Star opened her eyes and was startled by the difference between what her eyes saw and what her mind had been seeing. Then she gently pushed Wil away, as she stopped his hand's slow crawl down her belly. "What's wrong?" he asked.

"Nothing," Star told him. "It's just *hot*. Have you ever done it in the water?"

"Once," Wilbur told her. "Is that what you want to do?"

At this point, Star was honestly feeling bad for Wilbur. She was well acquainted with the pangs of unrequited desire, and did not want to be the cause of such. As Wil watched, she removed her clothes, and showed him the intense beauty of a moonlit Star. Then she backed away from him into the pond, saying, "Are you coming?"

Wil was out of his clothes in a flash. Star couldn't help but notice that he was very ready for her. But when he got himself chest deep, Star looked him in the eyes and said, "Do you feel that?"

Finding himself unable to move, Wil could definitely feel what Star's Naiadae were doing to him, and he moaned.

"It's going to get a lot better in a minute," she told him. "But first, I want you to listen to me. By now you probably understand that I'm an Apprentice."

"Yes," he squeaked.

"Good. Then you know you don't want to make me angry."

"No," he gasped.

"And I'm *not* angry with you. Not at all. I'm making you feel *good*, aren't I?"

"Yes," he moaned.

"Well, like I said, it's only going to get better. But when it's done, you're going to go home, and you're going to tell Janie that you had a hot old time with Star down by the pond. Okay?"

"Okay."

"You're going to tell her we did it twice...no, *three* times, and that Star was just happy as pie about the way you did it to her. So, what are you going to say?"

"Three times," Wilbur managed to croak.

"And...?"

"Star liked it! Oh!"

That's right. And if you ever say anything different, I'll have to come back here, and I'll be angry. This is what you get if I like you...and I *do* like you, Wilbur," she said, giving him a little peck on the lips. "But you definitely wouldn't like it if I was mad at you. Now just relax, and I'll give you something special. Something you'll never forget."

Star got out of the water, and sat naked on the blanket. Waiting to drip dry, she caused Wil all manner of lovely distress, and listened to his moans and cries. When she was dry enough to dress, she told him he could come out, she was leaving.

But Wilbur was far too taxed to move yet. Not wanting to get wet again, Star fetched him with a mag-line and lay him on the blanket. Then she gave him a little kiss, and said, "Remember our deal." I have no doubt that Wilbur never forgot that night.

The day after Star's aborted initiation, we left Smith's, heading south to look out over the Florida. It was a beautiful morning, and we decided to hike a while. Here and there, we stopped to pick wild blueberries and blackberries. With her lips beautifully stained, Kimmy kept our conversation coming back to crocodiles. Finally, I said, "You don't need to be scared of crocodiles, Kim. We aren't going to set foot in the Florida."

"Star said y'all are gonna ride me out over it on the lines."

"You don't have to do that if you don't want to."

"Oh, I *want* to. I just keep thinkin' 'bout how tiny I am and how big them crocs get out there. I'd barely be a hushpuppy in one of them big ol' gullets. I got a feelin' I'm gonna see a big 'un, too. You know how I can find a big fish? Well, I keep gettin' the same feelin' 'bout a big crocodile."

Kimmy had been on about the crocs for some time, and I think Star was getting tired of it. Finally, she grabbed Kim around the shoulders and said, "If a crocodile even *looks* at my little sister, I'll turn him into a nice pair of shoes and a big, wide belt."

"Actually, you're *my* little sister," Kimmy told her.

"How so?" Star asked.

"Yer thirteen, ain'tcha?" Kimmy said.

"Yes."

"Well, I'm fourteen, and that make me the big sister. And if a crocodile comes for you, I'll turn him into a nice stew."

"So, you were telling me the truth the first night we...met," I said.

"I ain't never lied to you, Spearl, nor to Star. I know I ain't much, but I'm honest."

"You *are* much," Star said, squeezing her tight and kissing her cheek. "Now forget about the crocodiles, Big Sister. Let's ride the lines for a while."

Once we had on a gauntlet each and our lodestone out, I grabbed hold of Kim and said, "*First*, I want to taste those blackberry lips!"

"Go right ahead," she agreed.

When I finished that kiss, I found Star waiting in line. "Try mine," she smiled.

I gave her a little peck, licked my lips and said, "You two should eat blackberries every day."

It was late afternoon when we reached the Southern Edge. The sky was clear, and the view of the swamp was excellent. "I'm ready to see those crocodiles," Star said through an excited smile.

"That's right, you've never been here before," I said.

"Now when would I have come down here?" she asked me, her hands on her hips.

"I ain't never come down here, neither" Kimmy said.

I tossed Kim both gauntlets and said, "You ride out with Star. Father took me for a ride when we were down here. I'll sit and watch you two."

Kimmy looked at Star with wide eyes and said, "I just *know* we're gonna see a big 'un."

"Well, let's go see him," Star told her.

Star was even better with the lines than Father. After a few fast runs, during which I could hear Kimmy screaming with laughter, they settled into a slow crawl no more than five meters above the swamp. At one point, they came to a tiny island of sand about thirty meters across. Above this little beach, they stopped on the lines, and I could see Kim pointing. There in the water, swimming toward that beach, was an enormous croc at least six meters long. I sat up straight and found myself wishing Star would take them up a little higher. I did *not* get my wish.

Very suddenly, Star let out a horrific, elemental wail. Her back arched, and the wail became a scream of pain and anguish.

Next thing I knew, the girls were off the lines, falling onto that tiny island. Kimmy tucked and rolled, coming up on her feet. Star lay as if dead on the sand. "Spearl!" Kimmy screamed, just as I noticed the crocodile was about to step foot onto that spit of sand. His eyes were locked on the two people I loved most in World.

"Spearl!"

If I'd called lines and Star's Zephrae, the girls would not have survived. It would have been too slow. I was very nearly panicked, when I saw that Gryn was in my hand. Where the words came from, I do not know, but I pointed Gryn toward the sky and shouted, "Linea Clipses terran heah!"

Immediately, the ground shook, and this time I was sure I saw those green flashes above me. In an instant, the island the girls were on rose up ten meters, and threw the big croc off like a duck shaking water off its back. I slid Grin into my belt, as I wasn't wearing my scabbard, and could feel that it was very cold. Then I summoned lines and Star's Zephrae, and headed out to crocodile island.

I felt like it was taking forever to get there. Star's Zephrae seemed sluggish, but it could simply have been my anxiety. I wanted to be out with them *now*. When I finally arrived, Star was unconscious and cold. Her lips looked blue, but it could have been the blackberries. Kimmy grabbed me into a hug so tight it squeezed out my air. "Not now!" I gasped. Then I calmed myself, called up three lines and said, "Help me get her onto my back!"

Kim was still wearing my gauntlets. The lodestone was back in my pack. "Take one of the gloves," she said.

But I told her, "No time!" and we, slowly, rode out of the Florida.

I'd placed my inside hand on top of Kimmy's gauntleted one, but my outside hand was unprotected. I knew, with Star on my back, that I was going to have a problem.

Our interminable ride brought us out to where our packs were waiting. I immediately checked to see if Star was breathing. She was. Then I felt it, just as Kimmy cried out, "Your hand!"

The palm that had ridden out and back without protection was deeply split down the middle, and blood was oozing through the skin around the split. My other hand was red, and burned a bit, but it was my right one that was truly in jeopardy. The pain was intense. I could still feel the very cold blade of Gryn in my belt, so I took it out and laid it on the wound, hoping to at least ease the pain a bit.

Somehow, and immediately, Gryn closed the split. The pain was gone, and other than a thin, red line where that gaping wound had been, my hand seemed fine. Having no idea what I was doing, I laid Gryn on Star's forehead. Nothing happened. When I looked up, Kim had Star's wine jar in her hand. "Give her some," she said.

I dribbled a little of the wine onto Star's lips. In a moment, she licked them and her eyes fluttered open. "Take a drink," I said.

Star took a gulp. Her eyes began searching, as if she were lost. Suddenly, she seemed to understand where she was. She looked into my eyes and said, in a low and pitiful voice, "They have Mama." Then she grabbed hold of me and wept into my ear, "They have Mama and Papa."

XIV
Traces of Horror

Although I can, I rarely enter Mother's traces. It has nothing to do with experiencing from female eyes. I've never been bothered by that when I'm in Star's. Mother, you must understand, was a being unto herself. Star, of course, was also, but Star was *born* as she was, whereas Mother was more or less *made*. I can enter Mother's early traces and look out through the eyes of a mute shykik, a girl who knew certain possibilities were coming, but was unsure which would arrive. She was also a child pawn in the schemes of the mighty Fierae—schemes that took her mother and her voice.

But that child was transformed into a powerful Female Apprentice, enhanced by a merging with the Fierae. Then she was changed again, when she added another dimension to those Fierae schemes, to their surprise and dismay, by joining with Blitz' other half and existing for a time on the high air as charge. When she returned she was, again, something different.

As if this weren't enough for one mute child, she was then imprisoned on her own mind-sca, afraid for the lives of her unborn children and for World itself. Many times, as children, she told Star and me that story, which always ended with, "But your father and the Universe saved me, and in turn saved my precious twins."

Mother's traces, especially those after all these transformations, are hard to experience, because she simply wasn't human, and I just couldn't settle in. You can't relate to that kind of perception. In fact, I've always found Star's traces to be much more human.

Father's traces were easy, and the first, other than Star's, that I found my way into. Most of my account of Father and Mother's journey north, and subsequent ordeal at the hands of the Masons, is taken from Father's traces. But in order for me to know the entire story, there were excursions that had to be made into the strange and baffling traces of my mother. In this case, they were traces of horror.

Mother and father waited two days after Star and Kimmy and I left before beginning their journey north. Their hope was, the farther south Star traveled, the less likely she would be to pick up on their departure. Before they left, Grandfather Tool said to Father, "You be extra careful. I gots a bad feelin'. Had a bad feelin' all dem years ago, and y'all got cotched by dem slavers. Remember? Gotta bad feelin', Spaul. Don't get cotched by nothin'."

Father *did* remember Tool's warning all those years before, but he and Mother felt very self assured. They had been through, and *come* through, so much together, that surely a few nitwits from across the sea wouldn't pose any problem. When they left, they were like life-mates heading off on a vacation—a little time away from the children. Their first stop would be the beach for reminiscences of first love, then on to Ginny, where they hoped to pick up the Mason's trail. They never made it to Ginny.

Spaul and Pearl dropped their packs, shed their clothes, and ran out into the inviting ocean. They swam and talked, and just for a moment, Pearl danced a school of Naiadae over Spaul's body, causing him some concern. But she stopped after a moment and smiled. "Only kidding," she said. "I want it to be like our very first time, high in the clouds with the stars over us."

"After some clams and fish?" Spaul asked.

"More hungry for food than your poor, neglected lover?" Pearl pouted.

"How about this?" Spaul proposed. "Just like the first time, but with a glorious, day-lit blue sky above, *then* clams and fish, *then* high in the clouds with the stars over us."

"Sure you're not too hungry for that first part?" Pearl smiled.

"I have *never* gotten over being hungry for you. Maybe I should put more twins in your belly."

When he said that, Pearl grew pensive. Finally, she said, "I haven't allowed it all these years because I don't know what another child would be. Blitz is gone, sailing Star's sea as Starshine. What Fierae I am now is my own, is what I brought back with me from my time aloft with Blitz. I'm a very strange being, Spaul."

"Strange and wonderful," he told her, drawing her into a hug. "Maybe we'd have a human child?"

"It's not something I can think about right now," she told him. "I'm very worried about Star. And I worry about Spearl carrying that gollam knife."

"Short sword," Spaul told her.

"It's too powerful, Spaul. I've been through trace after trace of arcane knowledge just trying to determine how she made it, but I can't even figure out what it is."

"The twins are far to the south," Spaul said. "Spearl has found someone very special to him. Who knows, maybe Smith will come up with a handsome nephew and Star will..."

"Will what, Spaul? I fear a child for myself, what might Star bear? It all worries me so much."

After a little silence, Spaul said through a suggestive smile, "Let it go for now. Call up your Zephrae while I've got you naked on this beach." After a moment, Pearl smiled and a chorus of Zephres surrounded them.

Joined in love, just like the first time, Spaul and Pearl rose high into the beautiful day. So intent were they upon one another, that they didn't notice, just a klick to the north, the ship snuggled into a little harbor. Nor did they see the huge tent pitched just onshore from that ship.

But they themselves were very visible high above the beach on that clear day. And though Pearl couldn't hear it, or feel it, the mark on her hand that she'd received when she'd smashed Fargus' villainous bottle, was singing loudly to those who knew how to listen.

When their play had exhausted itself, Pearl's Zephrae deposited the lovers on the wet sand at the water's edge. Spaul's arm was around Pearl, and her head was on his shoulder. When she said, "Ouch! Something stung my back!" Spaul leaned his own head back and saw the little dart stuck below her right shoulder. "There's a..." he began, until he was stung as well. Before he could say anything else, he felt Pearl go limp beside him. Then his vision blurred, and World slid away into blackness.

Though she could feel consciousness returning by degrees, Pearl could not move. When she managed to open her eyes, she could make out what looked like a huge tent over her, rippling in the sea breeze. Then she realized she was looking at it through a ceiling made of glass. She could also hear a strange, chugging sound. She listened intently for Spaul's thoughts, but heard nothing. Then a curiously accented voice asked, "You are awake? I think so. You will not be able to move, though the drug will allow consciousness. We are truly sorry this must be done by force, but we are desperate. Fargus believed you could survive a fusion with a Fierae charge. If this is so, you could be the mother of a new race of powerful Apprentices.

"You are encased in glass. An engine is pumping fresh air into the enclosure through a filter made of spun-glass fibers. It is keeping the elementals out of the enclosure. There is nothing in there with you, you will not be able to summon any elemental magick."

Pearl was fully conscious now, and knew that the speaker was mistaken. Though it was true there were very few Zephrae and Naiadae in the enclosure with her, there were some. Those that were making it past whatever "filter" was being used were heading immediately for the outflow vent that allowed air to circulate. They did *not* like being enclosed in glass.

But Pearl reached out to the Zephrae who were with her and persuaded some to stay. Seeing with their eyes, she looked down on herself, lying naked on a raised pallet covered with a thick, woven mat. Copper threads had been wound onto her fingers and toes. These filaments ran like shiny strings through a tiny hole in the glass cage and out to a contraption with two large cranking handles.

There were not enough elementals inside her cage for Pearl to completely neutralize the drug coursing through her, but she tried nonetheless, and found herself able, though barely, to speak. "You will die," she managed to say, and she felt a tear slide down her cheek.

As soon as she spoke, the man went to the contraption and began turning those cranks, which seemed to engage a wheel of some sort. When the wheel was spinning at a high rate of speed, the man toggled a switch and Pearl screamed with all the voice she could muster.

It was cold, dead fire that had jumped through the copper strings connected to her. Like a lifeless, mindless Fierae bolt, it seized every muscle in her body. Then the man threw the switch again and Pearl went limp. Though still conscious, she retreated to her sea, which had changed from a white-capped fury to dead calm in an instant. From her flat, silent mind-sea, Pearl watched as the man entered the glass enclosure and raped her.

XV
Fierae Blood

"They have Mama and Papa," Star wept into my ear as I held her. Then I could feel her body tighten, and she held me away by the shoulders. Her eyes were glowing, and the grim look on her face frightened me. "They've drenched her in Fierae blood, Spearl. They've burned her with that fire and then..." Star's body shook violently, after which she stood as if gravity had no effect on her. Looking down at me, still sitting where I'd held her, she said, "Then they raped her, Spearl."

"Father?" I managed to ask.

"I don't know."

"What are you going to do?"

"Take Kim and go to Smith's. Leave her there and then follow me as best you can."

Kim was standing behind me. So dire had Star's demeanor become that I'd actually forgotten about her until she shouted fiercely, "We *all* go! You *need* us, Star! And if they did those things to Mama...well...*somebody's* gonna get their necks wrung!"

What happened next surprised me. I half expected Star to simply rise up with her Zephrae and leave us. I certainly didn't expect her to throw back her beautiful head and laugh. Then she said, her elemental voice charged with lectrics, "Now I know why we love you so much! Do you trust me, Big Sister?"

"Yes!" Kimmy told her without hesitation.

"Then mind your fear! Brace yourself with rage! Get your hands gauntleted and the lodestone between you! We're going to go *fast!*"

When Kimmy and I were ready, Star cocooned us all in Zephrae. Then she rose us up and out of World. "It's too high!" I called to her. "When the Zephres release us, we won't be able to breathe!"

But Star only grinned savagely, as World continued to fall away beneath us. Finally, at unfathomable heights, she looked at us and shouted, "This is going to hurt, but not for long. Bear it!"

Instead of releasing us from their cocoon, the Zephrae collapsed onto us, some pressing tight against our skin, others rushing into our mouths and noses, filling our lungs painfully with air. I could see Kimmy trying to scream, but the storm of Zephrae rushing into her silenced it. Then we fell on the lines, pointed north. Star had constructed a windscreen in front of us, and had a tremendous chorus behind, pushing. We were moving so fast that sparks and tendrils of flame were flying off that shield. From the ground, we must have looked like a falling star.

As we fell, the Zephrae that had packed themselves onto and into us slowly left, easing the agony involved in their keeping us alive. When we finally reached an altitude at which we could breathe, Kimmy screamed, "Gol*lam*it that hurt!"

"You are a fierce little warrior, Sister!" Star called back to her.

"*Big* Sister!" Kimmy grinned.

Needless to say, I was worried about what Star would do, and at that point I was worried about Kimmy as well. My two girls seemed very much to be itching for a fight. I was thinking about what I could say to talk Star down from her fury when she cried out to me, "I see our destination through Zephrae eyes! Spearl! I'm sending you a half-second back into my trace. Do you see the big boat?"

Surprising Star and me, Kimmy and I shouted in unison, "Yes!"

After a moment, Star let out a burst of elemental laughter and cried, "What *are* you, Big Sister?"

"I don't know," Kimmy yelled back, "but whatever I am, I'm pissed!"

"Star!" I said, hoping to calm things a bit. "We can't just drop in there raining down fire and helluva! Remember Mother and Father! We don't know their circumstances. It's *stealth* we need. If there must be retribution, let it come *after* we've freed our parents!"

"Tribulation!" Star called to me. "But I'll set us down a klick away and listen to you. Gather you thoughts, construct your plan, but be quick. For all I am Fierae, I have none of their patience! Not now! And for all that *you* are *Apprentice*, I see you've strapped on your sword!"

"What choice did I have?" I shouted. "It would have followed me, anyway!"

"Choices!" Star shouted back. "You *chose* to wear it!"

In another moment, Star set us down. Just before she did, we could see the big boat and tent with our own eyes. As soon as our feet touched the ground, Star moaned and collapsed in a heap. Kim and I ran to her, and I dropped to my knees to cradle her in my arms. But she recovered quickly, looked up into my eyes and said, "Both our parents are soaked in it now! Fierae blood!"

The sound of Spaul's thoughts rose Pearl from her sea. Actually, it was a single thought, "Pearl!" and it was very close. He was in the enclosure with her.

"I'm here," she said, her voice weak.

Then she heard that strange voice say, "This one is your hoosband, is he not?"

"You *will* die," Pearl said again. "You have no idea what dread you've called down. It's on its way."

"Then we will try again, quickly," the man said. "Perhaps the bond between you will facilitate the fusing."

Spaul was just recovering from the drug, and managed to get to his feet. "We came here to *save* you," he said, looking through the glass at the man standing by his vile contraption.

"Maybe you will," he said, as he turned the handles and made the wheel spin. "Mate, now, with your weef."

"Go to helluva," Spaul spat.

But the man toggled the switch, on and off again rapidly, and Pearl screamed. "Do anything but what I tell you and she may die," he said.

"Stop it!" Spaul screamed. "How can I do it like this? I'm not able."

"Find a way," the man told him.

"Spaul," Pearl said. "If you let me, I can come to your mind and make you ready. Relax. Let me do this. The pain of this dead fire is terrible. I can't take much more."

"Do it," Spaul said in his thoughts, but to the man he said, "When she arrives, I won't save you."

It was strange, how Pearl chose to make Spaul ready to love her. In his mind he was suddenly on a white beach at night, stars ablaze overhead. Beneath him, she was soft and pliant, and shivered at his touch. "Beon min hus," she whispered, as he felt himself release into that love. Then the fire came, that Fierae blood. Every muscle in him tensed and cramped, and he could feel Pearl beneath him seized in agony. He wanted to scream with her, but managed to restrain it. As soon as it ended, he felt nothing, as he retreated to the silence of his sea.

"Alright! I said as resolutely as possible. "Can you tell me where Mother and Father are?"

"They are in the tent," Star told me, slowly getting to her feet.

"Are *you* okay?"

"Yes."

"Then let's see if we can scare them. Rise up over them in a cocoon and call down in your most terrible elemental voice to release Mother and Father. While you're doing that, Kimmy and I will make our way to the tent. If they haven't released our parents by the time we arrive there, burn that ship! That should get their attention, and distract them so Kim and I can rescue Mother and Father."

Star smiled. "It's a good plan," she said. "I especially like the part where I get to burn something."

"Well, indulge yourself," I told her. "Make it spectacular. Hopefully, they'll all come running out and leave our parents unguarded. Kimmy, I'll lead the way, you stay at my back and keep a constant lookout behind us. If you see anything, call out. I'll have Gryn in my hand, and I've a feeling it will strike out at any danger we perceive."

"What's perceive?" Kimmy asked.

"That we know about," I told her.

"Danger in our demesne," she said, smiling.

"That's right," I smiled back.

Donning a terrible grin, Star summoned her Zephrae and rose. Even though the ball had not yet set, she was glowing brightly. "Release your prisoners!" she roared so loudly it made Kim cover her ears.

"Come on!" I called, and we ran like helluva toward the tent.

I had no doubt that Star knew precisely where we were. When the tent was no more than ten meters away, the great boat burst into flames as Star washed it in sheets of fire. "Release them *now*!" she roared.

I touched Gryn to the tent, and opened up a slit in its wall. As I peered in, I could see people running out to see the conflagration at the ship. I could also see, all the way on the other side, the glass cage holding Mother and Father. "Let's do this," I said to Kimmy. "Keep low, watch my back. Stay with me, okay?"

"I'll be your perceiver," she told me.

Somehow I couldn't restrain a short yelp of laughter as I said, "Gollam, I love you!"

I opened up the side of the tent with Gryn, and Kimmy and I made our way in. We were almost to the glass cage. I could see that Mother was on her back, and Father was just climbing off of her. They were both naked, and horrible thoughts began conjuring in my mind. Then Kimmy pointed and said, "There's a big 'un right out there on the other side of the tent."

"What's he doing?" I asked her.

"I don't know, but he's there."

Kim was pointing in front of me and to my left. Mother and Father were ahead and a bit to the right. "Keep an eye on him," I told her.

"He's cut a hole!" Kimmy screamed. In a flash, she was in front of me, just as a dart fired through that hole. It caught her square in the chest, and she went down.

Gryn was gone from my hand in an instant. I can't say whether I threw it, or it simply flew of its own accord. In a moment, it was back in my hand dripping blood, as a big man with a blowgun tore through the tent and lay dead on the ground. The next thing I knew, Star was in the tent with me. I had Kimmy cradled in my arms. "It was drugged," Star told me. "You've got to get her out of here. I'm neutralizing it as best I can, but it was a big dose and she's so small. She's in shock. It's dangerous."

Suddenly, a dire looking man dressed in dark clothes entered the tent with several armed men behind him. Star walked directly to him and said, "I am what you seek. Let all these others go, and I will sit in your glass cage."

"No!" I shouted, but Star looked back at me and smiled. Then she said to the man, "Do it now, or I'll burn you where you stand."

"Get them out," the man said, pointing to the cage. Then, to Star, he said, "But you must go in."

As Mother and Father were being released, Star said in my mind, "Don't worry, that glass can't hold me. Once I know you're all safe...well...it's going to get ugly. But first I want to find out about their blood machine before I give them a taste of it. Go home. Care for Sister. Don't let her die, Spearl. I love her."

"That dart was meant for me," I wept in my thoughts.

"She took it because she loves you too much, as I do."

Mother and Father were well abused and weak. Still, they were able to call lines and start us on our way home. I insisted on carrying Kim on my back. We were going very fast, but at one point Mother stopped us and Father told me to let him carry her for a while. "No!" I insisted. "She's mine."

Grandfather Tool was waiting in the yard when we arrived. He looked like he hadn't slept in a week. "Got cotched, didn't you?" he hollered. "Nekkid as jay-birds and got cotched! Don't nobody listen to ol' Tool!" Then he saw Kimmy unconscious on my back, saw the look on my face and howled, "Oh no! Not dat baby! Not dat darlin'!"

"She's alive!" Mother told him. "But she's in shock. She needs tending. Get a bed ready! Fetch some corn!"

Grandfather turned and ran. I was right behind him, carrying Kimmy in my arms now. In a moment, I was putting her down on our bed, as Grandfather handed Mother and Father each a robe. "You two looks like sheet," he said to them. "What dey done to you?"

"Nothing good," Mother said.

"Where Star?"

"Dealing death, I'd imagine," she told him.

"Death too good," Grandfather growled.

Mother took the jug of corn Grandfather had fetched and dribbled some onto Kimmy's lips, but it ran down her cheek. "She took that dart too near her heart," she said. "Star neutralized it, all of it, but the dose came too hard, too fast. There's nothing else I can do. Now we must wait."

For three days I sat with Kimmy's hand in mine. I didn't sleep and I didn't eat. Whenever Mother or Father tried to get me to rest, or eat something, I silenced them with a look. I have never been so grim in my life, as I sat there watching my love die. Watching her die for *me*. On that third day, I felt her heart stop. I was on the very verge of plunging Gryn into my own, when I heard Star say in my mind, "Don't despair! I'm here!" A few seconds later, she flew through the door with the strange contraption that had tortured our mother and father. "Stand back!" she told me, her voice commanding and elemental.

Suddenly, a chorus of Zephrae began turning the cranks and spinning that wheel. Star took two copper threads coming off the contraption, one in each hand, and placed her palms on Kimmy's chest. "Throw that switch—that little lever, there," she said, pointing with her eyes. "Two seconds—on, then off. Got it?"

I did as she told me, and watched as Kimmy's back arched up off the bed. After a moment, Star said, "Again! Two seconds!"

I toggled the switch a second time, and again Kimmy's body jumped. Then Star took her hands off her chest and kissed her on the forehead. In a moment, Kimmy's eyelids fluttered open, and she said in a tiny, harsh voice, "I saw him, Star. He was a big 'un." Then her eyes closed, and I could see that she was sleeping. I could see that she was alive.

Whether it was my three days without food or sleep, or the sheer relief of having Kim back after watching her die, I can't say, but I collapsed into Star's arms sobbing like an infant. "Thank you," I wept, over and over. "Thank you."

I think Star was a bit overwhelmed by my condition, and said nothing for a while, letting me cry myself out. Then she held me by the shoulders, the way she so often did, and said, "You didn't think I'd let my Big Sister die, did you? Or *you* for that matter, though I don't think Gryn would have gone willingly into your chest."

"How long have you been in my thoughts?" I asked. "I never felt you there."

"Your mind was sorely occupied. I've been with you pretty much since you left with Mama and Papa. I was afraid for Kim. I could feel her ebbing away as you held her hand. So I searched through some ancient knowledge and found a use for those Mason's torture device."

"Did you know it would work?"

"It *did* work, Spearl! Sometimes you ask the gollamest questions. She'll recover, now, but it will take time. Take care of her. Keep her in that bed until she screams at you to get out."

"You sound like you aren't going to be here."

As I said that, a commotion started outside the door, and I heard Mother say, "Spaul! No!"

Then Father pushed past her into the room. He had an ax in his hand. "You know what that thing is!" he said fiercely to Star.

Believe it or not, Star actually chuckled, and said, "They thought they were putting a Fierae charge into her, Papa. They have all this knowledge, but they're ignorant. They have lost nearly all their Apprentices, and know next to nothing. I'm educating them."

"So they're still alive?" I asked, quite surprised by Star's revelation.

"Yes," she smiled. "I've been...magnanimous. I've been *merciful*. And they're such marvelous *tinkerers*. I've decided to put them to use."

"I've got a bad feeling," Mother said.

"I'm destroying that evil thing!" Father growled, staring daggers into Star's eyes.

"Fine. But take it outside. Kimmy's not well enough for that kind of ruckus. Here, I'll help." With that, Star picked up the contraption with a line and had Zephrae scoot it out the door. Father was in a rage. I'd never seen him like that. He immediately followed the Fierae blood machine, and in a moment, I could hear him out in the yard breaking it to pieces. "It was too small, anyway," Star said.

"Where..." I began.

But Star stole the thought from my mind and answered, "I can't tell you now, Spearl, but I have to go. When like Fierae charges find themselves, they *must* join. If I stay here, I'll eventually lose control. I can't do that to you, and I won't do it to Kimmy. So I've found something to divert me."

"What are you doing, Star?" Mother asked in a hushed tone.

"I'll tell you when I'm sure, when I'm certain. But you don't have to worry about those Masons anymore. I've been merciful, but I had to punish them for what they did to you and Papa. Now they do as they're told. They want no part of further punishment."

"Star..."

"Enough, Mama! I am what I am! And you know I can't stay! You *know* what would happen! Now I have to go. Just being here this long is a burden I no longer wish to bear."

Star turned and grabbed me into a hug. "Be careful with Gryn," she whispered to me. "If you'd tried to force it into your chest, it may have broken in order to stop you. I'm not sure what would happen if it breaks, but it's possible World wouldn't survive— at least not as we know it."

"Star!" I said, amazed at how casually she'd spoken those words.

Releasing me from our embrace, she smiled and said, "It's only a world, Spearl." Then she turned and left.

I could say nursing Kimmy back to health took all my attention. I could say I didn't miss Star because I didn't have the time. But the fact is, I wouldn't *allow* myself to miss her, or even think of her, because every time I did the pangs that rippled through my chest were unbearable. I had missed her terribly when Father and I took our trip, but I knew I'd see her again soon, and it was bearable. This was different, and I finally understood how badly Star needed what I couldn't, or perhaps it would be fairer to say *wouldn't*, give.

So I put her out of my thoughts, exiled her to a place beyond the sea of my mind. If Father or Mother mentioned her name, I left the room. Kimmy understood, or at least she pretended to, and never spoke of her Little Sister. But I could see that it hurt her, and one morning she said to me, "Today, Spearl, I'm getting out of this bed, right after you love me *two times*! And as soon as my legs start workin' right again, we're goin' to find Star. I know we may have to leave her again, but she's gettin' a visit like it or not. I swear, Spearl, 'fore I keep you two apart, I'll share you with her. If that's what has to be..." then she fell silent, and I saw her chin quiver.

"Don't you dare cry," I said softly. "When you're stronger, we'll go find her. And there won't be any *sharing*. Next thing I know, you'll be wanting to rent me out."

When I said that, Kimmy grinned and said, "I got two pieces of silver saved up for you right now. One piece for each time yer gonna do it to me."

"Is that all I'm worth?" I asked.

"Well," she said through that grin, "I guess I could owe you a couple more."

XVI
A Long and Winding Road

I managed to keep Kimmy in bed all of two weeks, until that day she "rented" me. At first her legs wouldn't hold her, and I carried her around on my back for at least ten days, though I suspect she could have walked much sooner. She loved whispering into my ear as I carried her, "Git along, pretty muley."

I found excuses not to go look for Star, and Kim found places *everywhere* for me to love her. She had come back from death insatiable, and I'd be lying if I said I minded one bit. But there came a day, as we lay exhausted on a hay pile in the barn, when she said, "Tomorrow!"

"Tomorrow what?" I asked, trying to catch my breath.

"We'll tell Mama and Papa we're goin' to the beach—and we *will*, so we won't be lyin'—then, after some fishin' and lovin', we'll go find Star."

I was ready to argue, but Kim rolled over onto me and planted a kiss that took my breath away again. Then she smiled and said, "Well?"

"Tomorrow," I conceded. She'd won the argument the minute she dragged me into that barn.

That night, at dinner, Kimmy and I told Mother about our plans to go to the beach. Without so much as a pause, she said, "You're going to try and find Star."

Kimmy and I looked at each other, and I finally asked, "How do you know that?"

"Your grandfather told me," Mother smiled.

"Grandpapa!" Kimmy scolded.

"Didn't say *nothin'*!" Grandfather protested. "Didn't *know*!"

Then Mother laughed, and Kimmy said, "You're bad, Mama."

"Perhaps," Mother told her. "But I'm not stupid. And there will be *no* argument. Your father and I are going with you."

"But *Mama*," Kimmy whined. "We really *were* going to the beach first, and we..." then she stopped, and blushed.

"You two still can't keep your hands off each other, can you?" Mother grinned.

"Let me see," I said. "How is it that you and Father came to be captured, *naked*, at the beach?"

"Yes!" Grandfather said, slapping his palm on the table. "How come *dat*?"

"Okay," Father laughed. "You two go to the beach. See if you can tell what happened at the Mason camp after we left. Your mother and I will go to Ginny and see if she's there, or if anybody knows where she might have gone. We'll give you three days to...go fishing, and then you meet us in Ginny. Okay?"

"I like fishin'," Kimmy blushed and grinned.

"Nekkid as jay-birds, and got cotched," Grandfather grumbled.

Kim and I made it to the beach as fast as Star's Zephrae would carry us. We wanted as much of our three days of "fishing" as we could get. As soon as we arrived, we surveyed the Mason's camp...well...almost as soon as we arrived.

The boat was a burned out hull. Other than that, there was nothing except a melted slag of glass that had once been my parent's prison. "She told me it couldn't hold her," I said to Kimmy.

"I wouldn't want to be the ones *tryin'* to hold her," Kim smiled.

"I wonder where she's gone," I mused.

"We'll worry about that when we git to Ginny," Kim told me. "But right now, we got three days and a whole beach for our demesne. So you better start perceivin' what I'm wantin' and get to it."

"Are you wanting a fish?" I asked, crouched and coming for her.

"Nope!" she giggled, turning and running halfheartedly away.

"Are you wanting a *spanking*?" I called, coming for her in earnest.

Yelping with laughter, Kimmy ran for the ocean, tossing away her clothes as she went. "I'm wantin' *somethin'*!" she squealed.

Kim loved it when I chased her like that, and thoroughly enjoyed wearing me out once I caught her.

The morning after we arrived at the beach, we ate a little fish left over from the night before, after which, Kimmy dug something out of her pack. "What *is* that thing?" I asked her.

Grandpapa made it for me," she said, holding up what appeared to be a small, folding shovel. "See here, how it works," she said, showing me where it was hinged. "Once you straighten it out, you push these two pins through these two holes and it keeps the handle straight while yer diggin'."

"Digging for what?" I asked.

"Last time we was here, I was perceivin' little pieces of metal here and there under the sand. Some of them might have been silver, and I'm sure one was gold. I knew we was kind of in a hurry to get Star those livers, so I didn't make nothin' of it. But come right over here to where I'm standin'. If'n there ain't somethin' gold about a meter under my feet, I'll take a *real* spankin' without so much as a whimper.

"I wouldn't *really* spank you," I smiled.

"You might," she told me, "since yer doin' the diggin'."

It was quite a ways down, and by the time I dug it out, the hot ball had me sweating to beat all helluva. But what we found, what Kimmy had *perceived*, was indeed a treasure. It was a very large, very heavy ring made of gold, with a big garnet stone in the middle. There were letters around the stone, mostly worn away. What I could make out said, "Univers out Carolin."

"It must be sayin' somthin' 'bout Two Carolines," Kimmy said when I read it to her. "Maybe there was a time when people from Two Carolines thought they was the whole universe."

"Whatever it means, it's a beautiful treasure. We'll find a chain for it in Ginny, and you can wear it around your neck."

"I ain't wearin' that heavy thing," Kimmy told me. "I ain't all that fond of wearin' *clothes*, much less sparklers. We're gonna sell it in Ginny and get a nice pile of silver for it."

"Mother and Father would give you some silver, Kimmy."

"I know they would, and I'm grateful. But this will be *our* silver, and we can put some of it into my savin' box. You know, Spearl, there might come a time when you'll be wantin' to put a bun in my oven." When she said that, Kimmy's cheeks turned red as beets.

I laughed and said, "I've *been* putting buns in, but they don't seem to bake! It's been making me wonder, considering all the love you've been getting."

"You been gettin' it, too, you know," she said, squinting her eyes at me. "And I ain't some barefoot and dumb, knock-me-up hick, neither. My mama was a Madama. I can find fish, bad men, and gold, and the minute one of yer little swimmers takes hold, I can tell that, too. Mama taught me 'bout herbs and weeds to take when that happens to make it quit. I've already had to stop it twice, Spearl, and it ain't no picnic. Gives me the cramps somethin' awful."

"Why didn't you just...let it bake?" I asked.

"We're so young, Spearl. I thought, maybe we should wait a bit. Now don't get me wrong—you say the word and I'll grow us a baby. But I just thought we should see a little more of World and the way of things first."

"Well," I said, and there might have been a touch of anger in my voice, "you should have talked to me about this. You said you've never lied to me, but this is a kind of lying, Kimmy."

I think I expected Kim to be contrite when I said that. Instead, she became angry. "I'm tellin' you *now*, Spearl! And didn't I just say I'd do whatever you want here on out? That's a big thing to give! It ain't yer belly gonna blow up like a melon, and have me pukin' every mornin' for weeks! This thing *ought* to be up to *me*, and I just give it to you, stock and barrel!" Then she started crying, and I felt like World's biggest shite.

When I took her into my arms, she made a halfhearted attempt to shrug me off, then cuddled up close. "It wasn't no lie, Spearl," she whimpered.

"I know," I told her. "I'm an idiot. But I don't like you taking those herbs and weeds if we can help it. If you can tell when one of my *swimmers* takes hold, maybe you can tell what times we shouldn't love. You know, when you'd be most likely to make a baby."

"I already know that," she sniffled.

"Well, we'll just avoid those times till were *both* ready for a baby. Okay? We'll *both* decide."

Kimmy wrapped her arms around me and whispered in my ear, "Might be hard not to, some of them times."

"Well," I smiled, "I can think of a few games we could play to take our minds off it."

Kim laughed in my ear and said, "Not Old Maid, I hope."

"Not Old Maid," I told her. "Let's go for a swim and I'll show you."

By the time we left for Ginny, Kimmy had perceived—and made me dig up—six pieces of silver and a little box full of small, copper coins. "Them's pennies," she told me. "I've seen them before. People finds them here and there. The ancients musta made a gazillion of them. Ain't worth nothin', but I ain't never seen nothin' like this box."

I searched my memories, but couldn't find anything resembling the smooth, hard material that box was made of. "Looks like a tiny treasure chest," I told her.

"It can be my new savin' box," Kimmy said.

"I don't know," I said. "It looks like it may have been made by the ancients. Father might not like it."

"If'n he say's I can't have it, I'll 'bide by that. Till then, I'm puttin' it in my pack."

"Let's get dressed," I told her. "It's time to head for Ginny."

"Let's not," she said, with a wicked grin that reminded me of Star. "It's so *hot*! Let's ride like we are for a bit."

She wasn't lying about the heat. It had been a long summer, and seemed not to want to end. "But what if we come across somebody?" I asked her.

"Star was right," she laughed. "You *are* bashful."

"Am not!"

"Oh yes you are!"

"You're going to end up riding with a red bottom if you don't quit," I told her.

As usual, Kim won the argument, and we started out from the beach with Star's Zephrae blowing over our naked, suntanned bodies.

We hadn't gone ten klicks when I shouted, "Star says stop!"

"What is it?" Kimmy asked.

"Some perceiver *you* are," I said. "Look! There's a big muley cart with two men on it just north of us. They're heading inland, too, and in about a klick or two, our paths are gonna cross!"

"Bashful!" Kimmy teased.

"What if they ask me to rent you?" I told her.

"Maybe we should get dressed," she conceded.

Once we were clothed, we continued on our way, but stopped when we met up with the muley cart. Two men were driving it, both as brown as grandfather, and the cart was loaded with huge, earthen jars with tight fitting lids. What really caught my attention was that those jars seemed to be covered with *frost*.

"Ha dee?" one of the men hollered.

"Good!" I hollered back. "And you?"

"Real fine," he answered, smiling. "Y'all 'Prentice, ain'tcha?"

"Sort of," I told him. "But I don't think I could frost jars like that."

"Yeah, dat sumpin' ain't it? Keeps fish and such cold till we gets 'em home. Missy Star majicks 'em."

"Star?" I asked, suddenly excited.

"Real name DreadStar, daughter to Drea. But she say, 'Jus' call me Star.' Don't seem right, though, so most calls her *Missy* Star, or *Lady* Star. De bad men call her Witch Queen, but not to her face. Oh, no! Scared of her, dey is."

"The bad men?" I asked.

"All de bad men dis here girl' color. Ain't sayin' peoples dat color bad, but all de bad men dat color. Talk funny, too. Y'all headin' for Ginny?"

"We were," I said. "But we're actually looking for my sister, whose name is Star."

"You Spiral?" the man asked, surprise in his voice. "Yeah, I sees it now. Same skin, same kinda eyes, though not de same color. You Spiral!"

"Spearl," I told him.

"Yes! Spiral! We goin' to Star City now. Y'all come, too! Take you to Missy Star!"

"We got to go to Ginny, Spearl," Kimmy said in an anxious voice. "We promised Papa."

"I know," I said, "but..."

"Ain't no buts, Spearl. We know where she is, now. We'll find Star City, I promise, but Mama and Papa will worry fierce if we don't show up. They're liable to tan our hides."

"I don't think they'd tan our hides," I smiled.

"I was yer Papa, I'd tan ya, you broke yer promise," the man on the cart laughed.

"See," Kimmy said, anxiety showing on her face. "And, anyway, we got to sell our treasure."

"Can you tell us how to get to Star City?" I asked the man.

"I *could*, but Missy Star makes everybody promise not to. I believes you's Spiral, but I still ain't breakin' that promise. Take you with me is best I can do."

"I've got an idea," I told Kimmy. "Give me the ring."

Without a word of dissent, Kimmy handed over the Universe ring. "Can I trust you to give this to my sister?" I asked the man.

"We honest folk," he told me.

"Yup, we honest," the other man confirmed.

"Anyways, Missy Star would know. Wouldn't be surprised she know we talkin' right now."

"Actually," I told him, "neither would I. You tell her that's Kimmy the Perceiver's ring, and we're coming for it. Can you remember?"

"Kimmy de Seever," he said.

"*Per*-ceiver," Kimmy corrected.

"Purr-seever. Kimmy de Purr-Seever's ring, and y'all's comin' to get it back."

"Good. I'm sure Missy Star will give you a reward."

When I said that, the man laughed. "Don't need no ree-ward," he said. "We rich. We fish mongerers. Fresh fish in Star City make a man good'n rich. People all gots plenty to pay, too. Missy Star keeps her peoples real good. She *ought* be called queen, but she don't like it. If'n she did, people'd make her queen tomorrow."

I thanked the men again, and as they were ready to leave, the first one said, "Y'all git to Ginny, now, 'fore y'all gits whupped!" Then, through cackling laughter, he added, "Might ought to keep yer clothes on!"

Kimmy smiled, but she also blushed. I think I did, too.

Once we were back on the lines, Kimmy asked, "Why did you send Star our ring?"

"I've got a hunch," I said. "You found that ring once, and I think you can find it again. Can you tell where it is now?"

Kimmy closed her eyes and wrinkled her brow. Finally, she said, "Feels like it's in that man's pocket, but I could just be guessin'. I don't know. But you might be right. We get to lookin' for Star City, I'll see if I can't get a feelin'. I got a real good picture of it in my head. Who knows? Even if it don't work, it was a good idea, Spearl. We ever do have a young 'un, I hope he's smart like you."

"You are very smart, too," I told her. "So our child is sure to be a genius."

"Don't poke fun, Spearl. I'm 'bout dumb as a post."

When she said that, I stopped us in our tracks. "Don't you *ever* say that again!" I yelled at her. For some reason, putting herself down like that made me very angry. I think my tone surprised her, and she teared up. "Now, don't cry. I didn't mean to yell at you. But, honestly Kim, you're just as smart as I am, and it makes me madder than all helluva to hear you say such things."

"I can't even read," she said softly, those tears welling into her eyes.

"Reading has nothing to do with being smart. You can't read because nobody ever *taught* you to read. When we get to Ginny, we're going to buy all the books we can with our six pieces of silver, and when we get back home, I'll teach you to read. I don't want to hear you putting yourself down again. I wouldn't love a dumb girl, only a very smart one."

"Least smart enough to get the best lover in World," she smiled.

"How many others have you tried?" I asked.

After punching me on the arm, Kimmy blushed and said, "You *know* you was first. And I know yer the best for me. I know it like I know my own toes."

"And you have such *pretty* toes," I told her.

"Ain't they just," she said, looking down at her bare feet.

Mother and Father were waiting for us on the road that led from the east into Ginny. We were already off the lines and walking when we spotted them. "See," Kimmy said. "Now what do you suppose would've happened if we didn't show up?"

"I knew you were right," I told her. "Which is why I listened to you. See, you were smarter than me."

"Smarter than *I*," Kimmy said, showing me a grin.

"Have a nice time at the beach?" Father called to us through a smile that made Kim blush.

"Star melted that glass cage into a puddle of slag," I said, changing the subject.

"There's a rumor in Ginny about a place called Star City," Mother told us. "But nobody seems to know where it is. We even met a man who said he'd been there, but when we asked him where it was, he just went blank. I can't be sure, but I think his mind may have been addled on that subject."

"Star could do that," I said.

"Your mother's been doing it for three days to keep people from recognizing her as Queen Starshine. We even saw Rosie at her inn."

"Star *is* in Star City," I said. "Apparently it's *her* city."

"How do you know that?" Father asked.

I told Mother and Father about the fish mongerers Kimmy and I met on our way to Ginny. "And they said her name is DreadStar?" Mother asked.

"Yes, but they call her Missy Star or Lady Star. I'm guessing the 'bad men' they referred to were the Masons—white men who talk funny."

"Are you sure that's all they said?"

"That's it," I told her.

"No," Kimmy interjected. "They said she was DreadStar, daughter of Drea."

"That's it!" Mother said, grabbing Kimmy into a hug. "Drea! She's at *Tara*!"

"You two did good coming to meet us," Father said. "I'm half surprised you didn't follow those fish mongerers to find your sister."

Kimmy didn't say a word, but I felt like I had to. "I wanted to," I told him, "but Kim wouldn't let me."

"Of course!" Mother laughed. "It's why the Universe sends good men even better women—to keep you out of trouble." Father laughed and shook his head when Mother said that. "Are you saying *I'm* trouble?" she asked him with a smile.

"*Sweet* trouble," he laughed. "Very sweet trouble."

We decided to stay the night in Ginny, buy a few supplies and head out for Tara the following day. Mother and Father went back to the inn to get Kimmy and I a room, while we went shopping. Kimmy had given me the six pieces of silver and told me to go find books with which to teach her to read. "What are you going to do?" I asked her.

"Don't be nosey," she told me.

Whatever she was up to, if she didn't want me to know, I'd never get it out of her, so I took the six silver and left her to the bobarkers. I was pretty sure her "savin' box" was back home under our bed, so I didn't think she would be buying me a present. But after I found her again, and showed her the three books I managed to purchase—talk about expensive—she showed me a fine, sturdy, braided gold chain that certainly cost much more than I'd paid for the books. "How?" I asked her.

"Pennies!" she told me. "I was tryin' to see if I could get anything for that strange box we found."

"I thought we were going to ask Father about that!" I said.

"Oh, don't be a fussbudget! World won't end 'cause we dug up a little box. And, anyway, I still got it. The bob wasn't going to give me but half a silver for it, and I told him where he could *put* his half a silver. But when I opened the box, and he saw all them pennies, he said I could have anything on his table. He says there's a man comes through here right reg'lar lookin' for anything copper, and he pays real good for it. So I traded him for this chain."

"I thought you didn't care for sparklers," I said.

"Well, I like *this* sparkler, 'cause it's gold and gold'll sit good in my savin' box."

I had to smile. "Why don't you wear it till we get home," I told her. "It'll look very pretty with your gold hair. Here, let me put it on you."

As I clasped the fine chain around Kimmy's pretty neck, she said softly, "Yer wishin' you could see me wearin' *just* this necklace, ain'tcha?"

"Oh, no!" I said, feigning surprise. "Now *you* can hear my thoughts, too!"

"Sometimes I almost can," she told me.

I didn't tell her that she'd heard my thought exactly. That night, in our room at the Ginny Stud, I got my wish.

The next morning we loaded our packs with biscuits and hushpuppies and jerky, then made our way out of Ginny. "Shall we ride the lines down the Ninety-five and then head west?" Father asked.

"The weather's cooled a bit," Mother said. "Let's just hike south, southwest and at some point we should cross the Tara Road."

"Do you think you can find it?" Father asked.

"Don't be silly. I can look through Zephrae eyes for that creek where I found my Naiadae voice."

"And I got my wolf eyes," Father said.

"They still glow a bit at night," Mother smiled. "But not like they used to."

"Sometimes I miss your Naiadae voice," Father told her. "But I'm glad the lectrics faded from *this* voice."

"They're still there," Mother told him. "I just don't let anybody hear them."

"How do you do *that*?" Father asked her.

"Now, Spaul, a girl can't tell *all* her tricks and secrets, can she, Kimmy?"

"Gotta keep somethin' for a rainy day," Kim smiled.

"I love your new necklace," Mother told her. "Did Spearl buy that for you?"

Kimmy just grinned, and Mother grinned back. "Well," she said, "it looks very pretty on you, but then, I think you could make an old shoelace look good."

"Spearl likes to see me wearin' it," Kimmy said, blushing at me.

"So," Mother laughed, "it was really a present for *him*!"

Hiking to the south and west took us through mostly wooded areas, so there was no riding the lines. Late that afternoon, Mother seemed puzzled. "What is it?" Father asked.

"I've been seeing that creek. We should have come to it by now."

"Isn't that a road down there?" Kimmy said, pointing.

Mother squinted her eyes, looking hard at that road, and said, with her hands gone to her hips, "That's the road into Ginny! We're back where we started!"

"How is that possible?" Father asked.

"Star!" Mother said in an exasperated tone. "I'm afraid she doesn't want us to find her."

"But how is she doing this?" Father asked.

"Could be any of a hundred different ways. She could have the Zephrae in on it. She could be fiddling with our thoughts and perceptions. Even if I knew exactly what she's doing, I doubt I could counter it, Spaul. We might as well go home."

While Mother was talking, I noticed Kimmy sitting against a tree with her eyes closed. Suddenly, she opened them and said, "I think I can take us to her."

"How?" I asked.

"If I'm still, and concentrate, I can feel that ring."

"What ring?" Mother asked.

I told her and Father about the Universe ring Kimmy had perceived, and how I sent it to Star with the fish mongerers. "And you can feel that ring now?" Mother asked Kim.

"*If* I'm still. *If* I concentrate. But I think, if Spearl carries me on his back, I can keep track of it."

After hearing all this, Mother went to Kimmy, took her face in her hands, and looked hard into her eyes. Finally, she said, "What *are* you, sweetie?"

"I'm yer son's..." she started to say, but stopped.

"She's your son's life-mate," I said for her.

Mother smiled, and actually seemed a little choked up. "Are you?" she asked softly, lifting Kimmy's chin with her fingers.

"Long as I draw breath," Kim told her.

After spending another night in Ginny, we started out fresh the following day. Kim rode on my back with her chin resting on my shoulder. Every once in a while she'd correct our course by whispering, "Left," or "Right," or "Straight now."

At midday we stopped to eat something and Mother asked, "Are you sure about this, Kim?"

"Oh yes," Kimmy told her. "It's gettin' stronger. Long as I concentrate, I can feel it. I can *almost* see it. Don't get me wrong, it ain't easy. Can't be nothin' else on my mind. I sure as helluva couldn't do it and walk at the same time."

"I think you just like me carrying you," I told her with a grin.

"You'll never know," she grinned back. "Can't give away all our tricks, can we, Mama?"

Once we'd eaten we got underway again. But after a couple of hours, Kimmy whispered in my ear, "Better stop."

"What's wrong?" I asked.

"Can't keep my mind on it right now."

"Why not?"

"Ridin' you has all of a sudden put somethin' *else* on my mind."

"Oh!" I laughed.

"What is it?" Mother asked.

"Kimmy needs a break. We're going to just wander off a bit and let her rest her noggin."

"Rest her *noggin*?" Mother said.

Kimmy and I both laughed, and Mother shook her head. "Just don't wander off too far." As we were walking away, I heard her say to Father, "Won't be long till those two make grandparents out of us."

Kimmy heard it too and giggled, but the grin left her face when I said, "No more herbs and weeds, no matter *what*!"

As a rule, I don't go into detail about the love Kimmy and I made back then—those moments of ecstasy and shenanigans were, and still are, keepsakes of a private nature. But I will mention how special our encounter was that afternoon on the way to Tara.

Once we believed we were beyond Mother and Father's hearing (Kimmy was sometimes...noisy) my pretty little treasure hid herself behind a big oak and told me to wait. After a few moments, she peeked around the tree and said, "There's a dryad waiting for you on the other side of her tree."

When I scooted around to see this "dryad," I found Kim wearing only her necklace. In her hands she held small branches full of leaves, and she'd contorted her body into the prettiest little impersonation of a tree. The dappled light through the oaks and sycamores played on her beautiful, taught body, as she looked up at me shyly through her lashes. "It's an iffy time to be forbiddin' herbs and weeds," she said in a dryad voice so sweet it guaranteed I'd love her regardless. Then she lay back on the loamy floor of our silent woods and said, "Swim into me, darlin'. Right now, I need you more than breathin' air. You're the bright spot in my nighttime. Come bring me somethin' worth rememberin'."

Thinking back on that afternoon, I have no doubt whatsoever that she knew—*knew*—that we were about to make Mother's words come true.

We tried to press on that day, but in less than an hour Kimmy stopped us for the night. To me, she whispered, "I just can't get that lovin' you did to me out of my head!" To Mother and Father, she said, "It's *awful* exhaustin', all this concentratin'. But it's close, I can tell. I'd bet silver 'gainst hushpuppies we'll find it tomorrow."

I thought Kim would want to "wander off" that night, but she didn't. Lying between our two thin blankets, she said, "Just hold me close, Spearl. I'm still simmerin' from this afternoon. That's a memory I'm gonna hafta put in my savin' box."

Less than an hour after we set out the following morning, we came to a road. "This is it," Mother said. "This is the Tara Road, and we're darn near the end of it. If we'd gone more southerly we'd have run into it sooner and not had to hike through these woods."

"I don't know 'bout more southerly," Kimmy told her. "I was just goin' ringerly."

"I know, sweetie," Mother said, giving Kim a hug. "You did just fine. Much better than I did! I don't know how it is that Star's tricks don't work on you as well."

"Maybe I can't *perceive* her tricks," Kimmy told her. "If she's trickin' with Zephres, it'd be wasted on me."

"Or maybe," I said, "she isn't aware of the power of Kimmy the Perceiver!"

"Stop it!" Kim told me, but she couldn't restrain her smile. I think, at that moment, Kim became aware of her worth—something I already knew.

Once we were on the Tara Road, Father wanted to call up lines and ride in, but I had a bad feeling. When I looked at Kim, I was surprised to see her face mirroring my reservations. "Maybe we ought not," she said.

"What is it, sweetie?" Mother asked.

"I just think we ought to surprise her. If'n y'all start fiddlin' with elementals, well, Star *is* an elemental, and she's gonna feel it. For all we know, she could take off soon as she can tell we're on our way."

"She's right," I said.

"Of course she's right," Father told me. "How could I be so stupid not to realize that?"

"Might have somethin' to do with you wantin' to see yer little girl so powerful bad," Kimmy smiled at him.

For a moment, I thought I saw a tear in Father's eye, but only for a moment. Then he said, giving Kimmy a squeeze, "My *other* little girl."

Mother and Father both agreed that it couldn't be more than a klick or two before we'd be looking down into the valley that had once held Tara, and was now home to Star City. We were about to start out down that road, when Kimmy said, "Carry me, Spearl."

I'd carried Kimmy a *long* way, and was somewhat achy. "You're taking a toll on my back, Kim!" I said. "Haven't you ridden enough?"

"Come here, Kimmy," Father said. Then he dropped his pack and knelt down. "Climb on," he said. After Kim was situated on Father's back, he said to me, "You can carry my pack."

After giving me a smug smile, Kim rested her chin on Father's shoulder and closed her eyes. We walked like that for about five minutes, then Kimmy opened her eyes and said, "Stop!" Climbing down off her new "muley," she said, "I can see the ring! Star wrapped string around the bottom of it so it would stay on her finger. She's wearin' it. It's special to her. So special it's almost like it's *part* of her. I can *feel* her through that ring."

"Are you sure, sweetie?" Mother asked.

"*Very* sure. And I'm sure of something else, Star can't hear my thoughts. And she hasn't been listenin' for y'all's. She thinks we gave up tryin' to find her after she sent us back to Ginny. I can tell cause of the feelin' of it—it's kinda makin' her sad. But she *will* leave if she hears y'all comin'. We get close enough, she's gonna hear you and bolt.

"Y'all got to stop thinkin', and we need to wait till night and sneak in. Honestly, I'm surprised she hasn't seen or heard y'all already. I'm guessin' she's got somethin' else on her mind or she would have."

"I think I can keep her out of *our* thoughts, Spaul, but there's nothing I can do for Spearl. They're too close."

"I can stop my thoughts for a while," I said. "But I don't know how long I can keep it up."

"I'll help you," Kimmy told me.

"How?" I asked.

"C'mon," she said. "Let's all slip back into these woods and sit quiet and concentrate till dark."

"Do it," Mother told us.

Kimmy and I sat against a big tree, and she took me into her arms. "Just listen, and don't think. Okay?"

"Okay," I agreed.

Very softly, very sweetly, Kim began singing to me. "Hush li'l baby don't you cry, Mama's gonna sing you a lullaby..."

A few minutes later, I felt her gently shaking me. "Wake up, darlin'," she said. "She might hear you dreamin'. Stay awake and listen."

"Okay," I told her, "but try not to sing me to sleep."

When she started singing again, it was a song I'd never heard. Later, she told me her mother used to sing it to her, and told her it had come from the time of the Ancients. I can't tell you on how many occasions over the years I asked her to sing it to me. It truly suited her sweet, sweet voice. "Today is just an endless journey. Tonight is only a crooked trail. But tomorrow will be such a long time, if loneliness comes between you and me. Could that be my true love there a-waitin'? Could that be his heart a-softly poundin'? If only he would come and find me, and hold me in his arms once again."

That night, as we crept down the Tara Road, Kimmy was perched on my back and singing her lullaby in my ear. But when we came up over a ridge and looked down into that valley, I don't know how I managed to keep my thoughts at bay. It truly was a Star City, and it was lit up brighter than the heavens over us.

"That's not lamps or candles," Father said.

"No," Mother told him.

"You know what that is, don't you Pearl?" Father asked.

"Yes."

"It's ancient teck, isn't it?" he said angrily.

"Spaul," Mother said, looking intently into his eyes. "I don't ever want to see you in a rage the way you were the night Star saved Kimmy. Listen to those words, Spaul—*Star saved Kimmy,* and you were in a rage."

"I..." Father began, but Mother stopped him.

"*Listen* to me, Spaul. Whatever Star is doing, rage will only drive her farther into it. Remember why you came here. Remember how much you've missed your little girl. Remember how bad you felt that the last time you saw her you were angry. Calm your sea, sweetie. Let's try love, okay?"

Father took a deep breath and said, "Yes. This trip was for love. But I *am* an Apprentice, Pearl, and at some point I will have to be true to that."

"I know," Mother told him, "but *this* trip, you are a father."

All the time Mother and Father were talking, Kimmy was singing her ancient song into my ear, but it was getting hard for me to concentrate. Finally, Kim stopped singing and said to them, "Y'all need to come to terms quick. Spearl ain't made of stone, you know."

"Let's go," Mother said. "As fast as we can. Do you know where she is, Kim?"

"She's at the south end where the light stops, in a big house of some sort. It's noisy in there—she don't like the noise. And there's smoke! She don't like the smell, either."

"I can smell something now," Father said. "I've smelled that before. When I was a boy, Thirest found a family burning coal one winter. Though he didn't make them stop—it was a very cold winter—he wasn't happy about it. We stayed three days chopping wood for that family. "Coal's bad for you," he told them, "and bad for World. Don't burn it if you can help it." When we left there, he said to me, "If I find out who's selling coal to these people, I'm going to gollam bury them in it."

"Follow your nose, then," Mother said. "Let's get down there and find her."

As we made our way into the valley, we could see that a road ran down the center of town from north to south. Along this road, alternating from side to side, were a line of poles, on top of which sat round globes full of light. The poles were all connected by smooth, dark ropes. The light didn't flicker, and I could see no flame. On either side of the road were small, square buildings, each with a little globe on a short pole burning brightly in front of it. Behind these square buildings were houses constructed mostly in line with one another, and behind these, fields full of crops. Through the windows of the houses, we could see the same kind of steady light. Then, suddenly, *all* the light flickered, went dark then came back up again. Kimmy stopped singing to me, and after a moment said, "That's what's on her mind. She's tryin' to keep all this light burnin'. She's in there," she said, pointing to a big, white building with a large chimney belching black smoke.

Suddenly, Kimmy jumped off my back and said to Mother and Father, "Y'all run 'round to the back! Me and Spearl's goin' in the front! Hurry! She's found us out!"

Mother and Father went around the building, one on each side, in a flash. There were steps leading up to a big door in front, and Kimmy and I ran up them with Kim leading the way. Just as she reached the top of those stairs, the door flew open and Star ran out. But Kimmy grabbed her into a bear hug and shouted, "Gotcha, Little Sister! Like it or not, we come for a visit!"

I'm not sure what I was expecting, but Star burst into laughter, hugged Kim and said, with tears starting to leak from her eyes, "I *wanted* you to come as much as I didn't." Then she looked over at me and began sobbing in earnest. Kim let her go, and Star ran into my arms. Soaking my shoulder with tears, she said, "All I could do was try not to think of you. I tried *so hard*, Spearl. I tried so hard."

For some reason, all I could think to say was, "You're taller."

Star laughed through her sobs and squeezed me tighter. Then Mother and Father appeared, and hugs and kisses were shared all around. When our emotions finally settled, Star put her hands on her hips and said, "*How* did you find your way here? You must have some majick I need to learn!"

Mother sneaked a smile Kimmy's way and said, "We can't give away *all* our tricks."

Then Star seemed to remember something. Slipping the big ring off her finger, she held it out to me and said, "My fish mongerers said you'd be coming for this. I expected to be wearing it a lot longer."

When Star held out the ring, Kim went to her, unclasping her necklace as she did. Then she took the ring from Star and threaded it onto the chain. "Turn around," she told her.

Star did, and Kimmy fastened the chain and ring around her neck. "That's from me and Spearl," she smiled. "We found it at the beach, and said it was too pretty for anybody but Star. It goes real good with yer eyes."

Star choked up again, and took Kimmy's face into her hands. She was leaning in to kiss her, but stopped and looked hard into her eyes. "You're..." she began, but Kim put a finger on her lips.

"I know," she said, "but don't nobody else. Let it be our secret for a day or two."

XVII
Star City

Before long, I had an arm around Star and the other around Kim. Star kept her head on my shoulder, and both arms around my waist. I knew how she felt. Being with her again was sheer joy.

After a bit, Mother asked, indicating the building Star had run out of, "You don't live here, do you?"

"Oh, no. I'll take you all home as soon as I'm done squeezing Spearl."

"Don't squeeze him dry," Kimmy told her. "You save some for me."

"I know he's all yours, Big Sister. Don't worry."

Then Father asked, "What's in this building?" and Mother gave him a stern look.

"It's okay, Mama," Star said. "Any good Apprentice would question what I'm doing here." Then, to Father, she said, "I call it my lectric farm. It's where I grow the lectrics to fill all those globes with light. I think the Ancients called it a 'power plant' or some such. I like lectric farm better. What I grow in there makes my people happy. They just toggle a switch and they can light up the night without worrying about fire. Right now, my tinkerers are working on a box that glows and gives off heat. If it's ready by winter, think of all the trees that won't be burned to keep my people warm."

"*Your* people?" Father asked.

"*Yes!*" Star said, adamantly. "You *ask* them if they're my people. You might find a few contrarians, but most of them *love* me."

"We love you, sweetie," Mother said.

"I know," Star told her. "But I think I need a *lot* of love, Mama. Just wait till tomorrow, wait till you see how much I'm loved. Wait till you see how happy everyone is."

"What about these 'tinkerers'?" Father asked.

"I think you know who the tinkerers are, Papa."

"Are *they* happy?" he asked.

"As long as they do as they're told, I treat them well," Star said, a touch of anger in her voice.

"I've heard that before," Father said, "in this very place."

"Do you remember what they did to you and Mama?" Star asked, her voice tinged elemental. "They had a choice between this and being burned alive. They chose this. If they'd chosen the other, I'd have gladly obliged them. But I don't want to talk about *any* of this. You apparently went to great lengths to find me. Did you come to argue and scold?"

"No!" Mother insisted, giving Father a look that would have chilled snow to the bone. "We came to visit. We came to be with you because we love you and missed you terribly—especially your father, though he hides it, and forgets it."

"I'm sorry," Father said, taking Star away from me and hugging her close. "I *did* miss you, more than I can say. No more arguing. Show us your home."

"Good!" Star smiled. "And I'll feed you! My fish mongerers came back not long ago with fresh seafood and a very beautiful ring. I'll never take it off, I promise!" she said, giving Kimmy and me each a kiss.

"Let's go, then," Mother smiled.

"Seafood sounds good," Kimmy said. "I'm *hungry!*"

Then Star whispered something in Kim's ear and they both laughed.

"Secrets?" Mother asked.

"Yup!" the girls giggled.

Star walked us south down what she called the Center Road, through the light of her globes. "The town was laid out this way when I arrived," Star told us. "But most of these shops weren't here, just the houses behind them. I encourage people to run little businesses, to sell and trade what they grow and make and catch—and to provide services. This bigger shop houses the garbagers. Every fourth day they ride their muley carts to all the houses and pick up the refuse."

"Where do they put it?" Kim asked.

"Most goes to a compost pile east of town, since our prevailing wind is out of the west. Things that won't compost are buried. Every house and shop gives half a silver a week for this service, which they can easily afford, and the garbagers make a good living."

"Sounds like you've got it all worked out," Father said.

"Actually, I just fine tuned that service. It was already in place, though not as scheduled and efficient as it is now. I believe it was originally Ilsa's idea."

"Ilsa?" Mother and Father said almost at once.

"Yes, Father, she's here," Star smiled. "I believe there was a time when she had a bit of a crush on you, and Mama as well."

"How is she?" Mother asked.

"Still beautiful. She was pretty much the Queen Bee around here until I showed up. Still called the place Tara—actually, *The People's* Tara. But it fell to pejoration and reverted to simply Tara."

"What's pee-gerashin?" Kimmy asked.

"A change for the worse," Star told her.

"Pee-gerashin," Kim said softly to herself.

"I'm afraid Ilsa is one of those few who aren't happy with my administration of things, although I will say she's fair about her opposition. When she agrees with something I'm doing, she says so as loudly as she denounces my 'follies,' as she calls them. I'm sure you'll see her tomorrow. She comes around almost every evening for tea and an argument. I could say she's simply jealous that I've usurped her leadership, but that wouldn't be fair."

"*Tea* and an argument?" I chuckled. "Sounds pretty friendly."

When I said that, Star giggled, a sound I loved and missed hearing. "We're a little more than friendly," she smiled. "Ilsa loves me almost as much as she loves her Tara, and I love her. We've become the closest of enemies."

As we neared the north end of the Center Road, we could see a big, dark house, two levels high with a nice porch. No lectrics shined around or in it, but over the door a strange little globe burned a deep blue. "What *is* that?" Kimmy said, pointing. "It's so pretty!"

"It took the tinkerers quite a while to figure out how to get just that color for me. I think they said cobalt and something else goes into the glass. They call it 'extra-violet' or some such. I call it the Dark Star, and only I'm allowed to have one. I know it's silly, but this *is* Star City, after all, and if I want a light of my very own, I'll have it. Ilsa says it's the beginning of despotism."

"What's despotism?" Kim asked.

"A despot is a bad, absolute ruler who will tolerate no opposition. So that *can't* be me. I don't think Ilsa could say I don't tolerate her."

Star giggled again, and this time it bothered me. Suddenly, a very ancient word came to mind. The word was "fey."

Once we were inside the dark house, Star said, "Up, my pretties," and dozens of candles sparked to life. Over us, a chandelier full of them burned. Oil lamps shone brightly on the mantle of her fireplace.

"No lectric globes?" Mother asked.

"Actually, the line that carries it hasn't made it this far yet. Copper shortage. The Deliverance Billies up in the hills dig me plenty of coal, but copper is harder to find. I have people out searching for it all the time."

"My pennies is gonna light Star City," Kim whispered to me.

"Don't tell Father," I whispered back.

"Then how does your Dark Star burn?" Mother asked.

"A battery. The tinkerers change it every other day. There are two, I believe, and they take the spent one to the lectric farm and fill it back up for the next change. Honestly, I don't think I'm going to even bother running the line all the way here just for my house. There are other places I can use the copper. I'm rather fond of real light, anyway."

"So, the lectric light isn't real?" I asked.

"Oh, you know what I mean," Star pouted. "And my people can't light a hundred candles with a thought to the Fierae. It's much easier for them to toggle the switch. Now! I've a fire going in the stove, let me cook for you."

"I'll help!" Kimmy told her.

"So will I," Mother said.

"Sounds like it would be too crowded for us, Spearl," Father smiled.

"Nobody'd want to eat anything I cooked, anyway," I told him.

When the girls were gone to the kitchen, Father said, "I can actually cook very well, but don't tell your mother. Between her and your grandfather, I eat like a king without lifting a finger."

"You're *bad*, Father," I told him.

"Nobody's perfect, Spearl," he smiled. "So you might as well enjoy your imperfections."

Once we'd eaten, the exhaustion of our journey caught up with us. "Come upstairs," Star said. "There are extra rooms, but tomorrow I'll take you to the guest house. There's a lot of bustle and business here during the day. You'll be much more comfortable in your own little cottage."

"You have a guest house?" Father asked.

"For visiting dignitaries, though I didn't expect you so soon."

"But you built it just in case?" I smiled.

"And thought of you all the entire time it was being built."

The following morning, we found out what Star meant by "bustle." It was just dawn when I heard her downstairs carrying on an animated conversation with two men. I quickly dressed, leaving Kim still sleeping soundly. I was curious to see what Star was up to.

As I made my way down the stairs, I could hear her saying, "I *understand* that you can drill it, and I understand what you mean by a pumpless well, it's also called an *artesian* well. But *how* are we going to get the water from the side of the mountain to Star City?"

I was almost to the bottom of the stairs when I heard Mother, behind me, say, "Pipes, sweetie."

Star chuckled, looked up at Mother standing at the top of the stairs, and said, "Yes, but what *kind* of pipes. Where would I get the iron? And even if I could, I'd have to build a huge foundry first to turn it into pipes!"

"Terra cotta pipes," Mother smiled.

Star went silent and closed her eyes. After a few moments, by which time Mother and I were standing beside her, she opened them and said, "Clay!"

Star hugged Mother, looking happy as I'd ever seen her. Then Father's sleepy voice came from up on the stairs. "You're helping with this, Pearl?"

"Bringing water to people is a *good* thing, Spaul. Not everything the Ancients did was stupid. They *breathed*, you know."

"They breathed ruined air," Father told her. "But I'm sorry. I'm still half asleep."

"See," Star said. "*This* is why I'm taking you to the cottage. So don't you dare say I'm trying to get you out from under foot. I'm being a good host." Then Star turned to the two men with whom she'd been conversing. "This is Thomas, and this is Hardy," she told us. "Thomas, Hardy, these are my mother and father and brother Spearl."

"Dis Spiral?" Thomas asked. "Heared a lot about you, son. Yer sister's bringin' great prosperity to Ta...I mean, Star City."

Star gave Thomas a hug and said, "You can call it Tara if you like, Thomas. It makes no difference. Tara and Star City are the same place. Now I want you to go ahead with your drilling. Just let me know what you need and how you'd like to be paid. And if you see the Chief Potterer, tell her to come see me, and to bring a few of her students. We're going to make clay pipes to carry the water."

"Nice to meet y'all," Thomas and Hardy called on their way out. "Spend some time with yo' family, Missy Star," Thomas added as he left the house.

"I recognize Thomas," Father said, once the two men had left.

"He was a servant of Rufus Bowagad," Star said. "Thomas is a very smart man. Ilsa taught him to read."

"Who taught Ilsa?" Father asked.

"She taught herself all those years ago reading Rufus' books, though he never knew. Ilsa is a treasure. I just wish she wouldn't fight me so, although there *are* times when her vehemence is welcome."

When Kimmy finally got up, sleeping late after her exhausting journey riding on my back, Star took us to the cottage. It was a beautiful little house with three small bedrooms, a nice kitchen, and a fireplace room that contained a small dinner table. "It's beautiful," Mother said.

"I just want you to be comfortable," Star smiled. "Right now, there's a pump in the yard. *Hopefully*, there'll be water going right into every house in the valley soon. I just have to figure it out with my potterers, and whichever other craftsmen can come up with ideas."

"I'll join you when you see the potterers," Mother told her. "I'll help when I can, but you know I won't when I can't."

"I will always listen to you, Mama," Star said. "But in the end, I will be Star."

"My beautiful daughter," Mother smiled.

Star showed us around, said food was being delivered, and then left taking Mother with her to meet the potterers. "There's a tub in here!" Kimmy squealed, finding the bathing closet. "Let's heat up some water, Spearl!"

"I saw that tub," Father smiled. "How are you both going to fit in there?"

"Oh, we'll manage," Kimmy told him. "Lessin' you want to go first, Papa. I'll heat yer water if you do."

"Maybe I will," Father said. "You two get in there, your water's liable *never* to get cold, and I'll have to wait all day."

"Now, Papa, you be good," Kimmy blushed as she went to fetch water.

"I'll help," I told her. "And, by the way," I added. "Father's a very good cook, you know."

"Really?" Kimmy said. "Will you make us some pancakes while we take *our* bath, Papa?"

Father scowled at me, but said, "Of course I will, Kimmy. And I'll put berries in yours if I can find some."

"No berries for me?" I grinned.

"You *might* get *stones*," Father told me.

Our water never got a chance to get cold—Kimmy and I splashed that little tub dry. "Now look at the mess you made," Kim scolded as we untangled and got out of the tub.

"Me?" I asked.

"Oh, just find me a mop and a bucket," Kim said. "I can't let anybody see this mess we made."

"They'd probably wonder what we were doing to make such a mess," I smiled.

"Stop it!" Kim blushed, tossing a sopping washcloth at me. "I'll be glad when we're home and I've got all my secret places to love you in."

"Bashful?" I grinned.

"Go find that mop!" Kimmy growled.

The mess got mopped, everybody got berries, and Mother returned with an old friend. "Spaul!" Ilsa squealed as she ran into Father's arms. "And this must be Spearl!"

"This is Kimmy," I told her.

"Your Mama's right, you two are cute as bunnies together."

"Bunnies!" Father grinned. "Exactly!"

"Where's Star?" I asked.

"Still with the potterers," Mother said. "Then it's the messagers, the schoolmarm, and after that she's promised to stop by for a minute and say hi."

"She is a busy bee," Ilsa said. "I just wish some of that busy would slow down and think."

"Me, too," Father agreed.

"We should talk," Ilsa told him.

"We should *eat* something," Mother insisted. "I'm hungry."

"Papa made us berry pancakes," Kimmy said with a satisfied smile.

"Were they edible?" Mother asked.

"Best berry pancakes this side of Smith's crossing." Kim told her.

"She's just being kind," Father assured Mother. "They were terrible!"

"Were not!" Kim protested.

"C'mon," I said, taking her by the arm while trying not to laugh. "Let's you and me go fix some for Mama and Ilsa."

"But they *were* real good!" Kimmy insisted as I dragged her off to the kitchen.

As soon as we were out of the room, Ilsa said, "Sometimes Star reminds me of Rufus, Spaul, and at the same time she's everyone's fairy godmother. She needs help. Her poor mind is like one of her light globes—so bright, but so fragile. The least little stone comes flyin' and it's gonna break and that light's gonna go out."

"Are you sure you're not exaggerating, Ilsa?" Mother asked. "I understand how close you and Star are. Could that have something to do with it?"

"It definitely has somthin' to do with it, Pearl. Much as there's things I wish you knew...well..."

Ilsa fell silent, and Mother took her in her arms. "You love her too much, don't you?" she whispered.

Ilsa placed a sad little laugh on Mother's shoulder and said, "When she needs it."

Kim and I came in with the pancakes, and there was a silence. They spoke no more of Star while I was present, but they didn't need to. I could see it on their faces. Then that word, "fey," popped into my mind again, and just as it did, Star walked through the door.

"All my favorites in one small room," she smiled. "Talking about me, I hope. The good and the bad? Ilsa knows about the bad, don't you, fair lady."

"What's wrong, Star?" Mother asked.

When Mother said that, it seemed as if Star lost her train of thought. After searching for words, she finally said, "I smell pancakes."

"I'll go make you some," Kimmy said, turning and scooting off to the kitchen.

"Come and sit with me and talk, Star," I told her. "Let these old folks reminisce."

Star laughed when I said that, but it was a laugh that didn't seem to be sure of what was funny. "They're not so old," she said.

Star and I talked, and before long she seemed recovered from whatever spell had come over her. Mostly our conversation consisted of childhood reminiscences. We laughed, embarrassed one another, and told tales bout Grandfather. I could tell Star missed him terribly. But after a while, she began talking about her "work," as she put it. About training schoolmarms and printing books and getting water to every house. "And all of that," I told her, "I agree with. I'd be happy to stay and help. But the teck you're using to light your globes was a big part of what nearly destroyed us."

"Us?" she asked me. "Humans, you mean. And, yes, I know about the teck. But things were different then, Spearl. The problem wasn't the teck, it was *greed*, and the fact that there were too gollam many humans. I'm not going to upset World providing for these few people. Call it an experiment. Let's see what happens. The people of Star City are *good*, and deserve a chance at happiness."

"I understand, Star. I only hope you can understand me. The Apprentices have kept humankind from going back to the ways of the Ancients for four hundred years. The air is clear, the water is sweet again, and humanity is back from the brink of extinction. But we're still very few, and if we excite the elementals again and lose contact with them, we're finished.

"The first Apprentices had a saying, 'Low teck or no teck.' What they were saying was, 'Low teck or no teck because we'll all be dead. Abandon the lectric farm, Star. Let's invent *new* teck low teck. No shortcuts. Let's do it right."

For a moment, Star seemed to be considering it. Then her eyes narrowed and she stood. "I've got to go meet the Chief Schoolmarm. Then I need to sleep. I'll come back to you tomorrow, in the morning."

As she walked out, Star said, "I'll see you all tomorrow. Sorry today was so busy." Then she stared hard once into Ilsa's eyes and headed out the door.

That night, I sat thinking, my concern for Star becoming a burden to my mind. When I finally went to our bedroom, Kim was fast asleep. I smiled, but wondered if I'd too quickly made light of her "exhausting journey riding on my back." Perhaps finding the ring *had* been an ordeal. She certainly seemed to be sleeping, and eating, more than usual.

I was about to get undressed, when the urging of my concern overwhelmed me. Pulling my shirt back on, I headed out of the cottage. I would go talk to Star.

Her house was unlit, except for the Dark Star. My intention had been to knock, but the door was open. Star's bedroom was on the first level, but the darkness had me bumping around. Before long I heard a door open, and saw lamplight coming down a hall. Someone asked, "Who's there?"

"Spearl," I said, seeing the lamp lit concern on Ilsa's face. "I came to see Star. I didn't mean..."

"It's okay," Ilsa said, setting her lamp on a table near some chairs. "Come sit."

"Is Star here?" I asked, realizing what a stupid question it was.

"Yes," Ilsa told me. After a long silence, she added, "She's tied up."

"With what?" I asked.

Again Ilsa was silent for a long spell. Finally, she said, "You're like her, aren't you? Not so young as you seem."

"Yes," I assured her. "We're as much alike as we are different."

"I'm sure you must have realized today that Star and I are lovers."

"It occurred to me as a possibility," I told her, "but, no, I didn't realize it until now."

After another of those silences, Ilsa said, "Star is tied up with ropes, Spearl. Her back and bottom and legs are full of angry welts where I've taken a strap to her. She's resting now, but she'll call for more soon. And when I'm done, even though she could cure those welts and that pain in a minute, she'll lie there on her stomach all night while I hold her hand and listen to her moan. Our love used to always be gentle, and often still is. But every few weeks she needs *this*. This punishment. And tomorrow she'll cure the damage and you'll find her much more herself, and less...what's the word?"

"Fey," I told her.

"Her mind is fragile, Spearl. I tried to tell your parents, but they don't see it. I know you do. You being here isn't helping, either. I've had to do this almost every night since your ring arrived. All this 'work' she does is to keep you off her mind."

Without even thinking, I said, "I'll love her. I'll go to her *right now!*"

Ilsa showed me a sad smile and said, "It's much too late for that, Spearl. These goings on are the result of guilt. She punishes herself just for *thinking* of you, imagine if she allowed herself to do what her whole life has become an endeavor to avoid. And this guilt, Spearl, it's an addictive thing, as is the punishment it insists on. I only hope, once you're gone, that I can settle her again. Even my opposition, our arguments, are meant to distract her. I fear for her mind, and I fear what she will become as it fails her. We'll see how she responds to war. Perhaps it will be a beneficial diversion."

"War?" I asked.

"Your father won't allow her lectric farm. He'll be compelled to destroy it. He'll debate and anguish over the decision, but in the end he'll destroy it the way he and your mother destroyed Rufus."

"Do you blame them for that?" I asked.

"No. He was mad. When your sister becomes mad, she won't be so easy to destroy."

"I know you love her, Ilsa. How can you do this to her?" I asked.

"Love should be played for wants, Spearl, for desires. It is often difficult when it must satisfy need. I'm sure it sounds insane, but I do it to protect your sister's sanity. I fear what she'd do to herself if I didn't."

I wanted to cry, and I wanted to shout my anger. The thought of Star being beaten made me feel sick. Finally, I said, "Kim and I will leave. We'll come and say our good-byes in the morning."

"Don't come," Ilsa said. "If it weren't for the pain, and the need of it, she'd know you were here now. She'd know what I've told you. I'm afraid she'll find out no matter. Your visit to Star City was ill timed, Spearl. I had her somewhat settled before the ring arrived. I just hope I can bring her back from this edge she's leaning over."

It was then that I heard Star wail and it shivered my spine. "Ilsa!" she howled. "More!"

"Go, Spearl. Go before you hear anything else."

I said nothing, and turned to leave. As I walked out, I heard her again cry, "Ilsa!" and my tears blinded me.

I didn't know what to tell Kim. I didn't know what to tell Mother and Father. Fortunately, I spoke with Kimberly first. "We need to leave," I said, holding her in bed as the sun rose. I was surprised when she said nothing, and her silence made me ask, "Are you okay?"

"Yes," she said. "It's Star, I know. I can feel it, Spearl. I can feel it and it's bad, isn't it?"

"Yes," I told her.

"And you can't tell me everything you want to tell me, can you?"

"Once we're home I'll find a way, but right now, no. I don't know how to tell you."

"We'll tell Mama and Papa I'm homesick. Tell them I miss Grandpapa, and it won't be a lie."

"I want to do this as quickly as possible," I told her.

"Let's go!" she said, watching my tears begin to fall. "I've gotta get you out of here!"

I packed while Kim went and talked to Mother and Father. She stuck to her homesick story, but I'm sure her face and eyes told more. "Ride your lines down the Tara Road to the end," Father told us as we left. "Then hike due east to the Ninety-five."

Mother kissed me and held me tightly. She had the look of someone refusing insistent tears. "We'll come tomorrow, " she said. "I need one more day."

"Tell Star..." I began, but fell silent. Mother held me tighter and I whispered in her ear, "Tell her I'm sorry."

There is no describing the anguish I felt, and, yes, the guilt, as we rode the lines away from Star City. Couldn't I have loved them both? Couldn't I have found a way? After a long stretch of silently accusing myself, Kim said, "Yer too quiet, Spearl. I won't have it. I can't watch this eat you alive." Then she shouted, "Star says stop!" which shouldn't have worked, but it did.

"How...?" I asked.

"Even the Zephres know we're one, Spearl. You need to figure it out, too. You tell me, right now! You tell me everything till yer *empty* of it, you hear me? The good is ours and the bad is ours, *together*! Okay?"

It poured out of me like sickness. I cried it and shouted it, then fell weeping into Kimmy's arms. She couldn't help but weep with me until we were both so weak we couldn't go on. For some hours we sat against a tree and held one another. Eventually, Kim took a deep breath and said, "Come on, Spearl. Let's get home to Grandpapa. We dwell on this much longer, it'll take our soul."

The journey home was a blur, but at some point Kim said, "If I'd known...if ever it will help..."

But I stopped her with a sad smile and said, "This was *never* your fault."

"There *ain't* no fault," Kimmy said. "The Universe plays its tricks and we do the best we can."

Kim and I made it home without incident. Immediately after hugging us, Grandfather asked, "Where Spaul and Pearl? How Star?"

When I couldn't find my voice, Kim said, "They're comin' tomorrow, and Star was pretty as ever. Wait till I tell you what I found with the shovel you made me!"

"C'mon," Grandfather smiled. "I walk you 'round de yard on dat muley while you tells me."

"Okay!" Kim smiled. Then she looked at me and said, "I miss ridin' my muley."

There was something secure and comforting about sleeping in our bed that night. Even before Kim climbed in with me, I could smell her on the pillow. Though tears sometimes threatened us still, we ended up making the gentlest love. It was almost sad ecstasy, as though grief and desire had somehow come to terms. I woke the next morning to Kim leaning on her elbow watching me sleep. When my eyes opened, she smiled and said, "Good mornin', Papa."

"Papa?" I said. "You've never called me *that* before."

"'Cause you ain't never *been* one before."

I was still sleepy, and her meaning nearly escaped me. But as I leaned toward her for a kiss, I understood. Before our lips had a chance to meet, I sat up and took her soft shoulders into my hands. "You mean ...?" I asked.

"I can't tell what it is yet, though I know it'll come to me, but it's a baby sure as I got pretty toes!"

"Should we tell Grandfather?" I asked her.

"If we want to surprise him, we'd better. Sometimes I think he's got a little bird that tells him things."

"Let's go!"

Grandfather's joy was infections, and it lessened the burden of our trip to Star City. But there was always a stone of grief in my stomach that wouldn't leave. I tried to keep it from Kim, but knew I was failing.

Mother and Father arrived that afternoon. Almost immediately, Kim and Mother took a walk together. When they returned, Mother said to Father, "Kim and Spearl have news for us, Spaul." But before Kim or I could say a word, Mother very nearly shouted, "They're going to have a baby!"

Father jumped out of his chair, laughed and said to me, "See! See what happens!" Then he wrapped me in a hug and said, "You two are going to be wonderful parents. Yours will be a lucky child." Letting me go, he picked Kimmy right up off the ground and planted inspired kisses on each of her cheeks. "It's going to make you even prettier, if that's possible," he told her.

After a few more hugs and kisses, Mother said, "Kim and I have been talking, and we think she and Spearl should go down to Smith's Crossing and spread the news. It's perfect weather for traveling. They should go before it turns cold, or Kim turns too middle-heavy to stay on the lines. What do you think, Spearl?"

"I'm not sure what to think," I said, my companion grief stirring to anger. "I don't know what Father is planning to do about Star's lectric farm. I don't know how much you understand about Star's condition," I said, looking at Kim.

"I told her Ilsa was right about Star bein' fragile, Spearl. I told her I can feel it, and so can you."

"Now I'm wondering what you *haven't* told me," Mother said after listening to our exchange.

"Maybe we just haven't made it clear to you," I said angrily. "Star isn't well! Not at all! She needs love, not adversaries trying to destroy her."

"I would never hurt your sister," Father said.

"And if you oppose her, that won't hurt?" I yelled. "If you tear down what she's built..."

"We're *goin'* to Uncle's, Spearl," Kimmy said adamantly. "Mama has promised me that *nothin'* will be done until we come back. If we don't get away, Star's pain is gonna become *your* pain. It's already happenin'."

"You're too close," Mother said. "I believe you about Star's condition because I can see it transferring to you. I won't lose you both."

"We haven't lost Star!" I shouted.

"No," Father said. "And we won't. We'll find a way. But we'll need you, hale and hearty, to help. Go to Smith's. Rest. Watch Kimmy's belly grow. Come back to us when the weather starts turning cold. Come back to us *whole*, Spearl, and then we'll do our best to help your sister."

"I find it hard to believe you'll ignore her Ancient teck for that long, Father."

"I can't ignore it," he told me, "but I give you my word we'll do nothing until you two return. Your mother talked to Star at length before we left, and thinks we need to stay away from her for a while."

"Mother is wise," I said.

"She is," Father smiled. "Tomorrow morning, take Kim and go. She's becoming more beautiful every day. Let joy find its way back to you."

"Oh, he'll be gettin' some joy!" Kim said. "And he better be givin' good as he's gettin'!"

After saying that, Kim slapped her hand over her laughing mouth and blushed like a rose. Actually, we all did. Then Grandfather walked through the door and said, "Gettin' what?"

XVIII
Blitz' Prophecy

Shortly after we left for Smith's, Mother and Father hiked off to the big pond (away from Grandfather's hearing) to have an argument. It was animated. "You gave your *word*, Spaul!" Pearl indicted.

"And I'm not going to break it," Spaul guaranteed. "I'm simply going to find the other two Apprentices that are supposed to be in this neck of the woods..."

"*Neck of the woods?*" Pearl cried, throwing her head back and slapping a palm on her forehead. "Those other two are *somewhere* south of the line, and *somewhere* east of the Second Mountains. How in helluva are you going to find them?"

For a moment, Spaul was silent. Then he said, "I figured you'd help me."

"Well, you'd better check your math," Pearl told him, her voice tinged with lectrics. "I will do *nothing*, not plan, not scheme, not lift a finger against Star, until Spearl and Kim return. And even then, it's iffy!"

Spaul actually smiled and said, "I haven't heard those lectrics in your voice for some time."

"I don't *let* you hear them...most of the time."

Gently, Spaul took her in his arms. "They've had an affect on me," he smiled.

"Ah," Pearl smiled back. "Now that you're losing the argument you figure to have your way with me and soften me up."

"You're already soft," he said, nibbling her ear.

"And you know gollam well that you're going to *get* your way with me, don't you?"

"I do," he whispered, after which the conversation devolved into sighs and moans.

Lying by the big pond, their clothes scattered here and there, Spaul and Pearl held each other, glowing like the steadily sinking ball. "Are you softened?" Spaul asked.

"Yes," Pearl breathed. "But be careful. If you ruin this feeling by making me angry, there will be punishment."

"Will I like the punishment?" Spaul smiled.

"You will not," Pearl answered.

"I don't think this will make you angry. Will you speak with Blitz about Star? Just see what, if anything, he has to say."

"I've already tried, Spaul. Blitz has gone to ground. When he was in air, I could easily speak with him through the Zephrae. But now he's a ground charge, and he's retained the male aspect he'd taken to air. In other words, he's very sleepy. I can locate him, *maybe* get him to hear me briefly, but I'd be hard pressed to hear him unless a storm party was exciting him to join. Even then, the conversation would be cut short when I had to run for my life to avoid the bolt of their joining. Needless to say, if I came out of my body to converse, I'd end up joining and almost assuredly never return."

"Not even for me?" Spaul pouted.

"You've joined more than I have, Spaul, but you don't know what it's like for a female."

"It's pretty intense for a male," Spaul told her.

"But you can come back. I wouldn't be able to, even for you. Nor would I be able to miss you, and I would miss missing you," she smiled.

"Which is why you're not going," Spaul told her. "I want you to set up a meeting for me with Blitz. I'm sure we can influence a little storm party to come this way in the next day or two. Get the point across to him to come here and join. When he does, I'll converse."

"You'll *join*, I'll bet!" Pearl told him, trying not to smile.

"Puny humans mustn't bet with the likes of an aneke'lemental," Spearl told her.

Then they both heard laughter coming up over the ridge, and Grandfather Tool shouted, "Cotched y'all! Butt nekkid again, and *cotched!*"

Pearl located Blitz, apparently he was always nearby. "I know where he is, and I told him what we're doing," Pearl said to Spaul. "Whether or not he heard me, we'll know soon. I told him to wait for the storm by the big pond. So let's influence the weather and see if he shows up."

"Surely you can call a storm better and faster than I can," Spaul told her.

"You help!" Pearl insisted. "You'd better start honing your Apprentice skills if you're thinking about opposing Star."

"I hope I don't *have* to oppose her, Pearl."

"But you *will*, won't you? As an Apprentice you can brook no dissention when it comes to your almighty rules!"

"That's not fair," Spaul said softly.

"No, it isn't," Pearl told him. "None of it's fair. And if you *do* converse with Blitz, be sure he knows I hold the Fierae partly, if not mostly, responsible for my children's anguish."

"And their parents' anguish," Spaul said. "Did you never tell him that while he was still in air and you could speak with him?"

"I told him many times," Pearl said angrily.

"How did he respond?" Spaul asked.

"He always said, 'We know what we do'."

The day after Pearl contacted Blitz, the storm began its approach. It was late afternoon, and the big pond was glassy calm before the storm. "He's here," Pearl affirmed.

"I hear him chittering," Spaul told her. "I've never heard a ground charge say, '*She* comes.'"

"It's very rare. Air charges almost universally assume maleness. On those rare occasions when the female becomes dominant in air, I honestly think it's just curiosity, as if they're saying, 'what will *this* be like?' The charge Blitz joins with will probably be disappointed. Usually, female curiosity about air is quickly sated and she once again wishes to return to ground. But Blitz won't trade with her. Actually, I don't think he can."

"Why?" Spaul asked.

"Because he's dying, Spaul. He can't live without his other half. I'd be surprised if he lasts another hundred years."

"So he sacrificed..."

"Yes. Both his halves sacrificed. So far, I don't see that it was worth it. But the Fierae are nothing if not patient. We could both be long gone before any of this makes sense."

"I'll pose hard questions," Spaul said.

"Oh, you'll fawn and then join," Pearl grinned. "And you'll come back to me with wolf eyes wanting me to feed you liver."

"I'll *try* to pose hard questions," Spaul smiled.

"I have a pigs liver marinating in the kitchen," Pearl smiled back.

Some hundred meters from where Blitz was waiting by a tall pine, Spaul and Pearl set up two little folding stools and sat. "Take good care of my body," Spaul grinned.

"Come here. I'll hold you the entire time. When you come back, you'll be getting a kiss."

"My body is liable to sweat," he told her. "And...well...you know what the ecstasy is liable to cause."

"I brought a little washcloth," Pearl smiled. "I'll clean you up before I bring you home."

"It's been a long while since I've done this," he said a little nervously.

"I've often wondered why that is," Pearl grinned.

"Because *you* are my ecstasy," he told her.

"It's because *you* are *bashful*." Pearl told him. "You're shy of me watching you get loved like that."

"Not while it's happening," Spaul told her.

"But when you come back," Pearl grinned, "you might get teased unmercifully. Then I'll see my bashful boy."

For a dying Fierae, Blitz seemed mighty vigorous when he climbed into that pine, chittering maniacally, "Come here come here, she comes comes comes!"

"How long till she arrives," Spaul called from his light body.

"Spaul!" Blitz shouted. "Distraction obscured your presence! So long it's been! You will join, I will bet."

"No betting. Let's converse."

"Will you join?" Blitz persisted.

"I don't think I'll be able to resist."

"Why resist? Love is above all!" Blitz crackled.

"I won't resist, but I'll converse first, and as long as I can. I'm concerned about Star. She's creating and using Ancient Teck, and she doesn't seem well."

"No consequence, little Fierae human. Soon she will rest."

"What do you mean, 'rest'?" Spaul asked.

"She will be relieved. She will pause. She will wait. The trace is convoluted and does not sustain her with continuity. She slips off and then on."

"I don't understand," Spaul shouted, as Blitz stretched away from the pine.

"She comes!" he roared, then those two magnificent faces formed as Spaul had never seen them before—he from below, she from above. When they met, their merged voices screamed ecstasy.

"What about Star!" Spaul called to them, already feeling the joining tugging at him.

Again, that magnificent multi-tonal voice screamed passion, then their response, "Star heralds the coming! New Apprentices are here, more arrive! Less intimate with the elementals. Less aware, but still visible. Elementals will befriend them and grant favor, not response to request, but like wishes come true.

"They are female, Spaul, influenced in the womb when Star was conceived. Some are already here. You can not find or train them as you did the males. Nothing is apparent about them. They grow into their majick and will be independent, each with their own rules—the merit of which determines their awareness.

"The male Apprentices served well, Spaul. Be proud! We will honor you! But as rare as female Apprentices were, male Apprentices shall become! Now join! Come share this bed of delight!"

"But Star's not well!" Spaul cried, even as he was being pulled into the joining.

"No consequence, cute cute human lover. We know what we do. When it is time, you will bring her!"

Spaul returned to his soaked body, eyes glowing and spent. "My poor wolf," Pearl said, rocking him in her arms. "They certainly had their way with you. Will you fall off my lines if I try to ride you home?"

"A minute," he managed to say.

"All Fierae loved," Pearl sighed as she rocked him. "All Fierae taken."

Pearl managed to get Spaul home, and fed him liver. As he was spooning more applesauce, she said, "Can you tell me about it now? Are you somewhat recovered?"

"It was *strange*," Spaul told her. "It was a joining like no other. As if...I don't know. Maybe she from above made it different. But the things they *said*!"

"Can you tell me exactly?"

"No. Get me my ink and paper, and leave me alone for a bit. I'll get it all down, verbatim, but it'll take some time. I guess going into my traces would be pointless."

"The trace would be of me holding you in my arms. Light bodies don't trace, at least not that I can perceive."

"Then leave me with it, and I'll get it down. I've never heard them talk like that before, Pearl. It was almost...*human*."

It took Spaul a while, with a break for more liver, but finally he called to Pearl. "Okay," he said. "Here it is."

Pearl took the paper from him and began reading. "Rest," she said, almost immediately. "What do they mean Star will rest?"

"Keep reading and then you tell me."

"Off the trace and then back on? I don't like this, Spaul."

"Keep reading," he told her, getting into the leftover liver.

Pearl finished Spaul's account with an astounded look on her face. "I see what you mean about them sounding human. That explanation about these new Apprentices was...well, it was intelligible. This part about the new Apprentices being influenced in the womb when Star was conceived, could that work both ways? Could the Fierae have been influenced? Perhaps female air charges are *not* so rare anymore."

"I did think about that," Spaul told her. "I also thought of something else—actually, some*one* else."

"Kimmy!" Pearl exclaimed. "They said some are already here, they grow into their majick, and nothing about them is apparent."

"I've never detected *any* sign of Apprentice in Kim," Spaul said.

"Nor have I, and I've looked on more than one occasion," Pearl told him. "But I've wondered aloud what she is."

"Still wondering?" Spaul asked.

"Not so much," Pearl answered. "She's just a few months older than Star."

"Influenced when Star was conceived," Spaul quoted.

"Things are changing around us," Pearl said.

"Things have been changing around me since the day I met you."

"Changing for the better?" Pearl asked him.

"*Some* for the better."

"And the rest?"

"Too soon to tell."

"And did the Fierae leave anything for *me* tonight?"

"Yes," Spaul told her. "As long as it's she from above."

Kim and I rode the lines toward Smith's at a steady, but relatively slow, pace. Kimmy had become used to Mother and Star's speed, and said, "It's going to take us three days on these slow lines!"

"Talk to Star's Zephrae," I laughed.

"Please, lovely Zephres, could you push a bit faster," Kimmy smiled. Immediately, our speed increased by half at least.

"How did you do that?" I yelled through the wind in my face.

"I don't know," Kim called. "I wished us fast, now I wish they'd block the wind of this fastness!"

Again, Kim's entreaty was answered. "How?" I called, a huge grin on my face.

"I think somethin' just likes me, Spearl. I ain't done *nothin'*!"

"Can you see or feel the elementals? Are you aware of them? How about the lines, can you see them?"

"I ain't seein', feelin', or awarin' *nothin'*! But I'm thinkin' that somethin' just likes me. It's like gifts, Spearl, and I *do* feel somethin'. I feel real happy 'bout gettin' them! *Real* happy. Almost like sneakin' some of Uncle's Maria." A moment later, Kim shouted, "Star says stop!" and we came to a halt.

"What are you doing?" I asked.

Kim grinned and said, "All that happy made me want to give *you* some!"

"You're a sassy little thing," I grinned.

"And I'm feelin' my oats," she said, dragging me into a copse of trees.

"I wonder if I could train her," Spaul said to Pearl.

"Weren't you listening, or were you too enthralled by your Fierae lovers?"

"I know what Blitz said," Spaul told her, "but they don't live in this world, not the way we do. I'm here, I'm probably the most finished Apprentice left. Shouldn't I be what I am?"

"Even if you *could* do it, how do you suppose Spearl would feel if you started training Kimmy?"

"He'd feel like I was taking her away from him."

"And what are you going to do to avoid my becoming extremely angry with you for making my son feel that way?"

"Not train Kim," he said.

"You can be so reasonable when you want to," Pearl smiled.

"When *you* want me to, you mean," he told her.

"You wouldn't have been able to do it, anyway, Spaul. I understood what Blitz told you. There's nothing to train. There's no separated set of abilities. If you told Kim she's an Apprentice, she'd laugh and call you crazy."

"But what about Star?" Spaul asked, his face frowned with concern.

"Do nothing," Pearl told him. "The Fierae aren't the least concerned with her teck."

"The Fierae are not infallible, Pearl. You yourself blame them for Star's problems. I'll listen to them, but I won't be governed by what they say."

"They've been plotting this trace for a long time, Spaul. When the Universe monkeys with their plans, they plot around the problem. Whatever monkeying *you* manage will hardly even be noticed. They're too patient, too powerful, too intelligent, and now I think they have an even better understanding of us. Please leave Star be. The thought of her 'resting' soon, weighs on me. *Please*."

"I'll do nothing till Spearl and Kim return, that much I promised. The rest requires cogitation. And, of course, your concerns will influence that cogitation, heavily."

"It better," Pearl said. "Or she from above may come down heavily on *you*."

"That might be nice," Spaul smiled.

"Come on," Pearl said, her head tilted toward their bedroom.

XIX
The Tinkerers' Coup
(Traces of Pain)

They came in the night, all of them. Star was tied to the bed, and Ilsa was adding layers of welts to her already abused body. Through that pain, she never heard them coming. One grabbed and held Ilsa, while another thrust a dart into Star's red and beaten buttocks. "What have you done!" Ilsa screamed.

Star didn't trust the tinkerers, and had spies keeping an eye on them. Unfortunately, those spies uncovered the danger too late to stop it. But when they realized the tinkerers and all their men were skulking toward the Dark Star, they alerted the people of Star City.

"Our drugs didn't work on her," the head Tinkerer told Ilsa. "This was poison, enough to kill several cows. We'll dissect her now, and learn what we can. Then we'll find the mother again." Running a finger down Star's swollen back, he said, "I see she had strange tastes. That was convenient."
"No!" Ilsa wailed, falling to the floor. "No!"

The inhabitants of Star City, once the slaves of Tara, came as one—every man, woman and child. They came through the door like a river, and only one was injured before they swarmed the tinkerers like fire ants and beat them to death. Even the tinkerer Apprentice had no time for majick, and died beneath the people's clubs and axe handles.
"My poor baby!" Ilsa sobbed, as broken tinkerer bodies were dragged into the street and burned.

Ilsa gently untied Star. "My poor, sweet child," she wept.
"Don't cry," Star said in a harsh voice, causing Ilsa to nearly faint. "If you hadn't made such potent love to me, it would have had no effect at all. Hold my hand, my love, I have to finish dealing with this poison before I can heal. What happened to the tinkerers?"

"The people all came to save you, Star," Ilsa said through her sobs. "They beat the tinkerers to death and have burned the bodies."

"Then they saw me like this?"

"Yes. They were concerned. I told them the tinkerers did it to you. That's when they burned the bodies."

"My people came for me!" Star said, beginning to weep. "My people love me."

"We love you so much, Star. But this isn't love you have me make. I can't do it anymore. It tears at my soul."

Somehow, in spite of the poison and her ruined back, Star sat up and took Ilsa in her arms. "It's all right, my love. It will be nothing but gentle between us from now on. I didn't realize it hurt you so much."

"It hurt me terribly," Ilsa sobbed.

Then a voice came from the door, the speaker afraid to look in. "Thomas died," he said. "No one else harmed 'cept poor Missy Star."

"She's alive!" Ilsa sobbed.

"She's alive!" The man shouted, running out onto the porch. "She's alive!"

The people, Star's people, packed into the house. When they saw that she was still naked and welted and weak, they sent only the women into her room. "Fetch aloe!" one called.

"And corn, and herbs for pain!"

"Bring some light oil, too!"

"And clean bandages, and food for her to eat!"

Before long, Star had managed to neutralize the poison, but she didn't heal those last marks from Ilsa's hands. Instead, she let her people tend to her, let them kiss her and coo to her. Through it all, her tears fell, as she took all that love like sustenance.

The following day, Ilsa helped Star out of the house, for she would not heal her wounds. Twice a day women came and tended to them, which affected Star much the same as being strapped. The tinkerers poison was gone, but her own poison was taking hold.

Slowly, Ilsa walked her down the Center Road to where Thomas's funeral procession stood. "You look better, Missy Star!" someone shouted.

"Please be well!" another called.

"We're here for Thomas!" Star called back. "And how can I *not* be well with my people tending me so lovingly."

When she said that, everyone cheered. Star raised her hands, which caused her to wince, and the people immediately quieted. "Thomas was my friend," She said, "as *all* of you are my friends. But Thomas was a friend to the people of Tara as well! He called this place Tara because it was how he'd known it for so long. From this day forward, we will call our home Star City no more! We will call it Tara, and when we hear that name, we'll remember Thomas, who died to save me! And we will change the name of this road to the Heroes' Way, in honor of *all* of you, my heroes, who came to my rescue!"

When the people's cheers finally settled down, some of the women who'd been nursing Star went to her, and one of them said, "Let us take you home, Missy Star, and tend to you."

"Not until Thomas is laid to rest," she said stoically.

"Please don't tax yourself," the woman insisted. "Tara needs you. Tara needs her queen." Then she shouted to the crowd, "She don't want to go, but we takin' her home for tendin'! Y'all can tell her 'bout the funeral later!"

Star smiled as they helped her back to her house. "I *will* be your queen," she told them, "and let nothing harm you. But I like you to call me Missy Star, because we are friends."

When the women had tenderly redressed Star's wounds, and were finally gone, Ilsa said, "Please heal yourself, Star. I can't bear to see what I've done to you."

"When the women have healed me, I'll remove the scars," Star told her. "They'll love me more if they've nursed me back to health. I won't deny them tending their queen."

"Queen?" Ilsa asked.

"Let them think of me as queen, though I won't allow them to speak it to me. They *need* me to be their queen, and I'll give them what they need. But what am I to do now that my tinkerers are dead?" She said, almost pouting. "It was all I could do to keep the globes lit when they were still alive."

"Please don't fret, Star. If you won't heal yourself, you need to rest so your body can do it for you."

"My darling Ilsa. What would I do without you? Come here and let me love you, gently as we can. Let me tend to *you* a bit. I've put you through so much."

XX
The Apprentice

"Dey's a 'Prentice comin'!" Tool shouted in through the front door.

"Quiet, now, Papa!" Pearl scolded. "Spaul's still sleeping. And how do you know it's an Apprentice."

"He floatin' a pack 'longside of him. Mus' be a *rich* 'Prentice. Dress up in fine clothes!"

Pearl came to the door and looked out. Sure enough, a well dressed man with his pack on a mag line was coming toward the house. "Go invite him to breakfast," Pearl told Tool, "and then start cooking. I'll get Spaul up."

Looking sleepy and nervous, Spaul came out dressed in a robe to greet the Apprentice. After touching hands, Spaul said, "You're Forest, aren't you? Thirest called you the most well dressed Apprentice in World!"

Forest chuckled and said, "I'm glad you remember me, Spaul. You couldn't have been more than twelve last time I saw you."

"Well, you look exactly the same," Spaul said. "In fact, I think you look younger than I do."

"These particular looks *are* deceiving," Forest smiled. "We can stop the aging on the outside, but we do grow old. I feel it more every day. Won't be long till my time is up."

"Do you have someone to preserve you in your bunker?" Spaul asked.

"No," Forest told him. "It's not what I want, anyway. Most of those leaving want a pyre, as do I. I know Thirest wanted a bunker, and I'm sure you preserved him well, but things have changed. We're almost gone, Spaul. I know of only four others, and they're old as I am, though not as vain. They've all aged, as I see you're doing."

"I stopped it for a while, but you're right, it's cosmetic. I wanted to look as old as I feel."

Forest laughed and said, "If I looked as old as I feel, you'd start building that pyre right now." Spaul smiled, and Forest said, "I received your message, Spaul."

"Message?" Pearl asked, coming into the room with breakfast.

"Before we talked," Spaul told her, "I sent a pulse along the lines. I knew it wouldn't get far, and honestly didn't expect it to work."

"It was weak when I saw it," Forest said. "If I hadn't been coming east to investigate the rumors, it would never have reached me."

"Rumors?" Pearl and Spaul said almost at once.

"Rumors of what they're calling a 'witch' in Ginny, who made herself queen and then abused the people. They say she made all the women pregnant, and that one I've heard from more than one source."

"Those are very old rumors," Pearl smiled. "I've been to Ginny recently. There is no queen."

"There's also a rumor that the Billies in the hills north of here are digging coal—lots of it. When I followed your pulse, and found it came from not so far south of those hills, I cogitated that it concerned that rumor. Why *did* you send that pulse, Spaul?"

"You never told me you sent out an alarm, Spaul," Pearl said sadly.

"I honestly didn't expect it to be answered. I've done nothing else since we talked."

"Talked about what?" Forest asked.

Before Spaul could answer, Pearl said, "What information we give you, we'll offer. Don't think to interrogate us in our home."

"Pearl," Spaul said softly.

"Spaul!" Pearl said not so softly.

"We may be dying out," Forest said to Pearl, "but Apprentices are *normally* still respected." Then he looked at Spaul and said, "Perhaps the Apprentices here should speak alone."

Before Spaul was able to respond, Pearl said, her voice tinged with lectrics, "The Apprentices here *are* speaking, though I'd suspect the ability of any who can't tell one of their own."

Spaul shook his head and said quietly, "That's not going to help."

Forest's eyes went wide and his face pale. "What are you?" he said to Pearl.

"Something quite beyond your understanding," she told him.

Then Forest looked to Spaul and said, "What?"

Spaul snorted a little laugh, shrugged his shoulders and said, "What the helluva. Pearl is a Fierae-fused, shykik female Apprentice. Try not to piss her off."

"And those rumors out of Ginny?" Forest asked.

"That was a long time ago, and it wasn't Pearl. The Fierae she fused with took over for a short while, and...um...didn't play well with others. But that's all been straightened out."

"And this Fierae is still...*fused*?"

"Sort of," Spaul told him, "though Starshine passed into..."

"Spaul!" Pearl interrupted. "That's enough! Despite his appearance, this is a dying old man with just enough of his wits remaining to cause trouble. He's a relic! Remember what Blitz told you. Their time is over."

"You mean *my* time," Spaul said, hurt sounding in his voice.

Pearl went and took him in her arms. "No. Your time follows a different trace, a *new* trace."

Suddenly, Pearl could feel Naiadae condensing around her eyes. Immediately, she let go of Spaul, looked at Forest and said, "You little shite!" Within seconds, Forest and his fine clothes were soaking wet. Then his eyes rolled up in his head and he slumped to the floor. "He was trying to put me to sleep!" Pearl said indignantly.

Spaul shook his head and said, "I guess *that* fired back."

"Backfired," Pearl told him, placing a palm on his cheek.

"What do we do with him now?" Spaul said.

"What do I do with *you*?" Pearl asked him. "You called him here and never said a word to me about it."

"I didn't expect...I couldn't be sure...*okay*, it was a lapse in judgement! Will you forgive me?"

"Eventually," She told him. "But I wouldn't expect breakfast in bed for a while."

When Forest came to, he was sitting on a wooden chair out in the yard with warm Zephres blowing gently and steadily over him. The first thing he saw was tool sitting in another chair facing him. "You waked, Missuh 'Prentice?" Tool smiled. "Pearl dryin' you off, tole me to watch. You awake, I go get her and Spaul."

Feeling a bit disoriented, Forest said, "I'm leaving." But when he tried to move, he found himself being held in, or perhaps *by*, his chair.

Tool chuckled and said, "I go get them. She let you go after a spell."

Spaul and Pearl came out of the house and stood in front of Forest. "Are you going to be good?" Pearl asked him.

"Now see here," Forest said.

"You're almost dry," Spaul told him. "Do you really want to be hung out wet again?"

"Go back to wherever you call home, and live out your days," Pearl said.

"*World* is an Apprentice's home!" Forest growled.

"There are new Apprentices coming," Pearl told him. "They will make homes and keep them. World is about to experience a female touch. You've done your job well, the Fierae have told us that you will be honored. Except your honor and step aside. Don't end your time struggling against inevitable change. I'm sorry I knocked you out like that, but you shouldn't have tried to do it to me. If you'll leave peacefully, I'll give you a gift to make your last journeys easier."

"What gift," Forest asked, feeling himself being freed from the chair.

"Watch," Pearl told him. Then she called up two lines, situated herself on them, and had Zephrae blow her across the yard. "Do you see how it's done?"

"Yes," Forest told her. "It will take me some practice."

"Of course, you realize the lines will tug at your metals. Unless you can call to the Fierae to charge your hands, you'd best use it sparingly."

"Charge my hands?" Forest asked. "Can you do that, too?"

"Yes," Pearl smiled, "but you won't be able to. Now let us give you some food for your journey. You're welcome to spend a night here if you need more sleep."

"I've slept enough!" Forest said gruffly.

"I'm sorry I brought you here," Spaul told him. "It was all a mistake."

"Your mistake was getting involved with *that*!" Forest said, indicating Pearl. "Thirest was perhaps our finest, and you dishonor his memory. I've always thought it odd that such a great Apprentice should die so young. How did he die, Spaul? Was it before or after you met this witch?"

When Forest said that, an impressive spark snapped on his nose. Spaul shook his head and said, "You'd better go. You've pissed her off, and I'm pretty close to it myself."

Holding his burned nose, Forest called up a line, threw his pack down it, and hurried away. "That didn't go well," Spaul said.

"He's dying," Pearl told him. "Maybe a year. He knows it and is frightened. I feel sorry for him."

"Not so sorry that you wouldn't spark his nose," Spaul told her.

"No," Pearl said. "He called me a witch. I sparked his nose before you had a chance to punch him in it."

"That was sweet of you," he smiled.

"I'm sometimes too good to you, Spaul," she said. "But I plan on being angry with you for several days over this."

"I'm a little angry with myself," Spaul said.

"Trust me," Pearl told him, "my anger will be worse."

XXI
Traces of Pain Revisited

Other than blood relatives, Kimmy's are the only personal traces I've managed to gain access to. Now that she's gone, I very rarely go there. If I did, the temptation to return to them would become an addiction. Eventually, I'd be found dead, sitting in a chair with a smile on my face. Kimmy wouldn't want that. She'd want my memories of her to be tempered by time and seasoned by my missing her.

I mention my limitations with traces so you'll understand that I can't follow Forest as he made his way to the Billy's hills. But it wasn't long until he turned up there. One night, after a bout of tender passion, Ilsa told Star as gently as possible. "How do you feel?" she asked, running her hand down Star's smooth, silky back.

"Mmm," Star responded. "Don't stop. I love your touch."

"I have something to tell you, baby, but you must promise not to let it upset you."

"I promise," Star said dreamily. "I'm too relaxed for upset."

"I've heard there's an Apprentice up in the hills with the Billies."

"Yes," Star sighed. "I've heard that, too. I checked on it. It's just an old man hiding in a young face and fancy clothes. He's not even as strong as Papa. If he makes trouble, well, he's dying anyway. I may have to scoot him along."

"Can you talk so casually about killing someone?" Ilsa asked.

"Only when you rub my back like this," Star giggled. "Otherwise, I'd be more serious. Now come here and let me rub *you* a while. I have a spy amongst the Billies. I'm seeing her in the morning. Which reminds me, you're not to come here at all tomorrow."

"You've been keeping me away a lot lately, Star. What is it?"

When Ilsa asked that, Star became agitated and sat up. "Don't question me, Ilsa," she said, rubbing her temples as if her head suddenly ached. "I've too much on my mind. I haven't been able to run new lectric ropes, and can barely keep what globes there are lit without my tinkerers. That knowledge is so *tedious*! If you love me, you'll do as I ask. When I say stay away, just do it! In fact, you should leave now. I need sleep. Tomorrow I want you to check on the potterers' progress with my pipes. Do *something*, Ilsa, to help me!"

When tears crept into Ilsa's eyes, Star said, "Stop it, now. I'll not succumb to every little tear you shed. I'm not *yours*, Ilsa. I don't belong to your tears or this little bit of pleasure you dole me. Stay away tomorrow and it will give me a chance to miss you. Now kiss me, then go home to your bed."

The following day, a tall, muscular Billy girl arrived at the house. She carried a small pack, and when Star came to the door, she grinned, revealing a chipped front tooth. "You're early," Star said, unable to restrain a smile.

"Gonna give you a long day," the girl said through her wicked grin. "Now git on up them stairs. And I want *three* pieces of gold, now on."

"Or what?" Star said, smiling.

"Or you git nothin'," the girl answered.

"Maybe I'll give you *four* pieces," Star said.

"Three or four ain't gonna make no difference to *you*," the girl laughed. "Yer gittin *all* of it, no matter."

It was sometime after midday that Star became aware of Ilsa on the other side of the door. The sounds coming from that upstairs room had caused her to weep. "Let her in," Star said quietly.

"*Who* in?" The girl asked, mopping sweat from her brow.

"Open the gollam door," Star said.

A harsh "*crack*" sounded, and Star winced. "Say please," the girl told her.

"Please," Star moaned.

Ilsa was leaning against the door sobbing when it opened. She stumbled into the room and the girl asked, "You next?"

Ilsa looked up and saw Star chained naked between two poles, her arms and legs spread taught. Her back was to the door, and was a bloody mess. From the Billy girl's hand, a whip dripped crimson puddles onto the floor. "Take your gold and leave," Star told her.

Lacing Star's back with the whip again, the girl said, "Say, 'Thank you, Earline'."

"Thank you, Earline," she whispered.

Earline walked over to Star, kissed her neck, and said into her ear, "I'm gonna take a little taste with me." Then she ran her tongue up Star's bloody back and said, "Lordy, yer sweet! Next time I'll lash yer front and see how that side tastes."

When she said that, Star shivered once and said, "Please go."

On her way out the door, Earline looked at Ilsa, then to the whip in her hand, and said, "You wanna borry this?"

Once they were alone, Ilsa closed the door and said, "Why?"

"You know why," Star told her. "Because you won't. And even when you would, you held back your passion. See how fiercely Earline loves me? Even if you would, I could never go back to you now."

"Please let me take you down from there," Ilsa begged.

"Do you think I can't let myself out of these shackles?" Star laughed. "But I'll not waste Earline's tender ministrations. Come give me a kiss, Ilsa. Run your hands down my back."

"I can't stay here any longer, Star. I'm leaving Tara," Ilsa wept.

"You should," Star told her. "Go find Mama and Papa, they'll take you in. They'll *probably* take you into their bed. And you can tell them stories about how you used to take a strap to their little girl, and how she begged you to whip her harder."

When Ilsa fell to her knees sobbing, the shackles on Star's wrists and ankles released her. Slowly, the cuts on her back and legs began to close. Then she went to Ilsa and helped her to her feet. "Come," she said. "I want you to understand."

Ilsa found herself unable to resist as Star chained her between the poles. Then she took the belt from around Ilsa's waist, and tore the dress from her back. "Please," Ilsa managed to sob.

"That's what I always say, too," Star told her as she stroked red welts onto her flesh.

Though Deliverance Billies are usually tight lipped with strangers, an Apprentice willing to call them up gold from the ground made them talkative indeed. Before long, Forest knew all about Star's lectric farm, and most of what went on in Tara.

Eventually, it became apparent to the Billies that Forest was plotting against Star. This upset the diggers, whom Star paid well for their coal. When they made this clear to Forest in threatening tones, he said, "Wouldn't you rather dig gold out of your pockets than coal out of holes?" Then he tossed a sack at their feet.

After looking inside, the diggers smiled and said, "You need help with her, talk to Earline."

"And who is Earline?" Forest asked.

"Big, blonde moose with a chipped front tooth. Her daddy liked to bust her up some. Then she got big," the diggers laughed. "He's lucky she found somethin' else to keep her occupied."

By the time Star summoned Earline again, Ilsa was gone. No one knew where she went, but a rumor started that she'd helped the tinkerers beat Star, and was too ashamed to stay at Tara any longer.

Earline was supposed to come in the morning. That night, Star thought of Ilsa, and missed her. At dawn, she woke dreaming of Spearl. All morning she paced by the front door looking for Earline, who did not come.

Star didn't leave the house that day. She was very nearly in a panic. At one point, she drew a sharp knife across her palm—her eyes glazed and slightly crossed. Late that afternoon she heard Earline calling from the front of the house in a sing-song voice, "Where *are* you?"

Star ran to the door, desperation on her face and tears in her eyes. "Where have you been?" she said, weak and shaky.

Earline grinned demonically and wrapped an arm around Star, who trembled at the touch. "You missed me, didn't you?" Earline smiled. "That's good. Now git up them stairs. Since you missed me so much, I'm gonna take some time with you. Gonna take all night. I'm gonna taste yer back and I'm gonna taste yer belly. Fact is, I'm hungry, and gonna have a little taste of everything. Now git upstairs and outa them clothes. Time I git there you better be waitin' and sayin' please."

Forest and a small band of Billies waited until darkness fell over Tara. In her lamp-lit, upstairs room, darkness was also falling over Star.

One at a time—each plotted and drawn out first with a finger—Earline crisscrossed her body with long lacerations. The blind scream in her mind blocked out all thought and all perception except her beloved pain. She didn't notice when the light of Tara failed. Brute Billy strength and Apprentice majick were disemboweling her lectric farm.

As Forest's saboteurs finished their work, Earline took a short rest from the task she loved. Walking slowly around Star, she admired her ring and its chain, the only thing she wore during those sessions of dark love. Star's head was hung, her chin on her chest, but she raised it to look into Earline's eyes as she came around to face her. After crushing Star's lips with her own, she said, "Such a pretty li'l sparkler you wear. That stone's just the color of yer blood." She placed a finger on the ring, then pulled it away with a screech.

"That's much too hot for you to touch," Star smiled. "If you ever touch it again, it will burn away your hand."

Earline slapped Star hard across the face and said, "You'd miss this hand."

"I would," Star told her, blood running down her chin. "But you'd miss it more. Don't ever tempt me to reverse our roles, Earline."

"Fine!" the Billy girl growled. "You ready?" she asked, drawing a finger across Star's belly. "Here's a spot we ain't got to yet."

That short break in pain's infliction, that brief exchange of ire, perhaps even the slap across her face, allowed Star's elemental perception to peer out long enough to feel the lines called up and running the length of Heroes Way. From the lectric farm to the Dark Star, the only light still burning in Tara, they ran. An Apprentice, old and young at once, was riding them to her.

Earline's whip hand was cocked, her sinister eyes intent on Star's smooth belly, when the shackles fell away, and the whip blazed and fell to ash. Earline dropped backward onto her butt and hollered, "What the shite!" as the door flew open and Forest entered the room.

Star spun around to face him. Though her wounds were healing, stains of blood drew lines down her body. She knew, now, that the light of Tara had been destroyed. Her face was grim as she stared through slitted, glowing eyes at Forest. Her body also began to glow, and her molten flesh flowed, removing all traces of Earline's love. "What have you done?" she roared, her voice gone elemental. "Who taught you to ride the lines?"

Forest said nothing, as his face drained of color. Star came toward him, and he couldn't move. When she placed her hot palm on his forehead, he wanted to scream. "Say a name!" Star demanded.

Then she heard his mind say, "Pearl."

XXII
The New Apprentice

Spaul was surprised. He'd never known Pearl to stay angry with him for so long. It had been four days since Forest left. There had been no love from Pearl in that time. She'd been sleeping with her back to him, avoiding even his arms' embrace. On that fourth night, he said to her uncompromising posterior, "I miss you."

"I miss you, too," she said, not moving.

"Are you ever going to forget about this?" he asked. "No harm was done."

Pearl rolled over and faced him. "I'm afraid that's not the case," she said.

"I should have punched him in the nose," Spaul told her.

Pearl smiled and said, "I've been called worse than witch. Well, at least Starshine has. That's not why I'm angry, Spaul, if I even *am* angry, which I probably am, so don't count your chickens."

"*What*?" Spaul smiled.

"I'm *worried*!" she said. "I've been keeping a Zephre eye on your friend Forest."

"I wouldn't call him a friend," he said.

"No," Pearl conceded. "He's heading in the general direction of Tara."

"But how would he even know where Tara is?" Spaul asked.

"I don't think that's his destination. I think he's heading for the Billy hills that overlook Tara from the west. I think he's going to see why they're digging coal."

"But wouldn't Star feel him approaching and do what she did to us?"

"What little elemental majick he can manage wouldn't bring him to her attention. *Unless*, he's figured out how to use the gift I gave him. She'd notice someone riding the lines, and she'd expect it to be one of us. We are, or at least were, the only ones who know that majick. I shouldn't have taught it to Forest."

"If he's heading for those hills, there are very few places, if any, where he could ride. It's all wooded," Spaul told her.

"If he can't ride, and I know he can't do any *other* advanced majick, she probably won't notice him. Even if she does, she won't see him as a threat."

"*Is* he a threat?" Spaul asked.

"To himself!" Pearl answered. "There's no telling what he might try when he sees those lights. If he fires Star into an elemental rage, he, and who knows how many others, will die!"

"Shite," Spaul cursed under his breath.

"Yes!" Pearl agreed.

"I'm sorry," he told her. "I understand why you're still angry with me."

"Now that you do, I think I can let it go," she said. Spaul took her in his arms and smiled. "Don't smile like that," she told him, trying to keep the grin off her face. "I'm still very concerned," she said onto his lips as he kissed her. "I may not let you..." she tried to say as he kissed her neck. Then she *did* let him, and actually helped a bit.

"I really did miss you," Pearl said as Spaul held her after their love. "It was hard staying angry at you. But I'll manage it again if you don't agree with me."

"Agree with you about what?" he asked.

"We go after Forest," She said.

"I've cogitated that part," Spaul said. "I was expecting the particulars."

Pearl placed her palm on his chest and said softly, "You're not done with me yet, are you?"

"Tell me the particulars, first. Let me catch my breath."

"My poor, old man," Pearl said. "Two or three times and he's all worn out."

"The particulars," he reminded her.

"Okay. We know he's probably not riding lines, at least not once he gets into the woods. So he's going to be a while getting up there. Tomorrow, we go to Smith's and fetch the kids."

"I thought we were giving Spearl a *long* rest?"

"It's Kimmy we need," Pearl told him. "If Star detects us coming, and doesn't *want* us coming, we'll need our little ring hearer again. Hopefully, Star's keeping her promise to wear it always."

"You think she'll detect us?"

"She has an elemental perimeter set up around her city. It extends out quite a few klicks."

"You can tell that from here?" Spaul asked.

"Yes. It takes a little concentration, which I've been doing a lot of these last few nights."

"While you were angry?" Spaul smiled.

"Don't press your luck," Pearl smiled back. "It's a limited thing, this perimeter, designed to notice strong majick. It would probably notice me whether I was majicking or not. As an aneke'lemental, my presence tends to excite elementals a bit. I'm kind of a novelty. But I've also noticed that this perimeter shuts down completely, fairly regularly, for hours at a time. As if Star is working some very complicated majick, or is engaged in something equally as intense."

"Like what?" Spaul asked.

"I don't know," Pearl told him. "I could be anything. Even very intense love could distract her."

"Do you think she has a lover?" Spaul asked.

"You're kidding, right?" Pearl asked. "You honestly didn't get it?"

"What?"

"Ilsa, Spaul! Star and Ilsa are lovers! And if I start imagining how intense that love would have to be to distract Star so completely, well, you'd better hurry up and catch your breath."

When she said that, Spaul couldn't help but think back to the time at Tara when he'd imagined loving Pearl and Ilsa together. Hearing his thought, Pearl grinned at him and said in a sultry voice, "It's a shame we never got the chance."

"I've caught my breath," Spaul said, rolling over onto her.

Pearl laughed and said, "But for *who*?"

Though Kim wanted to spend most of our time searching for secret places to love, I insisted that Smith give us chores. "I'm gonna hafta be fair 'bout this, Spearl," Smith told me. "You want chores, and Kimmy wants, well, somethin' *other* than chores, I'm guessin'. So, bein' fair, like I said, I'll keep you two busy till lunch, and after that yer on yer own." Then he laughed and said, "I got a feelin' yer gonna be busy all day!"

I loved feeding the animals. It had been Kimmy's favorite chore, which was why Smith gave it to us. "See! This is fun!" I told her as we threw corn for the chickens.

"It is," Kim agreed. "But after this, we got shite to shovel. Why'd you hafta git him to give us chores?"

"We're eating his food and sleeping under his roof," I told her.

"I done so many chores 'fore you come along that he ought to feed us the rest of our lives!" Kim said.

"You go do something else, and *I'll* do the chores," I told her. "Go visit Janie."

"That ain't how it works, Spearl. And, anyway, it'd take you twice as long, and I'd *never* get any lovin'."

"I'd find the time," I assured her.

"And when I go visit cousin Janie," she told me through a pretty little pout, "yer goin' with me!"

After three weeks at Smith's, Kimmy insisted her belly was starting to bulge. Lying down by the pond early one evening, I placed my hand on it and said, "Flat as a pancake."

"Is not," she smiled. "It's swellin' up like all git out!"

Rolling over, I kissed her bulging-flat belly and noticed she was breaking out in gooseflesh. "It's getting cold," I told her. "Get dressed. Let's go share a mug of wine, then I'll tuck you into a nice warm bed."

"And tuck you into a nice warm me?" She giggled.

"You are truly insatiable," I said. "Do you know what insatiable means?"

"I ain't stupid, Spearl," she smiled at me.

"No," I told her. "But you are cold. Look here, you're all goose-pimply," I said, tickling her ribs.

"You could just rub that goosey off'n me!" she laughed.

Then I stopped tickling, stopped laughing, kissed her and said, "You better *not* catch cold with my baby in you!"

"*Our* baby," she corrected. "But yer right. Help me find my clothes."

That night, in bed, I said, "Maybe we should head home, Kim. It's starting to get cold."

"This is the first chilly night yet, Spearl, and if I hadn't been butt nekkid and sweaty, I wouldn't have got goosey like that. Three weeks ain't got Star off yer mind, I know!"

"Can you feel her from here?" I asked. "Can you feel the ring?"

"See what I mean!" she said, but I could see some concern other than for me on her face.

"Tell me," I said.

Kimmy said nothing, which worried me more. "What is it?" I asked. "The good and the bad, *together*, remember?"

"I *can* feel it, Spearl. It's like all that concentratin' I did when we found her the first time is makin' it a whole lot easier. But all I can tell you is…I don't know how to explain it."

"Try," I said.

"What you told me, 'bout what she was havin' Ilsa do, it's rattlin' her somethin' fierce. What I feel…well…I *can't* feel it. I have to make it stop when it's like that."

"Pain?" I asked.

"Maybe," she told me. "But if I kept up feelin' it, it'd make me…"

"*What?*" I asked, seeing what looked like embarrassment in her eyes.

"It'd make me do what *you* made me do down by the pond!" she blurted out. "Only not nice! It's like a bad feelin' takin' over and havin' its way."

"And pain is causing it?" I asked.

"*Maybe* pain. Maybe pain tricked into somethin' else. I don't *know*, Spearl, and it bothers shite out of me just thinkin' 'bout it."

"Then don't," I said, kissing her. "I don't think Ilsa can harm her with a strap. She can heal her body pretty much at will."

"Ain't her body I'm worried 'bout," Kimmy whispered.

"If it's cold tomorrow," I told her, "we should think about going home."

That night, I could have sworn I heard Mother calling to me in my sleep. In the morning, I told Kim about it and she said, "I heard somethin' callin' you, too. Coulda been Mama's voice."

"Maybe we should go home," I told her.

"Yer Mama ain't callin' you home, Spearl! It's just coincidentally!"

"A coincidence," I said.

"That, too, you shite!" she said, laughing and tickling me to beat all helluva. Then she stopped and said, "Hush! That *was* Uncle calling us."

"Kimmy! Spearl!" Smith was hollering up the stairs. "Guess who's here!"

"Janie?" I said to Kim.

"Mama and Papa," she told me, her smile disappearing.

By the time we came down, Mother and Father were eating breakfast. They didn't seem upset about anything, and I'd have been happy to see them had I not witnessed Kim's smile disappear so completely when she heard they'd come. Kimberly, my lovely, pregnant lifemate, was starting to exhibit abilities that I couldn't explain. Whether I understood them or not, I knew enough to pay attention to her.

Keeping as much concern out of their voices as they could, Mother and Father told us about Forest, and their intention to go after him to keep him from starting trouble. "So you're going to *protect* Star's lectric farm?" I asked Father, incredulity in my voice.

With a touch of anger in hers, Mother said, "There are bigger fish to fry than the gollam itty bitty amount of coal being burned to make a little light!"

Father started to say something, but thought better of it and smiled. Finally, he said, "I've had some communication with Blitz, Spearl, and there are definitely bigger fish. I won't oppose your sister, or her Ancient teck."

"These must be some awfully big fish!" I said.

"Apparently, there are a new kind of Apprentices coming," Father said, looking pointedly at Kimmy. "*Female* Apprentices. Some of them have already arrived, and could be as old as, say, *fourteen*."

Kimmy was *not* stupid, and Father's intimations weren't wasted on her. "Me?" she laughed. "Yer crazy!"

Mother also laughed, slapped her palm on the table, and said to Father, "I told you so!"

"You're a shykik," Father said. "Of course you told me so!"

"*What* is going on?" I demanded.

Father explained, as best he could, about the new Apprentices, after which I told him about the Zephres responding to Kimmy's requests.

"But they weren't really *requests*, were they?" Mother said. "More like wishes come true?"

"That's '*xactly* what they was, Mama." Kimmy said. "Them Zephres was just bein' nice and friendly, and tryin' to make me happy. I can't feel no elementals, or make silver come up outa the ground, or see what Zephres see!"

"Can't you?" Mother asked. "You located gold and silver at the beach. You seem to know the Zephres wanted to make you happy, and how do you feel, and even *see*, that ring? You're a *different* kind of Apprentice, Kim. You should except it and let yourself grow into your majick."

"Onlyest majick I'm growin' is in my belly!" Kim said fiercely. "And if you think yer takin' me off to git trained, there's gonna be fur a-flyin'!"

When Kim said that, a shock of fear ran through me. If she *was* a New Kid, somebody sure as helluva would want to train her. Father must have seen the fear in my eyes, and said, "Nobody's training Kim! Nobody's training any of the new Apprentices. Blitz, not to mention your mother, were very clear about that. These are *new* Apprentices, and we *old* Apprentices are to stay out of their way."

Putting two and two together, I said, "You certainly don't need *me* to help you stop Forest, which means you must need Kim. So you've come here to take my pregnant life-mate on a long journey into unknown danger. You're even thinking it would be best if I stayed behind."

"It *might* be," Kimmy said with an angry laugh, "but it ain't happenin'! I don't know 'bout bein' no 'Prentice, but it'll be all-fired bitin' and clawin' fer anybody tries to put a meter of air twixt me an' Spearl!"

I had to smile as I watched Mother's eyes widen with her grin. "You're such a *feisty* little thing," she said.

"Be careful," Kim told her, not ready to let go of her anger. "Feisty could get downright ugly!"

"Yes," Father said in a calm voice. "We did *think* about Spearl staying with Tool, but my Shykik lover advised me not to even broach that subject."

"Broach?" Kimmy asked, her ire dying down. "Ain't that a sparkler you pin on yer dress?"

"It also means..." I started to say, but Mother interrupted.

"Yes," she smiled. "It is. And that particular broach is staying in the drawer and not getting pinned-on. We aren't here to *make* you do anything, Kim. You and Spearl discuss it. It's your decision. But I am going to say this, Star needs us and we may need you to get to her."

"The Universe ring," Kim said.

"Yes."

"I guess there really don't need to be no discussin'," Kim said, looking me in the eyes.

"Oh yes there does," I said, standing and taking her by the hand. "Let's take a walk!"

I wasn't happy. I wasn't happy with Mother and Father's willingness to enlist my pregnant love in this dangerous adventure, and I wasn't happy with Kim's seeming willingness to go. When we reached the corral, I spun around and faced her. "You're gollam *pregnant*, Kim! There's a *baby* in here," I said, placing my palm gently on her belly.

"A boy," she smiled, looking up at me through her lashes.

"A boy!" I laughed, my anger quashed.

"Yes. But he's a long way off, and I'm fine."

Then my anger tried to return. "We don't have to do this, Kim. They're Apprentices, Mama's shykik and aneke'lemental. They'll figure this out without dragging you along."

"*Us* along," Kim told me. "You think they'd come all the way down here if they didn't need us. And if anything bad—shite, anything *worse*—happens to Star, how're you gonna forgive yourself? We *ain't* got no choice in this, Spearl, and you know it well as I do. You think I wouldn't rather stay here and dally with you in a pile of pretty autumn leaves?"

I had to laugh. "You've been thinking about that, haven't you?" I asked.

"I been watchin' them leaves turn brown," she grinned. "But the Universe has spoke agin. It just ain't givin' us no leave right now, and there's nothin' we can do about it. So we'll do the best we can, me and you. And if the Universe ever decides to leave us alone, we're gonna hole up, make a passel of young 'uns, and git *fat*!"

I laughed and said, "I can't imagine you fat."

Kim took my hand and put it back on her belly. "Pretty soon," she said, "you won't have to."

When we went back into the inn, Mother and Father were drinking tea with Smith. He saw us coming, stood and said, "I got chores. Can't be jawin' all day. But *tonight*, I'm gonna give y'all a opportunity to beat me at cards!"

"Fat chance of that!" Father laughed.

"We could cheat!" Mother told him.

"Cheatin' starts," Smith grinned, "y'all *definitely* won't stand a chance!"

Kim and I sat. I kept my face grim and said, "We...*we*, will go with you until we're in sight of Tara. After that, we're heading straight back home."

"Fair enough," Father said. "And if we need our Ring Hearer, I'll carry her on *my* back."

"We'll see," Kim smiled.

"Neither of us wants this," Mother said, taking my hand in hers. "But we *need* you. And I swear, Spearl, I won't let anything happen to either of you."

"Don't swear such things," I told her.

"Okay," she amended. "I promise to bring all my majick to bear to keep you two safe." Then she smiled at Kim and said, "Bitin' and clawin' if I have to."

"I didn't mean to git so all-fired ornery," Kim blushed.

"You stay ornery," Mother told her. "The Universe can be a pain in the arse."

We spent two more nights at Smith's. Mother and Father didn't see a need to hurry. The second night, after learning how—or perhaps how *not*—to play cards, Mother took Kim and said they were going for a walk. "I'm going, too," I told her. Mother seemed put out, but knew enough not to argue.

"We'll all go," Father said.

We headed toward the pond, Mother and Kim leading the way. "Do you fish this pond?" Father asked me. I was trying to hear what Mother was saying to Kim and didn't hear him. I think he was trying to divert my attention from their conversation. *"Fish?"* he said, smiling at my blank expression.

"We pull a few brimlets out on cane-poles," I told him. "For fun, though Smith fries them up for us." Turning my attention once again to the ladies, I heard Mother quietly asking Kim, "You can feel it from this far away?"

"I feel more than I'd like," Kim told her.

When I heard that, I marched up to them and said, "What are you two talking about?"

"Just about my feelin' the ring," Kim answered.

Mother let out a deep breath and said, "Spearl, there's something you two aren't telling me, and I want to know what it is."

I said nothing, but Kim gave me a look that said, Maybe she needs to hear it. "I've never told you what Star didn't want you to know," I said. "This is *not* something she'd want me telling."

"Spearl..." she said.

"I can't," I told her.

"Kim?" Mother asked. When Kimmy wouldn't answer, she said, "How can I protect you two if I don't know everything?"

"Oh, I agree," Kim said. "I think we should tell you. But you know gollam well I ain't goin' 'gainst Spearl. I'll talk to him 'bout it, but he's stubborn, and I'm kinda partial to his stubbornness. I warned you 'bout trying to force anythin' twixt us. It'd be a mistake, I promise."

"Just look at that moon!" Father said, which was another way of saying, You will drop this, *now*! "Why don't you kids run off to bed. Let your Mama and me talk a while."

As I took Kim by the hand and headed back toward the inn, I heard Mother say, "It isn't talk you want, and I'm not in the mood."

"Let me soften you up," Father said. "You won't get your way with those two, but I'll let you have it with me."

"I suppose that's some consolation," Mother told him. Then I heard her giggling, and Kim and I hurried off.

It was getting cold, and we were heading north and west. We stopped home long enough to get warm clothes and quilted bedrolls. Apparently, Grandfather's little bird had been talking to him again. "Y'all goin' 'gainst somethin', ain'tcha?" he said. "Y'all gonna listen to me this time? You listenin', Pearl?"

"I'm listening, Papa," she said, kissing his cheek.

"Kissin' me ain't listenin'!" he insisted. "Now *listen*! Y'all ain't careful, somebody's gonna git cotched! Don't you *let* nobody get cotched, Pearl!"

The following day, as we were leaving, Grandfather gave us all hugs. But he grabbed me a second time and whispered in my ear, "You bring her back, Spearl. You bring her and my great-granbaby back."

For a while, we rode lines on the Ninety-five. But eventually, we started heading west, hoping to find the Tara Road. "What do you think, Pearl?" Father asked. "Is she misdirecting us?"

"I don't think so," Mother said. "I can see that creek, and I'm being drawn to it."

"Drawn?" Father asked.

"It's not an elemental thing," Mother told him. "It's shykick, and not something I can explain. But I don't think Star is doing anything. What do *you* think, Kim?"

Kimmy stood still and closed her eyes. At one point, she started leaning, and I was afraid she'd fall over. But she opened her eyes, caught her balance and said, "Feels like what I *been* feelin' from her most of the time. I don't think we're close enough for her to be perceivin' us, long as we're careful. O' course, that's all grain o' salt, if you know what I mean."

"I think just about everything's grain of salt these days," Father said.

"Let's not take any chances," Mother told him. "If we find the creek, we'll get Kimmy on somebody's back from there to Tara. Once we're overlooking the valley, Kim and Spearl can head back. You and I will warn Star about Forest, then go find him and convince him to leave. And I *will* convince him!"

"Let's find this creek, then, so I can ride my pretty muley," Kim grinned, playfully bumping me with her hip.

"I thought you were gonna ride your *old* muley," Father pouted.

"I'm sure you'll git a turn, Papa. I better git my rides while I can," Kim smiled. "Ain't *nobody* gonna wanna tote me once this belly pops out!"

That night, we camped in a little clearing. It was the coldest night yet. I was hugging Kimmy close, sitting by the fire. She was shivering, and I was about to get her into our bedroll when a warm breeze began blowing over us from all directions. "Do you think you should do that?" Father asked Mother. "Talk about advanced majick."

"I'll not have my children freezing," she told him. "If Star feels it, we'll go to plan B."

"Plan B?" Father asked.

"Kimmy the Ring Hearer."

"That's *you*, Mother?" I asked about the sudden warmth.

"Yes," she said.

"How do you *do* that?" Father asked her. "I can't even get the Naiadae to chill water, much less the Zephrae to warm air."

"You just have to pay attention," Mother told him. "You have to feel what I'm telling them and then feel how that makes *them* feel."

"Good grief," Father said.

"I know," Mother told him. "That's why I tell you I can't explain these tricks. You have to watch, and listen and feel."

"Or," Father smiled, "just get *you* to do it."

"Or that," Mother smiled back.

Kim was quiet during this discussion, though she'd stopped shivering. Then, in a strange, sleepy voice, she said, "They love me."

"Who?" I asked.

With a dreamy look on her face, Kim smiled, and the warm air blowing over us turned *very* warm "Mmmm," she said, closing her eyes. "That feels good."

"Is she?" Father quietly asked Mother.

"She is," Mother told him. "They aren't mine, anymore."

"How?"

"She doesn't know she's doing it," Mother whispered. Then she reached over and touched Kim's hand. "Kimmy," she said softly. "You okay?"

"I was just cold, Mama, and sleepy," she said, her eyes still closed. "I'm dreamin' 'bout a nice, hot summer day."

"Why don't you let Spearl take you to bed?"

Kim opened her eyes and the hot breeze ceased blowing. Smiling, she said, "Thanks for warmin' me up, Mama." Then she whispered to me, "Take me to bed, darlin'. I'm awful sleepy."

Once in our bedroll, Kim fell asleep immediately, but I lay there awake listening. "What *was* that?" Father asked.

"Making the elementals feel good is the key to these higher instances of majick," Mother told him. "Apparently, Kim was feeling what I was doing and amplifying it. It's all vibrations of one sort or another, and she was picking up on it. It was making her feel so good, the elementals shifted to her vibrations, and hers wanted warmer. It ended up relaxing her so much it put her to sleep."

"Do you think she could be taught to control it?" Father asked.

Mother chuckled and said, "Always the Apprentice! No, Spaul, I don't. I think Kim is attuned, but as Blitz said, less aware. I can see the wisdom in it. Instead of Apprentices working majick through the elementals, this is more like the elementals working majick through Apprentices. You know the Lesser Three are greatly influenced by the Fierae. It looks to me as if they want that same influence over us."

"Is that a good thing?" Spaul asked.

"'Good and Bad' isn't of great concern to the Fierae, though I've never detected any 'bad' in them equal to what I've found humans capable of. It's an *inevitable* thing, Spaul. It's done. And the Fierae waited until the old Apprentices were pretty much gone to do it. There's only one power in World left that *might* could interfere with this trace the Fierae have plotted."

"Star?" Father asked.

"Yes. And I think the Fierae would pull her out of World before they let that happen. 'She slips off and then on,' Blitz said."

"But what did he mean? Does he mean she dies, that her light leaves then returns in another life?"

"I don't think so, but I worry for her," Mother told him. "I think I understand what they're doing, though. I think World may become a better place, achieve a better consciousness, and I think that's what they want before humans become numerous again. They're trying to achieve a balance that will avoid the kind of human infestation that nearly extincted us. This may seem incongruous, but I think the Fierae are just coming to an understanding of human death, or at least suffering, and the fact that they caused an incredible amount of it."

"Fierae feeling guilty?" Father laughed.

Mother laughed as well, and said, "No, but perhaps a bit uncomfortable. Fierae live for love and ecstasy. Perhaps this new understanding of humans that came with Star's inception gave them an inkling of what suffering is. Perhaps Blitz sacrifice reinforced that inkling. Knowing the Fierae as I do, and even I can't claim to know them well, if they've become aware of suffering, they'll try to plot a trace without it."

"That would be good," Father said.

"I think so," Mother agreed. "Have you ever noticed how Kimmy can't seem to get enough of Spearl?"

"I think that's a mutual affliction," Father laughed.

"Yes, but Spearl, for all his humanity, isn't quite human."

"Maybe not quite *regular* human," Father said.

"No, it's more than that. He *is* Star's other half, Spaul."

"Her *human* half," Father insisted.

"No," Mother told him. "Her *other* half. I've told you how he's accessed the Linea Clipses."

"Yes, but that's *Star's* majick. It's the sword, Gryn."

"But he's *used* it, once when Star was unconscious. I managed to get into that trace, Spaul, and couldn't stay on it. When he called up those lines, I had to come out."

"Why?" Father asked

"Because it was calling up Drea."

"But Starshine is gone from your sea. How is that possible?"

"Starshine is on my sea in my traces. And while human traces are phantasms of a sort—call them enhanced memories, though that's not entirely accurate—Fierae *exist* as trace. There are traces of me in which a Fierae *lives*. Something similar lives in Spearl."

"You've lost me all to helluva and back," Father said. "And what does that have to do with their physical attraction?"

"Kimmy lives to love," Mother said.

"Are you saying she's Fierae?" Father asked.

"No. But neither are you, yet when you join with the Fierae, they *do* have their way with you, don't they? You have no choice but to love like a Fierae. I think Kim loves like an elemental, almost a *reverse* joining. Instead of us joining with them, they're joining with us. And because of what Spearl is—half of this Fierae version of human—he and Kim physically attract. I think the elementals who inspire her can't help but love Spearl."

Father shook his head and said, "We live in interesting times."

"Yes," Mother agreed. "And I think the elementals will establish the terms of these times through these new Apprentices, these *female* Apprentices. I think, for humanity, a game of role-reversal is about to be played."

"A *game*?" Father asked.

"It's what the Fierae do, Spaul. I think she from above is going to be the new order of things—the new game."

"Do you think *that's* a good thing?" Father asked.

"Men have had a very long turn," Mother mused. "Take a break. Let's see what happens."

"Do we have a choice?"

"No," Mother told him. "Now, let *me* take *you* to bed."

"Are we going to play a game," Father asked her.

"*I'm* going to play a game," Mother told him.

"Oh!" Father said.

"Yes!" Mother agreed.

I lay there thinking about the things Mother and Father said. One aspect wouldn't leave my mind—Star being removed from the trace. Had the Fierae made Star—and by extension, me—to initiate the arrival of the new Apprentices? Was her usefulness now over? Would they simply discard her? Then I thought about Gryn, and wondered how big an opponent it could fell.

The following morning, Kim seemed well rested and quite happy. While we were eating breakfast, she said, "Papa, will you carry Spearl's pack for just a little while this morning?"

Father smiled and said, "Yes. I have a feeling Spearl would rather carry you, today."

I laughed and said, "She's heavier!"

"Yes," Kim smiled, "but your pack won't sing to you, or nibble your ear."

"I'd carry you if you croaked like a frog and *bit* my ear," I told her.

"Be careful," she said in a singing voice.

Kim's frog imitation had me laughing, but when she bit my ear, I said, "Hey! Frogs don't bite!"

"This one does," she said, planting her chin on my shoulder.

"I'm pretty sure the creek isn't far," Mother said. "But I'm afraid to look through Zephrae eyes to be sure. We're getting close to Star's perimeter."

"Can you feel her," I asked Kim.

After a moment, she whispered to me, "Not now. It's that feelin'." Then she said aloud, "Go ahead and look, Mama. I don't think there's any primiter right now."

Mother paused, closed her eyes, then opened them and said, "She's right. What is she doing, Kim? Can you tell?"

Giggling, Kim said, "Not now, Mama. I got to pay attention to my muley lessin' he bucks."

"I *might* buck," I said, bouncing her on my back.

"I was *tryin'* to change the subject," she whispered in my ear.

"Change it to your *favorite* subject," I whispered back.

"You *are* my favorite subject," she sighed, and I suddenly realized there was more than one way to take that.

It was late afternoon before we heard that creek babbling. As soon as we did, Father said, "I think someone is there."

After a moment, Mother confirmed it. "It's Ilsa! She's hurt!"

Kim leapt off my back, Father tossed me my pack, and we all began to run. We could see Ilsa curled into a ball by the creek. But when we got close, Kim said in a hushed shout, "Wait. She's asleep and real scared. Don't startle her."

Quietly, we advanced. Mother arrived first and placed a palm on Ilsa's forehead. She opened her eyelids and it was as if they'd been damming a lake of tears. "I'm sorry, Pearl," she wept.

"Hush," Mother said. "You're hurt. Let me see your back."

"Please don't look," she said, but allowed herself to be helped to sit. Gently, Mother maneuvered her dress up until she could see the welts on Ilsa's body.

"Don't look, Kim," I said.

"I seen worse," Kimmy told me. "I'll tell you 'bout Mama's last bo sometime. That's when I went to live with Uncle, and it weren't long till Mama was dead."

"I'm sorry," I said. "Why haven't you ever told me this?"

"Didn't never come up till now," Kim said matter-of-factly.

"Who did this to you, Ilsa?" Mother asked, but there were already tears in her eyes, and I think she knew.

"My poor, sweet baby," Ilsa wept. "This is what I did to her. I thought I could bring her back, but she's gone." Then she looked up into Mother's eyes and said, "She's gone, Pearl."

"What do you mean, she's gone?" Mother asked.

Ilsa shook her head and said, "You're looking at it, Pearl. You know. This is what she wants. I couldn't do it anymore so she sent me away."

Mother cogitated, and shortly knew everything. "The children know this, don't they?" Mother said softly.

"Spearl knows," Ilsa sobbed.

"Why didn't you tell *me*, Ilsa?"

"Because I was ashamed, Pearl! Even though I thought I had to do it, I was ashamed."

I made my way to Mother and Ilsa and said, "Don't you blame her, Mother."

"I don't, Spearl, and I don't blame you either. This must have been a terrible secret to bear. I wish you *had* told me, I'm hurt that you couldn't, but I do understand."

"I'm sorry," I told her.

"He's sorry for both of us, Mama," Kim said, and I understood what she meant. She would have told her.

"See if you can find some aloe," Mother told us. "And there's some light oil in my pack. Set up camp here while I tend to Ilsa." Then, to Ilsa she said, "I need to know everything. I need to know details—her habits, how soundly she sleeps, *everything*. We're going to take Star home! I'm taking her home if it kills me!"

"Don't say such things," Ilsa told her. "She's gone, Pearl, and she isn't Rufus Bowagad. She's a force."

"I can be a force if I have to," Mother said.

"I remember Drea," Ilsa told her. "If that's all you've got, don't you dare fight her."

"I don't want to fight, I want to take her home!"

"You try to take her from Tara and that Billy girl she's getting this dark love from, and there will be a fight. She did this to me for walking in on them and crying at what I saw. Try to understand what I mean by 'gone', Pearl."

I had a feeling that Mother now knew something I didn't. For some time she knelt by Ilsa and cried. I had never seen her cry like that. Kim went to her and held her for a bit, but Mother took a deep breath, snuffed out her anguish like a candle, and said, "We have plans to make!"

It was Mother and Father and Ilsa who were making plans. "You two are going home," Mother informed us. "You'll start back in the morning."

"Y'all might need us," Kimmy said.

"We'll stay till you leave here for Tara," I told her.

"No! You two leave in the morning," Mother insisted.

"Mama," Kimmy said. "Me and Spearl not tellin' you 'bout Star's pain kinda birthed other secrets, if you know what I mean. I can tell when Star's doin' that dark love, and when she is, she don't perceive *nothin'* else. Y'all make yer plans. When yer done, you just wait till I tell you it's time, *then* you go to Tara, and *then* Spearl and I will leave. Just so's we both understand, I ain't *askin'* this."

Mother chuckled and looked at Father. "You were right," he told her, "she's feisty."

Mother threw up her hands and said, "How can I argue with the first New Apprentice?"

"'Prentice my arse," Kim laughed. "Kimmy the Perceiver I might go with," she said, smiling at me.

For two days we waited. Mother tended Ilsa's wounds, and Father told tales about Mother's Naiadae voice, and the Tara of Rufus Bowagad. On that second day, late in the afternoon, Kimmy whispered to me, "She's a mess."

"What do you mean?" I asked.

"She ain't occupied to where her guard's totally down, but all day I been gettin' panic and confusion. It's hard to stay with feelin' it." Suddenly, Kim's eyes closed and she winced. "That tears it," she said. "She's at it and I can't take no more." Then she yelled, "Mama! Y'all go!"

Ilsa insisted on going with Mother and Father, and when Kim gave the word the three of them scrambled to leave. "As soon as we find the Tara Road," Father said, "we call up lines and go! We'll put Ilsa between us with her hands on ours."

"That the plan!" Mother confirmed. "Then we take our baby *home*! And you two," she said to us, "go now! I know it's late, but put some distance between you and Tara. Hopefully, we'll be right behind you."

"You be careful, Mama," Kim said. "I hate to say it, but she really ain't in her right mind."

"Go!" Mother said. "You take care of my other baby!"

"Safe in my arms, Mama. I promise."

XXIII
Tool's Warning

By the time they found the Tara Road, it was dark. Spaul called up lines, and Pearl rallied enough Fierae to charge their hands. Up the Tara road they flew with Ilsa between them. "You okay?" Pearl called to her.

"It's a little startling," she said, "but I'm fine."

"You sure she'll be at the Dark Star?" Pearl asked.

"Yes," Ilsa told her. "In a room upstairs."

Before long, they were overlooking Tara. Those strange lights were burning whitely down the Center Road. When they dropped off the lines, Pearl said, "I could take us up in a Zephrae cocoon, and drop us onto lines. We could step off right in front of her house."

"I thought we settled this," Spaul told her. "If we make it this far without being detected, we go in as stealthily as possible. Don't take any chances, remember?"

"You're right," Pearl said. "We stick to the plan."

No sooner had she said that, than the lights went out in Tara. "Now what?" Pearl asked.

For a moment, they all stood, trying to see what might be happening, but the valley was black. "I can see the Dark Star," Pearl said. "It's the only thing lit."

"Then we stick to the plan," Spaul told her.

"Gollam!" Pearl cried out. "Someone's riding lines! It's that idiot Forest!"

"Where?" Spaul asked.

"From south to north, down the Center Road. See? He must have done something to the lectric farm."

"And now he's going for Star!" Spaul said.

"Jess help him if he finds her," Pearl lamented. "Shite on the plan! Come to me, both of you! We're going up!"

"*Pearl!*" Star screamed. "My mother sent you! And Papa! They're coming to destroy me!" Star closed her eyes and shook her head once, then said, "They're here! She's rising over Tara to destroy me! How do they come without my knowing?" Earline was in a shocked state, still sitting on the floor. "Get up!" Star told her. "Drea has come, and she'll kill us all if she can! Take this little Apprentice and throw him into the street, then come back up here and I'll protect you." Every Billy knew of Drea, and many had nightmares about her. Earline quickly did as she was told.

"It must be Spearl!" Star said to herself while Earline tossed Forest out of the house. "He must be able to feel me, to find me."

Earline returned and said, "I pitched his arse out. Please save me from Drea, Missy Star!"

With the back of her hand, Star slapped Earline hard across the face and said, "Don't you ever call me that again!" Then she went to the window and said, "Come look."

When Earline joined her, Star pointed toward the street. In front of the house, his body frosted with blue light from the Dark Star, Forest stood. "This should get their attention," Star said. Then Forest flared up like a lamp, his fine clothes a brilliant wick, his body the fuel of that combustion. Star looked at Earline and said, "I'm moving in with you."

"What?" Earline asked.

"Don't worry," Star told her. "I'm bringing my own house."

Pearl, Ilsa and Spaul hovered high above Tara, looking down in the direction of the Dark Star. Suddenly, a brilliant flare erupted and lit the road in front of the house. "What is it?" Spaul asked.

"It's Forest," Pearl told him.

"He wanted a pyre," Spaul said, his voice cracked with emotion.

"Call lines!" Pearl shouted.

But before Spaul was able, green stripes pulsed in the sky and the ground shook. Shock waves buffeted Pearl's cocoon, and she cried, "I've got to put down! I can't hold it!"

At an alarming rate, they dropped out of the sky. At the last moment, Spaul shouted, "Take one of her hands, Pearl!"

Pearl understood. Spaul grabbed Ilsa's other hand just as his lines came up under them. The angle was steep, and the lines were weak. They hit the ground rolling and tumbling. All three were bloody and bruised. The ground under them shook fiercely, as those lines of force flashed and strobe-ed up into the night—brilliant ropes between World and Moon's eternal tug-of-war. "She'll break World!" Pearl screamed at Spaul.

"Look!" he called. "The house is rising!"

So violent did the shaking become that the rescue party couldn't stand or even see. Lying flat on their bellies, they held onto World as if trying to keep it from flying apart. All they could do was wait and see if the quaking would stop, or shake them to pieces.

To Earline's dismay, Star began to glow again. Her flesh looked like lava circling the curves of her body. "Linea Clipses!" she cried, reaching her fingers toward the ceiling.

Into the cool autumn air, her house rose over the valley. It's whitewashed walls caught brief glimpses of strange green light. Up it went, while the valley below shook as if monster feet were stomping in a tantrum. When the house was barely visible from the ground, a great chorus of Zephrae assembled and slowly started it moving west. The chorus grew, and the house flew faster, away toward the hills. Inside, Star took Earline's face in her hands. "You'd better not be afraid of me now," she told her. "You'd better still love me."

As if in a trance, Earline said nothing. Star hauled off and slapped her, and her eyes focused. "You'd better love me," she said again.

Earline slapped Star so hard that she dropped to a knee. Licking blood off her lips, she looked up at the Billy girl standing over her and said, "Thank you, Earline."

Just when it seemed their bodies would come apart, the shaking ceased. Ilsa was sobbing, and Spaul helped her to her feet. He couldn't see Pearl, and called for her.

"I'm here," she told him. "I'm okay."

"I can't see you. Stand up," Spaul said.

"Actually," she answered, "I'm not *exactly* okay."

Following her voice, Spaul found Pearl sitting on the ground holding her leg. "It's broken," she told him.

"Can you heal it?" he asked her.

"Yes," she said, "but it's *broken*. I can't just blink my eyes, jump up and dance a jig!"

"How long?" he asked.

"Maybe a day, if I think of nothing else the entire time. I need someplace to get comfortable if I'm to do this double quick."

"My house," Ilsa said. "Not far from where Star's is...was. I think we should leave her be, Pearl."

"Can you call lines, Spaul?" Pearl asked.

"No. Look for yourself. World's mag-lines are disturbed as far as I can see. It's like they've been flattened. They're pulling themselves together, but it'll take time."

"Then get me up on your back, old muley. I'm not *that* much heavier than Kim." Spaul snorted a laugh, and Pearl said, "You're going to pay for that."

As the trio of Star's rescuers headed off to find the Tara Road, I loaded my pack, and Kim fetched her little one with our bedroll. "Let me put some of that in *my* pack," she argued, as she always did.

"No," I told her. "I'm a man and can carry a bigger load."

"What a crock of shite!" she told me.

"You're pregnant," I added.

"Can't argue with that," she said. "Look at this belly bulgin' out!"

Kim pulled up her shirt, and her belly was still flat as the big pond before a storm. I laughed and said, "Bring that big belly here and let me kiss it."

Kim dropped her shirt and said, "You start kissin' on me, we ain't gettin' outa here tonight. Let's go. I got a bad feelin', and I keep thinkin' 'bout Grandpapa. Those ain't two things that mixes real good."

"What do you mean?" I asked.

"I've learned that when Grandpapa tells me somethin', I need to listen. And when I start thinkin' 'bout him, I need to listen to *me*, and *me* is sayin' let's git gone!"

"Okay," I said. "But when we stop for the night, I want another look at that belly."

Kim giggled and said, "A *close* look."

Night fell on us pretty quickly. We had just decided to stop when everything started to shake. It was so bad, Kim and I couldn't stand. We ended up sitting and holding each other, wondering if it would ever stop. "I think I saw flashes of light in the sky," I said, pointing back the way we'd come.

"I don't see nothin'," Kimmy cried. "But it's got to *stop*, Spearl. It's hurtin' me!"

There was nothing I could do but cover Kim's body with mine to protect her from the limbs that were falling all around us. Then the shaking seemed to fade away until it ceased entirely. "What *was* that?" Kimmy said, tears running down her cheeks.

"Don't cry, Kim. It's over now."

"What if it shook my baby loose?" she said, crying harder.

"Son of Kimmy the perceiver?" I said. "It'd take more than a little quake to shake *him* loose."

Kim stopped crying, but I could see she was still shaken in more ways than one. Blood was running out of the corner of her mouth. When I told her to open up and let me have a look, she said, "I bit my tongue is all. It ain't bad."

"Show me," I insisted.

Then she smiled and said, "You first."

I stuck my tongue out at her, and she did the same. She was right, it wasn't bad. Then she said, as best she could with her tongue still out, "No use wastin' this," and leaned in for a kiss.

Star settled her house on a high peak behind a stand of pines that looked over a cliff and down into the valley. "They won't find me again," she said to Earline. "You stay here. That brother of mine is not far away. Apparently, he led them to me, then ran."

"You gonna kill 'im?" Earline smiled. "Stoke 'im up like that dandy 'Prentice?"

When Earline said that, Star became pensive. Finally she said, in a far-away voice, "What *can* I do?" Then resolve seemed to gain definition, and she said, "What I *must* do. What*ever* I must do. They're trying to destroy me, and I've done *nothing* to them." Then she left the house, rose high in a Zephre cocoon, and fell away into the night.

We were sitting on a log by a little fire. Kim had gone quiet, and I asked if she was okay. "Somethin's wrong, Spearl."

As soon as she said that, it dawned on me that Star had sneaked a quick peek into my thoughts. "It's Star," I said.

Kim remained quiet for a time, then said, "She's coming. She's mad, Spearl."

"Angry?" I asked.

"Angry *and* mad," Kimmy told me. Then she gasped and said, "She's here!"

Apparently, Star had ridden lines over the forest, something Mother wouldn't do. "Lines called up over a heavily wooded area," she once told me, "tend to have weak spots, as if the trees have grown into them. Pulling them out makes the weak places." Apparently, my sister had overcome that obstacle.

Star stopped herself on the lines over us, then came down in a Zephre cocoon. Kim and I stood when we saw her vaguely lit by our little fire. I think I was expecting joy at seeing her, but there was none. Before she even spoke, I could see that this wasn't the sister I'd grown up with. The way she stood, the tensions in her body and face, the feral look in those beautiful eyes, all screamed insanity. For a moment, she stood and glared at me, her hands balled into fists. Finally, she said, her voice touched with a lectric hum, "Running off home now that you've delivered your assassins?"

I tried to stay calm, but I was scared. I'd been afraid *for* Star, but never *of* her. As gently as I could I said, "What are you talking about, Star? We've come to help you."

She threw her head back, barked a laugh, then spun around with her hands thrown up. "Lies!" she yelled. "The first words out of your mouth! They've succeeded in destroying my lectric farm, does that make you happy, you phony little Apprentice? Now our mother and father are searching for me to finish it, to destroy *me*!"

"That's not true, Star," I told her. "They came here to take you home."

"Oh!" She laughed. "Home to more of Mama's therapy? More torment to get poor little Starshine under control? How did you find me, Spearl? I had Mama completely confused the first time you showed up. Is it something I can thwart? Is there something I can remove from your mind, or do I have to..?"

"Have to what, Star? Are you going to kill me? Can you do that?"

"*You're trying to destroy me!*" she screamed, her voice gone totally elemental and less than sane. Then her hands became balls of fire that flew away from her and exploded on the ground on either side of me.

When she did that, Kimmy cried out, "It's *me*, Star! I can find you through the ring!"

"She's lying," I shouted. "Kimmy, shut up!"

Star seemed to calm a bit, and the fires on either side of me stopped burning. Then she smiled and said, "She can't lie, Spearl. Haven't you ever noticed? She isn't capable."

Star walked toward Kim. I tried to move, but couldn't. Taking Kim's chin in her fingers, Star said, "What are you, Sister, other than my brother's knocked up toy?"

"I'm his life mate," Kim told her.

Star laughed again and said, "That could have been a short term proposition if you hadn't told me this truth."

"Could you really kill Spearl, Star?" Kimmy said softly.

"I'll do what is required," Star growled. Then her features softened a bit and she said, "But I'm glad I won't have to." Walking over to me, she took the ring from around her neck and fastened it around mine. "There," she said to Kim. "Now you'll always know where he is. I hope that's some consolation. Good-bye, brother," she said, kissing me on the lips. Then she walked over to Kim, and cocooned them both in Zephrae.

"No!" I screamed.

"I'll take good care of her," Star said in my thoughts. "But she's forfeit if you come for me again."

Before they rose, I could feel her ransacking my thoughts until she shouted in my mind, "You *know*! Who *told* you?" A moment later she screamed, so loud I could hear her even through the cocoon, "*Ilsa!*" Then she and Kimmy rose up through the trees.

"Star! Please!" my mind screamed back to her, but they were gone. Star's spell that had held me released. I fell to my knees, feeling more alone than I'd ever been in my life.

The little fire Kim and I had built was going out. I was alone in the dark with my anguish. Then, and suddenly, rage replaced my grief, and I noticed a green glow around me. It was coming from Gryn, which had found its way into my hand.

XXIV
Traces of Madness

Star set down with Kimmy in front of her high house. "Just past these pines is a cliff," Star told her. "Don't fall off. Be good and I'll be good to you. Someday, if they can find a way to assure me, or maybe when our mother and father die, I'll send you and my nephew back to him. Until then, we must love one another for your son's sake. We wouldn't want him to see me angry."

"Listen to yerself, Star," Kim said quietly. "This isn't my Little Sister talkin'."

"No," Star smiled. "It most certainly is not. Now come in and meet Earline. You won't like her. She's a little rough, but don't worry, I'll forbid her to harm you. And, who knows, perhaps you and I can spend some tender moments together. I often miss holding something soft at night."

"This'll all end bad, Star," Kimmy told her. "They'll never rest till you give me back."

When Kim said that, Star became angry. Grabbing Kim by the arm, she dragged her through the pines to the cliff. "See that, down there!" she yelled. "See that black hole that used to be my bright Star City! They're down there plotting my destruction! Soon they'll know I have you and won't dare try me for the sake of your child. Here, let's send them a message!"

Star pushed Kim to the ground, called up great spheres of fire and thew them down at Tara. As they burst into conflagrations below, Star cried, "*There* is my city! See it now? See my light? And when I find Ilsa, I'll make a torch of her so everyone can see the price of betrayal! If they come again, I'll burn them all!"

When Kim began weeping, lying there beneath the pines, Star's anger cooled. Gently, she helped Kim to her feet and said, "Let's go meet Earline, then we'll have some supper. Don't worry, I promise to take care of you. You can have anything you want, just tell me."

"I want Spearl," Kim wept.

"Now you know how I've felt all my life," Star told her. "And, just like me, you can have *almost* anything you want."

I left everything but Gryn at Kimmy's and my last campsite. The green light of its blade led me toward Tara, tugging me this way and that to avoid the trees my tear blurred eyes couldn't see. I was running in a blind rage through the deep forest night, my legs unable to carry me fast enough. Then I noticed my feet were no longer on the ground, and I grabbed hold of Gryn with both hands. I felt like a rag doll being dragged through the night by a huge, unthinking beast.

How fast we went I can't say, but I became afraid, at one point, that I wouldn't be able to hang on. Then I realized I couldn't let go if I wanted to. Gryn had me in its jaws, had become the expression of my rage. When we finally stopped, we were on the Tara Road. Down in the valley, I could see several fires burning in the darkened city. "Where are Mother and Father?" I said aloud, and Gryn shot a shaft of green light down into the valley. I followed it as quickly as I could, and before long came to a house with lamplight burning inside.

I noisily came through the front door, and found myself frozen in my tracks by elemental majick. "Shite!" I screamed, my rage getting the best of me. Then Gryn flashed and freed me.

Father came running in holding a lamp, and called back into the room he'd just exited, "It's Spearl!"

"He just defeated my majick!" I heard Mother say. "How?"

"What's going on?" I yelled. "Star has taken Kim! What are you *doing*?" Then I fell to my knees to weep, but Gryn pulled me to my feet, and returned my anger.

"Your mother's hurt, Spearl. Come in here and tell us what happened."

"And calm down!" Mother called from her room. "Sheath that sword and calm down!"

Gryn's sheath was back in my pack, so I took a deep breath and slid it into my belt. I had trouble letting go of the handle, but finally managed it. I looked at Father and said, "I'm sorry. It seems to be developing a mind of its own."

"It has no mind, but yours," Father told me. "Be careful."

Mother was lying in a bed with her leg elevated on some pillows. Ilsa was sitting beside her. "It's broken," Mother told me, "and not likely to heal unless I can get a little peace. What's this about Kim? I thought you two were going home."

"We went when you three left," I told her. "We'd just stopped for the night when the shaking started. Not long after it stopped, Star dropped down on us and took Kim. She believes you're trying to destroy her. What happened to her lectric farm?"

"It was Forest. He was more cunning than I expected," she said. "But he paid for it with his life. Now tell me, Spearl, if you were heading home, how did you get here so quickly? How did you find us?"

I told her about Gryn hauling me through the forest, and how it pointed to Ilsa's house. "It's changed, Mother. I can feel it."

"Star accessed the Linea Clipses to move her house up into the mountains," she told me. "That was the shaking you felt. Gryn is a construct of those lines, they are its power source. Star kept those lines strong a long time tonight. I was afraid she'd break World. I think Gryn took some of that energy, maybe that's why World *didn't* break. I don't know. But you've got to be careful, Spearl. It's why I never allowed Drea to rise again. Calling the Linea Clipses is too dangerous. Move the moon enough and it will cause havoc on World."

I snorted a derisive laugh. Gryn had found its way into my hand again, and I said, "I'm getting her back! The moon and World be gollamed!"

"Spearl," Father said.

"Where is she?" I screamed, and Gryn shot a light so fierce that it sliced a hole in the house, and pointed up into the hills.

"Please, Spearl, wait. We'll *all* go!" Mother cried.

Then I felt Father's hand on my shoulder. I looked into his eyes and he smiled. "We'll all go, Spearl," he said in a calm voice. "Your mother and I would gladly die to save her, don't you know that? Will you wait for us?"

I don't know if it was his voice, or the plea in his eyes, but my ire diminished, Gryn's light dimmed, and I said, "Yes, Father, I will."

Star took Kim into the house where Earline was waiting. "Kim, this is Earline," Star said. "Earline, you're to be nice to Kim. If you harm her I'll have to find another love, do you understand? No pain for her, she doesn't like it."

"She's a pretty little thing," Earline said, leering and grinning. Then she fixed her gaze on Star and said, "You look like *you* could use a little lovin'. I never did get to finish with you tonight."

"I know," Star sighed. "But I want to keep an eye on Kimmy for a bit. I'm not really sure what she is. Could you defeat my majick if I bind you with it, Kim?" she asked, cocking her head. When Kim didn't answer she said, "I just don't know."

"Bring her with us," Earline said. "She can watch."

"That might be fun," Star agreed. "A little voyeurism, Kimmy, would you like that?"

"I never wanted to see you hurt, Star, and I still don't. If yer gonna have this *thing* here paint bloody stripes on you, I'd just as soon not have to watch."

"Then you can close your eyes," Star said angrily. "Bring her," she told Earline. But just as Earline's grin widened, a brilliant shaft of Green light lit the house. The glass in the windows facing it cracked and fell out of their panes. Then the light vanished. When she looked out, Star could see a perfect hole through the stand of pines where the light had burned through. "What the helluva?" Earline asked.

"I don't know," Star told her. "Keep an eye on Kim. I'm going to investigate."

No sooner had Star left the house, than Earline turned her attention to Kimmy. "What's so special 'bout you?" she asked. "You a little plaything she once kept?"

"I'm her brother's life-mate," Kim told her. "So you'd better do as she told you."

"She said not to *hurt* you," Earline said through her wicked grin. "And I *ain't*. In *fact*, I might could make you feel real nice. What say we take them clothes off you and find out."

Earline came toward Kim, and suddenly it was as if someone had emptied a bucket of water over her. Soaked to the bone, Earline's eyes rolled up in her head, and she slumped to the floor. Kim stood over her, looked down and said, "Y'all must be Niads. Thank you." Earline started to snore, as Kim made her way out of the house.

"Ilsa," Mother said. "We need some planks to make splints." Without saying a word, Ilsa left the room.

"You need to heal," Father said.

"I'll do the best I can, but I'll do it while we're moving. Enough is enough. We take Kim back tonight! And Star is too dangerous. She may...I might..."

"You mustn't," Father said. "It would be the end of you as well."

"There will be a fight," Mother said quietly. "When it happens, take the children and go."

"If there's a fight," Father said to me, "take Kim and go. Your mother and I will hold her as long as we can."

Mother seemed about to argue, but she smiled and said, "Yes. I like your father's plan better."

"Of the three of us," I said, holding Gryn up for them to see, "I have the best chance of stopping her."

"You'll stop World, Spearl," Mother said. "And even if you didn't, and succeeded in destroying your sister to save Kim, you'd never forgive yourself. It would gnaw at you throughout the years until you found yourself resenting her and your son."

When she said that I felt my heart go cold, because I knew it was true. "I once thought I'd use Gryn against the Fierae if they tried to take Star. Now I'm thinking of using it against her." Tears burned my cheeks as I looked at Father and said, "Apprentices don't kill."

"Nobody's going to kill tonight, Spearl," he told me. "We'll find a way."

"Where is Ilsa with those splints?" Mother yelled.

When I looked out the door for Ilsa, I noticed fires burning in Tara. "She's not out here," I said, "but there are fires."

Ilsa never did return. Father and I ended up tearing boards out of the ceiling to splint Mother's leg.

Kim left the house and stood for a moment on the porch. The light still coming from the Dark Star seemed appropriate. "Blackest light for blackest night," she said. "Now how do I get off this mountain?"

When she noticed the dark hole that green light had left in the stand of pines, she thought, "That had to be Mama. Who else could do such a thing?"

Kim decided to go look again down into the valley. As she stood near the edge of the cliff, she heard Star say, "Where you going, Big Sister?"

Kim looked behind her and saw Star standing there, her eyes lit like little amethyst flames. "I ain't goin' back with you, Star. I'll step off this cliff first."

"Oh, you wouldn't do that," Star told her. "You have your baby to think of."

"I am thinkin' of him, Star. He ain't bein' born anywhere near you or this place or that thing you call a lover. I'll take his light and we'll both leave for the next go 'round. I've lived and loved and been loved back. There's plenty die old ain't seen none of that."

Star tried to call up a line to snatch Kim away from the cliff, but the line pulsed once, then relaxed again. "What *are* you?" She roared at Kim, balls of fire forming in her hands.

"I feel sorry for you Star!" Kim called to her. "This is *your fault*. You've done this to yer brother!"

Then she leapt away into the dark abyss, and Star cried, "*No!*"

After a moment of panic, Star followed Kimmy over the cliff. Though she didn't cocoon herself immediately, she had Zephrae guiding her downward flight. But she couldn't see Kim. Near the bottom, the Zephres formed her cocoon and eased her to the ground. Holding her hands like torches, she searched. "Where *are* you?" she called, looking up as well as around. "Why did you *do* that?" she screamed. Then she caught a glimpse of Spearl's thoughts. They were headed toward her. "They come!" she shouted. "They're as intent to die as Kim!"

"Thank you," Kim said, as she stood up in that stand of pines. As soon as she'd leapt off the cliff, the Zephrae had blown her back into the trees. Though bruised, she was fine, and had watched Star, with her hands ablaze, dive off the mountain after her. "Time to find a path down outa these hills," she said.

It was dark, and the going, slow. After a bit, she stopped and sat on a rock. Closing her eyes, she tried to find the ring. Suddenly, she could feel it and Spearl, who was still wearing it around his neck. "Oh dear Jess!" she said. "He's comin' for me!" Then she jumped up and tried again to make her way down in the dark. Occasionally, distant Fierae bolts gave her glimpses of the path.

All around Tara, a storm was gathering. Father called up lines for us. My gauntlets were back in my pack, but with all the Fierae activity around, Mother would have no problem charging all our hands. "Gryn pointed up there," I said, indicating the dark silhouette of a nearby mountain.

"Let's ride to the base of it, then I'll take us up," Mother said.

"How's your leg?" Father asked her.

"Still broken, Spaul, but you did a nice job of splinting."

"It must hurt," he said.

"Yes," Mother smiled. "It's keeping me alert."

"But what are we going to *do*?" I asked. "What's our plan?"

"Every plan we've made so far has been worthless," Mother said. "Shite on it! We'll just do what comes next and see what happens."

"Sounds like a plan!" Father laughed.

We climbed onto the lines, and Mother's Zephrae blew us across the valley at a tremendous speed. "Look!" I called through the wind of our passing. "Lights! Up ahead!"

"It's Star!" Mother cried as Fierae bolts from the storm drew nearer and grew more numerous.

"There's going to be a big storm!" Father shouted.

"Do you think that's a coincidence, Spaul?" Mother said. "They've come! I just wish I knew what they were up to."

Suddenly, the Zephres quit and the lines set us down. "What happened?" I asked.

"Nothing," Mother said. "Let her come to us. If she calls up the Linea Clipses, do you really want that mountain hanging over our heads? Come on, Star!" Mother cried. "Meet us halfway!"

As if she'd heard that summoning, we could see those lights, which were Star's torch hands, rising. As they did, the light flickered and went out. Then Star fell at us like a meteor shot out of the mountain. Just moments later, she was standing not twenty meters away—eyes lit and flesh glowing. "Such a lovely family gathering," she called in a lectric seared voice. "Even the Fierae have come! Why don't you and Papa go to them, Mother? Leave your bodies here before they're broken."

"Too late," Mother told her, patting the splints on her leg.

Immediately, those splints lit up and fell away to ash. "Better?" Star asked.

"She healed it," Mother said to Father. "Thank you," she called to Star. "We've come to take you home! Let us help you!"

"Ha!" Star roared. "You are destroyers!"

"Enough of this!" I cried. "Where's Kim?"

For a moment, I thought I saw a shining tear lit by Star's

glowing eyes. Then she said, "She chose death, by her own design. I tried to stop her, but she was adamant."

Some grief is too severe to endure, some rage too blind to contain. Such were the terrible states that mixed in me at that moment. My mouth was open to scream, but no sound came. My eyes were iced with cold, vicious tears. My hand drew Gryn from my belt, and its blade flashed.

I started toward Star, and for a moment thought it must have started to rain. Suddenly, I was drenched. Then World went dark, and my battle, my grief, and my rage were ended.

When I awoke, the Ball was risen and shining off the hills to the west. Kim had my head in her lap, and was smiling down on me. "They *really* put you to sleep, didn't they?" she said softly.

"You're alive!" I told her, tears rushing to my eyes.

"Bitin' and clawin'," she smiled. "I was on my way back to you a few minutes after she took me. But it was a long walk down off that mountain."

"What happened? Where's Star? Where are Mother and Father?"

Kim leaned down and kissed me, then whispered, "I'm sorry, Spearl. Star died. Mama and Papa have taken her body away."

Sitting up, I grabbed Kim by the shoulders and said, "How? Where have they taken her?"

"I don't know, Spearl. They said to wait at Ilsa's house until they return."

Then I asked, my voice a harsh whisper, "Was it me? Did I kill Star?"

"No, darlin'," she said, placing her palm on my cheek. "You were sleepin' like a lamb. That's all they told me. C'mon, let's make for Tara."

"Did you see her?" I asked.

"I saw her body, yes. She wasn't even mussed. She was beautiful as ever, and seemed truly at peace. I know what her mind had become, Spearl. I promise you, she needed that peace."

"Let's go," I said, standing and putting my arm around her. "Maybe Ilsa knows something."

XXV
Traces of Mystery

Human traces follow human bodies. History falters when humans come out of those bodies. I've examined Mother's, Father's, and even Star's traces over the years to try and discover what happened that night—what happened to my sister.

For a long time, my love for my parents was strained because I knew they were keeping secrets about that night. When I learned to enter their traces, I tried to follow them after they left the valley with Star's body, but it was as if those traces didn't exist. It's as if Mother and Father were not in their bodies, or were not alive, until they returned to Ilsa's three days later. That, or those traces have been erased. But what power in World could do such a thing? All these years I've wondered, and in all those years, only the Fierae have come to mind.

When Pearl and Spaul saw that blade flash, they both, at the same time, flooded their son to sleep with Naiadae. "Did you...?" Spaul asked.

"We both did. He'll be asleep for a long time, I'm afraid," Pearl told him.

"You should have let him come," Star called, walking toward them. "You should have let us finish it. One last embrace. We *belong* together! You *know* that, don't you?"

"I suspect it," Pearl told her. "But they were also meant, Star, Spearl and Kim. I know it doesn't make sense, but life just doesn't, sometimes, especially when powers like the Fierae go up against powers like the Universe." As Pearl spoke, Fierae bolts crashed around them, and terrible thunder echoed from the hills.

"She's gone!" Star cried. "She leapt from the mountain of her own accord! In time, he'll love me again! We can be together!"

"You can't be that addled of mind, Star. You know he'll never forgive you!" Pearl called.

"Then I'll *make* him love me!"

"And for that, you'll never forgive yourself!"

"Then what, Mama? *What?*"

Pearl's eyes filled with tears, but she squeezed them out and shook them away. "I can't let you live, Star!" she screamed, her voice broken with grief. "I won't lose you both!"

"Then let's go together!" Star roared in an elemental voice. "Let's see if World can survive a mother and daughter's final embrace!"

As Star moved toward Pearl, Spaul went to his love and stood by her side. Star laughed, as if the gesture were meaningless. Then Spaul collapsed, as though he'd been struck dead. Pearl caught him and screamed at Star, "What have you done?"

"It wasn't me!" Star said, bewilderment on her face. Then she collapsed as well, and a tremendous Fierae bolt landed between them—blasting Pearl into unconsciousness, extinguishing that trace.

Mother and Father returned tight-lipped, but happy to see Kim and me together again. Grabbing Kim into a hug, Mother said, "This one's too feisty to die! But you certainly convinced Star that you'd leapt off the cliff."

"I convinced *me!*" Kim told her. "'Cause I sure as shite *did* jump off. I wasn't 'bout to let that Billy monster of hers anywhere near my baby."

"You'd have left me?" I asked, the sadness of that thought in my voice.

"I honestly can't say that I *knew*, Spearl, but I *some* kinda knew that they wouldn't let me die, anymore than they'd let that creature have her way with me. I wasn't off that cliff a nannysecond 'fore they blew me up into them trees. Star was ragin' and pitchin' fits in the dark, and never saw me come back. She went over after me, though. She didn't want me to die."

"Do you believe you're an Apprentice now?" Father smiled.

"I think I'm 'xactly what I was when I jumped," Kim told him. "Just another thing blowin' in the wind."

When I asked about Star, all Mother and Father would say was that the Fierae bolt had killed her, and that they'd burned her body on a pyre. "She was badly scorched," Mother said. "We didn't want you to see her like that. Always remember her beauty, Spearl. None of it was her fault, and none of it was yours."

"But Kim said she wasn't scarred at all," I told her.

"She was sparing you, Spearl. Or perhaps she saw what she wanted to see."

I knew Kim wasn't "sparing" me. Kim wasn't capable of lying for *any* reason.

Years later, when I saw that last trace, I was convinced the truth of Mother's story was porous. I've looked time and again, and always see Star lying on the ground *near*, but not under the Fierae Bolt. It was Mother's trace, her eyes, through which I saw those final moments. When I confronted her with the discrepancy, she said, "I'm not sure what I saw that night, Spearl. Like eyes, even a trace can be deceiving."

Before we left Tara, we searched for Ilsa. When we couldn't find her, Mother lifted us all up to Star's house to look. Inside, we found the Billy girl, Earline, shot through the heart with an arrow. Someone had tied a ribbon onto the shaft of that bolt—a violet bow very nearly the color of Star's eyes. We didn't find Ilsa, and after seeing the dead Billy girl, we were afraid to search any longer.

XXVI
A Very Brief Summary of a Very Long Life

Kim had our son at Grandfather's home. She insisted we name him Toolkin, much to Grandfather's delight. Just after his seventh birthday, Grandfather had Toolkin up on a muley, and was leading them around the yard. Suddenly, Grandfather sat on the ground and said, "Climb down and fetch yer Grandmama, darlin'."

I saw it happen, and was the first to reach him, lying flat by then in the yard. When he saw my face hovering over him, Grandfather smiled and said, "You done good, Spearl. You brung 'em back to me. You done real good." Then he died.

With Grandfather gone, and my relation with Mother and Father still strained, Kim and I left. We lived happily for years at Smith's, and had another son we named Spar.

Not long after Spar was born, Smith died and left Smith's Crossing, which was growing and prospering, to Kim and his daughters. Kim bought her cousins out, then hired them to run the kitchen and do chores. Kim also did chores, which she didn't seem to mind so much now that the inn was hers and making us wealthy.

My love for Mother and Father eventually won out, with prodding from Kim, and I made my peace with them on a visit with newborn Spar. After that, we visited often. One night at the inn, when Spar was ten years old, I heard Mother's voice calling me in my sleep. When I opened my eyes, Kim was already awake, propped on an elbow looking down at me. "I heard it, too," she said. "Let's go!"

Leaving the boys with Kim's cousins, we dug out our gauntlets and lodestone, and headed north. We found Mother and Father sitting up in their bed, holding hands, looking much too young to be dead. There was a note on Mother's lap, in Father's handwriting. All it said was, "Build us one pyre. Don't grieve."

I kept busy writing my accounts, but I never stopped wondering what happened to my sister. Just a few years back, I held Kim's hand as her light left one Autumn day, while brown leaves blew into piles down by the pond. "I'll see you again," she said to me. "They love me, Spearl, and won't leave us apart."

"I know," I told her, trying to hold back my tears. But they fell on the hand I was holding, just as all the strength left her fingers.

XXVI
The Final Chapter

I left Smith's Crossing, heading for Thirest's bunker. My children protested that I was too old for the journey, but I laughed and told them, "Can *you* call lines, and Zephres to blow you along?"

I'm not sure why I made that journey. I hadn't been there since the time with Father, right after I first met Kim. But something compelled me, woke me at night and dreamed me in the day of going. My children, however, were right. I knew I might make it there, but doubted I'd ever return.

Thirest's bunker looked just as I remembered it. Flowers still grew on its mound. I wished I could open it and go inside, but I had no majick with which to undo Father's seal. A storm was coming, and I was too tired to make a shelter. I sat against the bunker door, where there was a little overhang, and waited to see if it would pass.

I was lamenting the pain such humidity instilled in my bones, when it suddenly vanished, and I noticed I was tingling or vibrating all over. Then I felt a jolt, and found myself looking down at my body. "Spearl!" a crackling voice spoke. "No more pain! No more questions! Answers are coming!"

"Are you Blitz?" I asked.

"Ah, you remember! So cute cute, human, such love!"

"What's going on?" I asked.

"Life is going on! World and sky and the Universe go on! And now she comes, is coming coming!"

Suddenly, I witnessed the Fierae join just as Father had described it to me so many times. The ecstasy of it was a palpable thing, and I could feel it drawing me in. But Blitz called to me in that screaming, ardorous voice, "No! Stand away, little cute cute human. They are coming for you! Stand away away! Mighty with the Fierae they've become!" I moved away from Thirest's bunker some twenty meters, and Blitz cried, "Good! Do not touch, little human, or your lights will swirl away!"

Suddenly, that throbbing Fierae bolt pulsed brilliantly and a form stepped away. It was Mother, very young and dressed in a short, silver tunic. I wanted to run to her, but she said, "Stay!"

Then Father emerged from that light, and smiled. "Have you come for me?" I asked him.

"Stay there!" he told me, as I had once again started toward them. Then a third light pulsed, even brighter than Mother and Father's, and out of the Fierae bolt stepped Star. The beauty of her light body was almost too much to bear. Again, my impulse was to run to her, to take her in my arms, but she called, "Stay! You'll end us if we touch! Go into the bunker, Spearl! Meet me there!"

The door to Thirest's bunker was open. When I stepped through I could see Thirest plainly, and beside him, perfectly preserved and so very beautiful, was Star's body. "I'll be able to answer all your questions now," Star said from behind me. I turned and was again tempted to embrace her. "Not yet!" she told me. "When I'm back in my body, and you are in Thirest's, we can touch. It's finally our time, Spearl. The Fierae are patient."

"They told me you'd died," I said.

"I know, Spearl. Mama and Papa hated the deception, but you needed to be free to live your life with Kim. The Fierae would have left me in World longer had I not threatened its destruction with the Linea Clipses. It seems even deviant patterns of love interested them, though in the end, they came to regret the torment they'd allowed. It was a seminal moment for them, that first and only instance of regret."

"They erased Mother and Father's traces after they left the valley, didn't they?" I asked.

"That's not all, Spearl. Look in my hands. See what I'm holding."

I looked at Star's body, and saw cradled to her breast something I hadn't thought of since that night in the valley. "Gryn! But I...I never..."

"That's right. Gryn was only safe with you or me, so they removed all memory of it from you and placed it here with my body. It will be yours again, and you will learn to use it to heal. But come now, quickly. Blitz must speak with you before we come back to flesh."

Outside the bunker, I saw Mother and Father just a brief moment more. "I'm sorry I had to deceive you," Mother called.

"She's sorry for both of us," Father smiled. Then they dove back into the Fierae joining and were gone.

"My time is spent, my traces run!" Blitz howled to me. "But I will give you my blood, little Fierae human, and tell you what you must know. There is another element, the elementals of which inhabit all. They are the Luminae, who as yet remain silent. When they reveal their will, all must attend! Now go! Another life! You will see Kim again in your daughter's eyes! A great Apprentice she will be! A new way to love, Spearl, love her anew!"

Then the Fierae joining ended with a flash, and I found myself opening eyes that were staring at the bunker ceiling. "How do you feel, my love," came Star's wonderful voice from beside me.

"Young," I said. "Though not so young as you," I told her, leaning on an elbow to look down on her magnificent face.

"I'll catch up to you, someday, so stay this young until I do. Thirest was a great Apprentice, and you have all his talent, and more to come. He left this body so long ago for *you* Spearl. He is mighty with the Fierae, a cogitator and plotter of traces. Now we need to go outside, quickly."

"Star took my hand and led me out of the bunker to where the Fierae joining had been. The storm was over, but a light, misty rain still fell. Suddenly, I felt a tingling all over my new body. "What?" I said, my voice crisp with lectrics. Then the sensation was gone.

"Blitz has died, Spearl, and given you his blood. You are the last, and finest, male Apprentice. You will, by example, teach our daughter to use her great gift."

"*Our* daughter?" I asked.

"Of course. We were always meant to be together. I couldn't live without you and remain sane. We are one, Spearl, your thoughts comfort me. We're beyond brother and sister, and if the idea of incest plagues you still, *Thirest* was not my brother."

"And this was the Fierae plan all along, the trace they were plotting?"

When I asked that, Star laughed, and the sound of her laughter touched me with feelings I can't begin to describe. "With many twists and turns, the ever patient Fierae have plotted their trace around the Universe' demands. Did they intend you to find Kimmy, or were they intrigued enough when you did to alter their plot to suit the occurrence? Even I can't know these things, and I've been with them all this time."

"Were you with Mother and Father?" I asked.

"I was floating on the great mind-sea of the Fierae. I was healing, Spearl, for I was sorely damaged by my life without you. It was my time healing on their sea that caused the Fierae that moment of regret. But I'm fine now, and love you more than I can say. Please tell me you love me, Spearl. Please make my long dream come true."

"I took Star in my arms and kissed her. Then I walked her back into that fragrant bunker, and onto the bed on which we awoke. When we left there, much later, I noticed for the first time that my old body was gone, replaced by a pile of ash. "Looks like they weren't giving me a choice of which body to be in," I told Star.

Through a little pout, she said, "Didn't you just choose to be in mine?"

"What shall we name our daughter?" I said, kissing her cheek.

"I'll leave that to you," she smiled.

Before they left their bodies for Kim and I to find, Mother and Father engaged the elementals to preserve Grandfather's home. Star and I have decided to live there, at least until our daughter is born. "Shall we make your old room, or mine, ours?" Star asked me.

"Both," I said. "At least until Kimikin is born. We'll fill both those rooms with love."

"I'll miss Grandpapa, I'm afraid," she told me, a tear in her eye.

"And Mother and Father?" I asked.

"We can see them again, Spearl, though they won't stay long in their light bodies. Once you're one with the Fierae, it's hard to stay parted for long. How Mama was able to return to Papa after her stay with Blitz still baffles the Fierae. They thought she'd go mad. But she went to her sea and healed."

"While Starshine raised helluva," I interjected.

"Yes, but she managed to return whole and sane. The Fierae call her the Great Lady Pearl."

"What of these Luminae?" I asked. "Who, or what, are they?"

"I don't know," Star told me. "I'd never heard of them until Blitz spoke to you. But I'm sure we'll find out. Blitz wouldn't have mentioned them for no reason."

We were about to call up lines and leave for home, when a little white dog with black spots came running up to us. "Where did *you* come from?" Star laughed as the dog jumped into her arms.

"Seems to me you got a puppy last time you were born," I smiled.

"Thank you, Grandpapa!" Star called to the sky.

And I could have sworn I heard somebody say, "Star is welcome!"

Out Now:
Women Writing the Weird
Edited by Deb Hoag

WEIRD
1. Eldritch: suggesting the operation of supernatural influences; "an eldritch screech"; "the three weird sisters"; "stumps . . . had uncanny shapes as of monstrous creatures" —John Galsworthy; "an unearthly light"; "he could hear the unearthly scream of some curlew piercing the din" —Henry Kingsley
2. Wyrd: fate personified; any one of the three Weird Sisters
3. Strikingly odd or unusual; "some trick of the moonlight; some weird effect of shadow" —Bram Stoker

WEIRD FICTION
1. Stories that delight, surprise, that hang about the dusky edges of 'mainstream' fiction with characters, settings, plots that abandon the normal and mundane and explore new ideas, themes and ways of being. —Deb Hoag

RRP: £14.99 ($28.95).

featuring
Nancy A. Collins, Eugie Foster, Janice Lee, Rachel Kendall, Candy Caradoc, Mysty Unger, Roberta Lawson, Sara Genge, Gina Ranalli, Deb Hoag, C. M. Vernon, Aliette de Bodard, Caroline M. Yoachim, Flavia Testa, Aimee C. Amodio, Ann Hagman Cardinal, Rachel Turner, Wendy Jane Muzlanova, Katie Coyle, Helen Burke, Janis Butler Holm, J.S. Breukelaar, Carol Novack, Tantra Bensko, Nancy DiMauro, and Moira McPartlin.

Out Now:
Bite Me, Robot Boy
Edited by Adam Lowe

Bite Me, Robot Boy is a seminal new anthology of poetry and fiction that showcases what Dog Horn Publishing does best: writing that takes risks, crosses boundaries and challenges expectations. From Oz Hardwick's hard-hitting experimental poetry, to Robert Lamb's colourful pulpy science fiction, this is an anthology of incandescent writing from some of the world's best emerging talent.

Featuring
S.R. Dantzler, Oz Hardwick, Maximilian T. Hawker, Emma Hopkins, A.J. Kirby, Stephanie Elizabeth Knipe, Robert Lamb, Poppy Farr, Wendy Jane Muzlanova, Cris O'Connor, Mark Wagstaff, Fiona Ritchie Walker and KC Wilder.

Out Now:
Cabala
Edited by Adam Lowe

From gothic fairytale to humorous pop-culture satire, five of the North's top writers showcase the diversity of British talent that exists outside the country's capital and put their strange, funny, mythical landscapes firmly on the literary map.

Over the course of ten weeks, Adam Lowe worked with five budding writers as part of the Dog Horn Masterclass series. This anthology collects together the best work produced both as a result of the masterclasses and beyond.

Featuring
Jodie Daber, Richard Evans, Jacqueline Houghton, Rachel Kendall and A.J. Kirby

Out Now:
Nitrospective
Andrew Hook

Japanese school children grow giant frogs, a superhero grapples with her secret identity, onions foretell global disasters and an undercover agent is ambivalent as to which side he works for and why. Relationships form and crumble with the slightest of nudges. World catastrophe is imminent; alien invasion blase. These twenty slipstream stories from acclaimed author Andrew Hook examine identity and our fragile existence, skid skewed realities and scratch the surface of our world, revealing another—not altogether dissimilar—layer beneath.

Nitrospective is Andrew Hook's fourth collection of short fiction.

RRP: £12.99 ($22.95).

Acclaim for the Author

"Andrew Hook is a wonderfully original writer" —Graham Joyce

"His stories range from the darkly apocalyptic to the hopefully visionary, some brilliant and none less than satisfactory"
—*The Harrow*

"Refreshingly original, uncompromisingly provocative, and daringly intelligent" —*The Future Fire*